THE
MUSEUM
OF LOVE

THE MUSEUM OF LOVE

STEVE WEINER

THE OVERLOOK PRESS
WOODSTOCK · NEW YORK

First published in 1994 by
The Overlook Press
Lewis Hollow Road
Woodstock, New York 12498

Library of Congress Cataloging-in-Publication Data

Weiner, Steve, 1947-
The museum of love / Steven Weiner
p. cm.
1. French Canadians–Travel–North America–Fiction.
2. Young men–Canada-Fiction.
I. Title.
PS3573.E3946M87 1994
813'.54–dc20
93-42546

ISBN: 0-87951-531-7
3579864

To
Deborah Weiner

ONE

In August that year a Lutheran farmer named Ed Gien shot a social worker in the cranberry bogs. Prison guards from HM Prison Swallowfield helped disarm him and take him to an insane asylum. My father drove me down to see the farm.

Ed Gien had dug up women from the Lutheran cemetery, brushed them with resin and beeswax, and dressed them in his dead mother's shawls. He made ash-trays of their joints and lampshades and upholstery of their skin. Vises held rotted women's limbs in steel ball-and-socket armatures. Hip, breast, hair and thigh twirled over our heads from black fishing wire.

'Woman,' my father whistled. *'Disassembled.'*

My father was a prison guard. I ate lunch with him. Gruel and Oberlander, the German, ate with us. My father was an ugly man. His hands were swollen and knotted with veins. His ears stuck out and his red hair was combed over a bulging forehead. His eyes were dark and hollow.

'All this rain, Jean,' he said. 'Where does it go?'

'To the air.'

'Does it?'

'So it can rain again.'

We ate fried bread, *ragoût de boulettes*, squares of liqueur-filled chocolates. The coffee from the thermos was strong and French, so thick the grains oozed down the sides of the cups. The fragrance of rich caffeine steamed up between his big hands. My father was very depressed.

'*Merde*,' he said. 'All this rain.'

Oberlander picked up his concertina.

'*O liebling, mein liebes Kind*
Das Schiff geht ab, das weisses Schiff . . .'

'My darling child,' Oberlander sang, looking at me by the rain of the window. 'The ship leaves, the white ship.'

My father and I climbed the E-wing stairway. The red-brick gothic arches, statues of previous governors, rose over the cobblestone courtyard. Somebody had inscribed *Dieu et mon droit* on the walls. Prisoners below marched around a dead well in the heavy rain. The rain whistled through the toilet pipes. We went on tour.

Grotowski, a jut-jawed Pole with a shaved head, bent under an electric bulb hot and white under a damp ceiling. The wind boomed through the ducts. My father banged on Grotowski's bars.

'What do you want, *mon capitaine?*' Grotowski yelled.

'You made a bad mistake, Grotowski, using a crowbar on old Gunther.'

'One makes mistakes.'

'You've got lice.'

'I shall change my soap.'

'Your hands are scaly.'

'I shall use lanolin.'

'Grotowski, you're rotting.'

'Not as fast as old Gunther.'

My father banged on the cell bars. Grotowski put his hands over his ears. We walked down the black corridor. Voisin lay on his wooden plank and stared at the dripping stone roof. My father shined his flashlight on a whitened face.

'Voisin, get your hands out of your pockets!'

Voisin jumped up, pale and sweaty, wiping his hands. My father spat. We went to see Schlegel. Schlegel scratched his armpits. He saw me and stopped.

'Who have you brought me, *mon capitaine?*'

'My son.'

'And a very nice son he is, too.'

My father grabbed the bars. His huge hands, his hairy hands, squeezed until the big knuckles went white.

2

'*Pederast.*'

My father rattled the bars.

'This Schlegel is a bad number,' my father warned me.

We went to the darkest wing of all. Barrault the Jamaican lay on his cot in the damp of the dark. His breaths congealed in blue vapour. His smooth chest rose and fell and his eyes were yellow as yolks. Blue vapour crawled along the chains, bars, causing mould.

'Leave me alone, Verhaeren,' he muttered.

'Ha. Who? I?'

'Every day you come make trouble.'

'Why did you beat up the Ojibway?'

'I needed money.'

'What for?'

'I don't remember.'

'*THE CINEMA!*' my father shouted. '*YOU WENT TO THE CINEMA!*'

My father wiped the bars where he had accidentally spat. Rapidly and excitedly he cracked his knuckles.

'This man is a Negro,' he whispered to me, breathing hard.

'Yes?'

'Observe the difference.'

'Which is?'

'This man contains *négritude.*'

My father collected weapons. It was his private black museum, kept in the annex lunch room. He had the lead shingle of Joseph Bidolski, the hammer of Bert Rideau, and the knives of Willy Leszek. My father laminated newspaper photographs of our criminals and kept them in a vitrine. He bought one of Ed Gien's lampshades.

We were the Verhaerens.

Our house was brown sandstone shingled with a dark black roof. Our neighbours were the Dybs and the Zylches. Our living room had a red divan, red easy chair, brass floor lamp and radiator. Leaves' shadows moved at our dusty windows. Photographs of dead relatives hung over our altar where black crêpe twirled down. Bowls of salt water represented tears for those left living. Upstairs was my bedroom. From it I saw a smokehouse, a graveyard with black spike chain, rose bushes, hollyhocks stunted by the lake wind. There was a broken sundial. Lilies-of-the-valley lined our driveway.

I was Jean-Michel Verhaeren. I was Catholic. I was twelve years old and wore a red and black hunting jacket. My hair was brushed up in front. I had a speech impediment. As I said, I was Jean-Michel Verhaeren.

It was August 1954. I remember because the hot yellow light streamed down the leaves of our broken trellis. Filaments of algae grew toward our coal-cellar. In the heat of that August snakes were born. Our mother chased them. My brother Ignace beat them with a broom.

'*Tue-lé*!' she screamed. 'Kill them!'

'*Y sont trop vite*!' Ignace yelled. 'They're too fast!'

'*Mon Dieu seigneur*! *En-dessous*! Under there!'

The snakes escaped to the lavender lilacs. She danced into the yard, over the yellow grass, our mother, her pretty legs under the whirling dress.

'AAAIIEEE!' she screamed. 'THE BASEMENT WINDOW!'

I threw two snakes out of the basement. My father scraped up the rest, splashed them with kerosene, and I lighted the fire. There was a *woosh*. The snakes suddenly fried, became skeletons in red ash, rubbery, even their teeth charred.

'JEAN!' my mother yelled, pointing behind me. '*Au garage*!'

I caught that snake, too, dipped it in kerosene, lit it and twirled it until it sparked like a Roman candle.

The Petit Croix River came down from Manitouwadge past the Pic, toward Lillala Lake. Then it dropped to St Croix on the north shore of Lake Superior. Rutherford and Coldwell were going to be on the new trans-Canada Highway 17 but St Croix was not. St Croix had 2535 people, two coal-mines, a bowling alley, five churches and thirteen taverns. St Croix was going to die. So were Gilbertsonville and Heron Bay.

Sometimes lake steamers stopped. The boats were long and white, cut very low on the blue water. The pistons ran so smoothly one heard only a liquid *tic-tic* under the wooden decks. Camshafts turned bright as a penny, with the sweetest smell of oil, like the hot sugary smell of plum *tartes*. From brass rails one watched St Croix passing: the bluffs, the stunted grape-vines dark green and dusty, raspberry bushes, apple trees, and pygmy oaks, the French and Protestant districts, Ojibway Flats.

Behind our stone breakwater and lighthouse was the Portobello Hotel. Kelbo's Fish Market sold fresh muskellunge. In a tangle of reeds and broken pier posts, Ojibway fishing nets obstructed the banks below Abattoir Road.

Above St Croix was HM Prison Swallowfield. Behind, *la forêt* and darkness.

There came days when nobody went near our mother. Those were the green days when she walked into our living room and smeared paste from her mouth on to the walls.

She soaked in long hot baths (she kept the hot water running and the plug out). She dreamed of the convent where she had been noviced, Our Lady of Trois Pointes over the St Lawrence Seaway. Cherry red and somnolent, wrapped in white, her pretty black hair in a white towel, she slipped barefoot over the linoleum and treated us with silent, smug condescension.

Oak leaves fluttered at the windows. One had expectations. I combed her hair after the bath.

She was pretty. She was petite, with sparkling black eyes. An hysteric, sure she was, and illiterate, but a fine Catholic woman. She had had two miscarriages between Ignace and me. They weren't even buried, but burned at the Rutherford hospital. She had no secrets, not from me.

'I had *chlorosis* in the convent,' she told me. 'I was green. They scrubbed me with hard sponges. It did no good. I was fifteen before I had my first period. When it came, blood trickled even from my ear.'

'And the rapids roared.'

'Yes. It was high over the St Lawrence.'

'But you did not marry Jesu.'

'No.'

'Though you had permission to.'

'I was affianced. One might say affianced.'

'You had a screw loose.'

'I worked in the kitchen. I washed the drain. The slits were always clogged with hair. I had to pluck them out with my fingers.'

'You were crazy.'

'The light came through a dirty skylight,' she said. 'I lay with Sister Veronica, who was cold, until she died. I sewed her burial slip.'

'That was mercy, not crazy.'

'The dark chambers of women frightened me. They stroked me and whispered in my ear. I prayed until my knees were sore.'

'Did it help?'

'Some.'

'Sister Alicia.'

'Sister Alicia started dying. I slept with her. Also Sister Patrice. At least she said she was dying. I washed Sister Germaine. The steam covered us like a silky soap. I cured diseases of the foot. I worked with aloes and jasmine. I bathed Mother Superior and cherished her knees.'

'Who made you crazy?'

'I was in love with Jesu. We all were. I wanted to be a saint. Is that so sinful? I became delirious. They sent me to St Bonaventure in St Croix. I served the fish fry at the Oddfellows Hall and met your father.'

'Was he ugly then, too?'

'*Y était ben laid*. Very ugly. He got me drunk on red wine.'

'There in the hall?'

'No. He took me out to the cinema.'

'There?'

'No. Instead of taking me to the cinema he walked me down the embankment.'

'There?'

'It began there.'

'What began? Exactly. In your own words.'

'He gave me sloe gin from a flask in his pocket,' she said. 'I became dizzy. I held on to the rails. Dirty waves splashed over my convent shoes. He took me to the Portobello Hotel. We went to the ballroom, danced, then he rented a room. We went upstairs and he took off my clothes and penetrated me twice.'

'But you loved him?'

'I was frightened. I took the bus back to Our Lady of Trois Pointes. They rejected me. I had become vulgar. I took the bus home and did not eat for two weeks. Jack Verhaeren found out where I lived, came with roses. He spoke to my father, took me rowing on Old Woman Lake and did it to me again in the rowboat.'

'In the middle of the water?'

'By the ferns.'

'You were impregnated with Ignace?'

She smiled.

'I had a dream on the night *you* were conceived,' she said. 'I was in an ossuary in Bavaria. Ribs, skulls, fingerbones, made arches on pure white chapel walls. Monks groaned in the basement. I carried a lantern down deep stairs, past iron rings and coffins. Skulls clacked on the stairs. Teeth rained from the rafters. But I never found the monks. I couldn't move. I woke. Your father was on top of me.'

'It was *his* groaning you heard.'

My mother became abstracted. She told me it was like hearing a far-away celestina, in a dark forest.

Excrement rained on St Croix. It happened this way. The Poniatowski night-soil wagon was leaving Swallowfield when a sudden wind came off the lake. The composted dust flew high, and suddenly the wind changed and at the same time a rain squall hit the bluffs. Brown liquid rained down the streets.

My father was having his hair cut at the time. He looked out the window.

'Just as I thought,' he said. '*Le bon Dieu* shits on us.'

★   ★   ★

It was an exciting time for the Catholic women of St Croix. Pius XII had just canonized Catherine Labouré. Like Catherine Labouré my mother had worked as a waitress. But she (Labouré) suffered a vision of the Virgin Mary on a globe. My mother only saw dirty windows where she worked at Kelly's Nursing Home. She mopped the drain, cooked rice and made Jello. Her black hair was in a net, her face sweaty, under the cafeteria lamps.

'Michel, play with Manko.'

I played *manille* in Room 113 with Manko Eliasis. Manko had Newington's Disorder. His skeleton was being dissolved by his own kidneys. He excreted his own minerals. Finally Eliasis moved on a trolley. As he died he became a legless embryo, singing Greek lullabies.

'La la lalla la.'

•

Death came any time. Death came in corpse-sized bags of muslin the Ojibways unloaded from Norwegian freighters. Death came from the United States and was trucked to the towns of the north shore. When we heard the foghorns we crossed ourselves because we knew that *le bon Dieu* had washed his hands of somebody.

Death was in Rutherford Meadows, fixing a harrow. One could carry bags of meal to the barn and fall dead like the Basque boy Billy Sher. You could be reading the *Diocesan Newsletter* like Edmond Pic even in a portable toilet and die of a runaway truck. Death drove the newly-weds' boat, collecting flowers and money. Death beat the tambourine behind the Lamb of God. Death was a champion at *la bataille*. He beat the bowlegged priest Father Gregors, who died of lake fever in the spring.

Death was a great traveller. He rode the trunk-line and knew the trans-Canadian schedule by heart. You could see his overnight bags anywhere. He sold pancakes at the fête and grilled kielbasa with the Poles. He was a hell of a swimmer and hauled down the toughest trawler man, even the Portuguese Pedro Laguin, who went overboard last July with his nets.

Death hid in cupboards and dived out of steeples. He jumped from manholes and crouched in the ovens of the baker Freddie Granbouche. Death made no appointments. He walked into the Rutherford hospital any time like he owned the place. We had about thirteen deaths per season, almost all Catholic.

My brother Ignace was born *né coiffé*. My mother had had the caul blessed and buried under our lilacs. Now he was fourteen and white-haired. He would be a saint. He kept a miniature religious theatre. The house filled with glue, plywood, muslin, gouache, wire, little cogs. He bought transparencies of the Virgin and his little Jerusalem glowed on bluffs where innocents were massacred. Ignace took the Greyhound to Winnipeg and studied with the Jesuits.

That August molars suddenly oozed up from the banks of the Petit Croix. We found fragments of shroud and knuckle-bones washed down from the poor people's cemetery. Salamanders came through brown watery dust. If a black spiral moved on the watery shade, Ignace skipped a knuckle-bone through the lily pads. *Plonk*, a dead salamander.

'*À l'attaque!*' he yelled. 'Attack!'

But he crossed himself.

St Bonaventure was my high school.

My friends came from Heron Bay, Gilbertsonville, Three Rivers, Struthers, and the Ojibways from Crow Hill, Kalaka Falls and Mount Barrois. The Poniatowskis, Lemiczes, and Kolakowiczes came from the farms on yellow Catholic buses and even the girls smelled like cow shit.

Pius XII's photograph hung over the clocks. We wore lanyards with Pius's photograph. Over the *papier-mâché tableaux* of Catholic missionaries in Burma was a pedestal with a book of photographs of Pius XII. There was a photograph of Pius XII in the gymnasium. For passing into the seventh grade I received a locket with Pius XII's photograph.

In Father Przybilski's office was a huge framed engraving, black and white: *Marquette Bringing Catholicism to the New World*.

Sun-shafts came through oak trees on Ojibways kneeling in gilded ferns. A medieval engraving, *La Crvuvteen faisant mourir les Catholiques*, was over his desk, figures boiled in cauldrons, noses torn by pincers.

It was dark in St Bonaventure. Whatever the cafeteria cooked it always smelled like boiled brussels sprouts. Father Ybert came to religion class and two older students unrolled the St Croix Mural, seventeen-foot long, crayon-resist images of St Croix.

'Here you see the dark *forêt* of infancy,' he said. 'Nature governed you without the Holy Spirit.'

We followed his pointer. A dog crapped by the Bon Garçon on the rapids.

'The dogs of ignorance excreted your souls.'

He tapped St Bonaventure's image.

'But you were received by the Church, which blasted out your natural corruption. You received the Blood and Body of Christ.'

Father Ybert wiped his spectacles and smiled.

'Old age stalks you, my friends, and disease, and Death. Insanity. For now you suffer only poverty, but Death – you see him here behind the red bus – will take you and you will die.'

James Queyser looked pale.

'This is your reward for the sadness and sorrows you will be afflicted with in St Croix,' Father Ybert explained. 'When you are dead, beetles will chew your brains. Worms will crawl inside your tongues.'

Suddenly he turned the lights off.

'You will see nothing. The darkness will be for ever.'

Marlisse Franck cried.

'Death already creeps down the walls of your homes,' Father Ybert said. 'Death watches in the leaves that fall. Death creeps down your chimneys at night and steals pennies. Death sees when you touch yourselves in an impure manner. Death lives with Lutherans.'

Peewee Zelich hid under his desk.

'You have one hope . . .' Father Ybert said.

He turned the lights on. In the flickering fluorescent lights we saw he had changed into a white surplice with gold trim. The two older students wore surplices, too, and held a censer and chrism box. They all smiled.

'*The Holy Roman Catholic Church!*' we shouted happily.

On the thirteenth day of school Jackson Higgins ran off the roof of St Bonaventure's old wing and dashed his brains against Father Przybilski's parking meter.

The pretty girls of St Bonaventure stood at the bicycle rack. Maple leafs blew into the transom. Claire Pic wore a gold locket with rosemary against menstrual cramps. Frances Grgic's crucifix opened and held a blessed violet against polio. Antoinette Hartmann wore a cameo on her red sweater. It contained jasmine, against atheists. These were the pretty girls of St Bonaventure.

'Look at Jean-Michel Verhaeren!' Frances Grgic called. 'Look! He talks to himself!'

I threw away my tangerine. I got confused.

'Maybe he has to go to the bathroom,' Frances Grgic said.

'He doesn't know,' Claire Pic laughed.

Frances tousled my hair.

'What a character!'

Antoinette gave me a kiss.

'What a little man!'

I ran a gang called *les buveurs*.

Paul Hartmann was Undeceiver-General. Danny Auban was Sergeant at Arms, Lawrence Otto was First Soldier, Roland Zelich and Herman Pic, my cousin, were Second Soldiers. We met in a railroad shack. From the window we saw the trunk-line station, Galtieau Cement Works, the bleach factory.

I was *buscher* (bossman). They sang to me in *patois*.

11

Oh a me buscher, in a me buscher garden
Me a beg a me buscher pardon!

Then I would let somebody do something, or not, depending if I felt like it. I was the jailer, and the jailer's son, and I stole a bagatelle billiards. The *buveurs* played *trou-madame* and *sans égal*. I was the *Policier*, and the *Capitaine*, the *Prince du Sang*, *La Putain* and the *Procuresse*. I spread my cards: *La Morte*, *Le Cadavre* and the *Prince Etranger*.

We dragged little Protestants into alleys and stuffed red chillies in their mouths. We drew women's breasts on their school. We caught a rabbit, two dogs, a pigeon, three sand turtles and a sick squirrel and made them pay to see our zoo.

We believed in Wild Bill Hickok, *shérif du quartier Deadwood*, *ville d'amour*, also Jean Gabin. The Deadwood Chair was in front of a poster of *Quai des Brumes*. We kept a blue bowl of lavender talc. The Deadwood whip permitted speech.

'Catholic girls,' Roland Zelich complained, 'become whores.'

'Protestant girls work for Prange's and get married,' Danny Auban said.

'Catholic girls walk afterward like they had bowling balls between their legs,' Herman Pic said.

'Protestant girls walk with their legs closed,' Danny said.

'Catholic girls have an extra hole,' Herman Pic whispered.

'And they say,' Paul Hartmann blurted, 'to stick it in – !'

I stood and proposed a motion:

'*The best is to keep your hands off and your mouth shut.*'

I visited Uncle Emil.

Emil was foreman of the bleaching factory. It was a yellow building where magnesium salts had corroded the concrete ramps. The drains were clogged with grey wet strands of cotton. Under dirty skylights boys climbed to the top of the huge boiler, the kier. They packed cotton in with bare feet. In the next room bleached cotton shot through rollers and Emil tossed cold water on the sparking hot copper plate.

Emil came into the kier room.

'*Awaye!*' Emil shouted.

Boys jumped out of the kier. Didi Ligne pulled a lever. Chemicals began percolating. Emil locked the hatch.

Emil we called *le marocain* because of his thick lips. He had red hair, like all the Verhaerens. He was impotent from the chemicals. When his wife became pregnant by her cousin Felix, he went into couvade anyway and lay in a shack on an island, groaning. I kissed his hand and put it against my cheek.

'Why aren't you in school?' he asked.

'Priests make me a diarrhoea.'

I kissed his knees.

'Stop that,' he said. 'You must want something from me. What is it?'

'I want to live in your house,' I said.

'You? You *buveur*? To steal from me?'

'My family makes me crazy.'

'Ah. You will put up with worse. *Tu m'comprends-tu là?*' Emil said. 'Much worse.'

Steam shot to the skylights. The chemicals, now shit brown, gurgled into the drain. But the cotton was white!

My cousin Estée died.

It was a freak. She choked on a safety-pin. We went to her house, a brown wood-frame house on St Pierre Street. Black crêpe covered the porch columns. Ferns hung in bunches, with black satin ribbon. The clocks had been taken from the house and now Estée's family sat on a blue couch. An electric bulb hung over the corpse.

'I learned of the great misfortune that has befallen,' my father said, taking off his hat. 'Who could have expected it?'

'I learned of the great misfortune that has befallen,' my mother said, lifting her black veil. 'Life hangs by a hair.'

'I learned of the great misfortune that has befallen,' Ignace said, touching Estée's mother's hand. '*Le bon Dieu* is terrible in his mercy.'

13

'I learned of the great misfortune that has befallen,' I said. 'Estée was a friend of mine, too.'

Estée's mother started crying. My mother shook the evergreen branch soaking in holy water so that three drops fell on Estée. I touched Estée's cheek.

'She's cold,' I said.

The Szegy mortuary took Estée in a hearse up the road. It was blowing hard. The *cimetière* smelled of wet sand, dead flies, plastic flowers, candle-wax. We marched into the Verhaeren vault. Below, the French quarter, dull roofs, stretched to the harbour. We buried Estée and sang *En voyageant sur la mer*. Estée's lamps burned out at seven o'clock, and we went back to her house. Her uncle René grilled sturgeon. Uncle Emil made *piquant* rice and okra. Uncle Bobo brought cigars. We had Ojibway corn, potatoes, grilled tomatoes, leeks and cider. Estée's brother Jim brought Ontario wine. Orange stain appeared on our father's fingers.

'What did you expect?' Jim said. 'You had impure thoughts of Estée.'

'The girl was only thirteen,' my father objected.

'Then you admit it.'

'I admit nothing.'

'We know you, Happy Jack, what makes you happy!'

Our mother became hysterical. She believed that birds flew upside down when they passed over the house of the dead. She heard Estée's voice. She became afraid of Estée. The wind shrieked up Isle of May Street. She drank too much wine and threw up on the porch. Estée's brother Allen accused our father of having touched Estée.

'I deny that!' my father yelled.

'Then you are a perjurer!'

Our mother ran around the living room. Ignace screamed from the roof.

'Estée!' he yelled. 'In the trees!'

We ran to the windows. Over steep dark roofs Estée's soul rose in the howling winds. In bare, black branches a lavender mist dispersed.

'Estée!' we yelled.

There was a fist fight. My father broke Gustave Verhaeren's nose. All night men were chasing men and breaking windows until the police came. By morning everybody was draped over the furniture and our mouths tasted like ash.

TWO

Bill Aubourg unlocked the St Croix fish museum. Bill's leg was crippled. It flopped down the slimy wooden floor as he fed the fish. The aquariums held six flounders, two dogfish, a silver dace, seven shiners, a kokanee, and a birdfish with gills where the beak should be, its eye twisted. Our museum, we believed, would be a tourist site during the September fête. *The Fisherman – His Music – His Museum.* That would be our theme in electric lights, an arcade visible over the north shore. There would be oils by Bill's wife: *Le Pêcheur au soleil levant.* My Uncle Georges would grill fish. My father would play the accordion. M. d'Aube would bring floodlights from the fisheries. St Croix would have *son et lumière.*

Americans would cross the International Border and lay our Catholic girls on gunny sacks.

We smoked pipes. We talked about the Canadian winter, Ojibways, Basques, lamprey eels and women, all the things *le bon Dieu* has seen fit to trouble us with. Those were the days, we had a future.

M. d'Aube leaned over.

'Who salutes standing in the morning, horizontal at noon, and bowing low in the evening?'

'*The three stages of erection!*'

He put an arm around my shoulder.

'Now you are twelve, Jean, with a *petit moustache.* You are ready to fall in love. I must tell you about women.'

'*Oui, Monsieur d'Aube.*'

'What is a woman?'

'A person.'

PACKING SLIP:
Amazon Marketplace Item: The Museum of Love [Paperback] by Weiner, Steven

Listing ID: 1106K515481
Purchased on: 11-06-2001 22:34:54
Shipped by: mhaynes@ee.net
Shipping address:

Ship to: Alex Shakar
Address Line 1: 4832 North Talman Ave #3
Address Line 2:
City: Chicago
State/Province/Region: IL
Zip/Postal Code: 60625
Country: United States

Buyer Name: Alexander M Shakar

- -

Here are the details of your completed Amazon Marketplace sale:

Printed for Michael Haynes <mhaynes@ee.net>

'They have certain anatomical features,' he said.

'Yes.'

'And these features contain the woman's nature.'

'There are many kinds of women on the earth,' my father interrupted. 'But the worst are the French. They trap boys in birdhouses and feed them double-pointed nails. Some fly in the air and become like owls and swoop down. *Ecoute bien.* In the meadows I have seen women with hair in their nostrils. They grind boys. They burn their heads with hot irons. *Tu m'comprends-tu là?*'

'*Oui, Papa.*'

Bill Aubourg showed me his pack of pornographic cards. White women in black leather straddled chairs with Negroes.

'Listen,' Bill said. 'When you come home from the tavern your wife shrieks. Well, the hell with that. Beat off her monkeyskin. Punch her in the stomach. Knock off her bearskin. Put a fist in her face. Knock off her catskin.'

'Yes.'

'When she hops out bleeding, bite off her rabbitskin. Belt off her muleskin. Drub her on the pigskin. If she falls on her knees smash her. Knock off the insect-skin. You got to bust through to the woman-skin. Then she'll put her tongue in your ear.'

'*Cé ça,*' M. d'Aube said. 'She'll put that tongue anywhere you want.'

My mother bought a breviary. It was painted with facsimile medieval illuminations. It had psalms, matins, vespers, lauds, patristic homilies, prayer schedules. It had a list of martyrs, which she painted.

Zena Courennes brought her a parchment from Lourdes. Zelda Zylch gave her a brass *pater noster* that told the hours. Old Woman Dyb got from my mother a Belgian amber with the Virgin Mary's fingernail. Father Przybilski could not stop the relics trade. My mother took me to a wrestling match, went to the parking lot, and traded a mother-of-pearl rosary for an oil portrait of Catherine Labouré.

This was the time of the decency crusade. Catholic women

marched into Hebbard's Stationers, ripped up the pornographic magazines, stole seventeen books by Zane Grey, and dumped stacks of *The Watchtower* off the embankment.

Zena Courennes came for brandied tea. Legs crossed, she sat on my mother's wicker chair. My mother was at the Dybs' and I came in from playing hockey. I felt uncomfortable. It was warm and no place to hide. Mrs Courennes had thick red lipstick and her smile looked rubbery.

'Would you like some cake, Michel?'

'Thank you, Mrs Courennes.'

'I hear you have become a bad boy at St Bonaventure.'

'Yes. Well. I am the theatre, I guess.'

I couldn't take my eye off her legs, which she knew, and refused to withdraw.

'Boys are cruel,' she suggested.

'And the girls.'

'Ah. The girls.'

'Especially the girls.'

'One hears Antoinette Hartmann is cruel,' she said.

'It is more a power.'

'Women have power, too.'

'They do, Mrs Courennes.'

'Right now, for example.'

It was suffocatingly warm.

'What do you mean?' I asked.

She laughed musically.

'Your legs are concrete,' she suggested.

'Indeed. I am paralysed.'

There was a movement outside. My mother waved through the window. She wore only an autumn sweater, carrot orange, braided. She was going down to the Bergs'. As she went away Zena Courennes poured a bit more brandy into her tea and luxuriantly ate her fruit cake. She carefully wiped her thick red lips.

'You skate?' she asked.

'I am a good hockey player.'

'But you are small.'

'I am a little rough one, as they say.'

'Your legs are strong.'
'Like concrete.'
'And do you go fast?'
'Nobody stops me.'
She laughed.
'I'll bet nobody stops you.'
She stopped smiling.
'So. Women have this power,' she repeated.
'Is it not so?'
'Even now?'
'Especially now.'
'Come here, Jean.'
'No. No. I mustn't.'
'For heaven's sake. It's good for you.'
'No.'
'I beg you.'
'No.'
She smiled.
'It's good,' she said.
'I know.'
'Very good.'
'It must be very good with you.'
'So very good – '
The door flew open. My mother, carrying a jar of Maxwell House instant coffee, came in from the cold, blowing.

'Jesu – it's cold enough to freeze a Norwegian's ass!' she said.

Zena Courennes turned away. We had tea with my mother.

Father Przybilski called me to his office. Pius XII looked down from the fireplace mantel. Father Przybilski had gained weight. The buttons of his cassock bulged. He must have had piles, too, because he couldn't sit still.

'You have been with a woman?' he asked.
'No.'
'Women are a source of venereal disease.'

19

'And many other things.'

'From women one obtains insanity, melancholy, delusions. Isn't that true?'

'It is.'

'And yet you think about women.'

'They have a strange sparkle.'

'Only to you.'

Father Przybilski beat me with a yardstick. I held tight to my vision of women.

I discovered Father Ybert.

He had a private chamber inside the chemistry stockroom. A baboon head was stuck on a red and white pole and a sign around its ears read '*Darwin*'. Over the head was an umbrella. Sharp sticks stood in a circle around the head. Father Ybert was shaking incense smoke at the baboon fur when he saw me in the doorway.

'Go away, Jean-Michel.'

That September Kelly's Nursing Home put in new black and white tiles. I found my mother kneeling, sponging up red from a broken bottle. She was so pretty, her cornelian glowing in a shaft of sunlight. Her hair was damp from perspiration, strands curled over her forehead. She saw me in the doorway.

'What are you staring at?' she asked.

'Nobody, Mama.'

She sponged furiously. The red did not come up.

'GO AWAY,' she said. 'YOU KNOW THIS HAPPENS ONCE A MONTH!'

In Kelly's Nursing Home old Dieter Veck went into convulsions. The nurse, Annie Fer, flipped open a trap in his throat, syringed out the fluid and flicked it on the floor.

'Nearly, nearly, dead,' she sang. 'Dead, dead, dead.'

Herman Lang lost his leg under a bus. The thigh was ripped open and they sewed it up in Rutherford hospital. Then he came to Kelly's to convalesce. After two weeks a strange callous formed. The doctors were astounded. The callous grew larger and larger. Finally, when it broke open, there was a rubbery little leg inside.

'*Mon Dieu merci!*' my mother said, crossing herself.

Our mother and Ignace fought. In the living room, the kitchen, the halls and the bedroom. From the basement my father and I heard bodies flying against posts, knocking tins off pantry shelves.

'*Maudit qu't'é fou!*' she shouted. 'You are a fool!'

'I am not a fool!'

'A hairless albino!'

'I am but blond!'

The ironing board crashed into the door. Our mother must have grabbed him because he squealed and there was a sudden flurry of falling hammers and screwdrivers. Then the chase was on again, up the stairs, Ignace yelling, our mother swearing. He ran through the bedroom and down the lattice into the driveway.

'Come back, Ignace!'

'No.'

'Ignace!'

'NEVER!'

He ran down LeClerc, his shirt streaming out.

'IGNAAAACE!' she yelled.

What did they fight about? It was their secret.

St Croix attended the Swallowfield *variétés*. My father played the accordion *québécois* style, keeping time with his feet on wood blocks. Oberlander sang German lullabies. Semml and Gruel put on puppet shows. Heads of Diefenbaker and Eisenhower, Cardinal Léger, Hitler, Pope Pius XII and Chief Pontiac bobbed in the miniature world. In the gangways after midnight priests ran up and down the corridors keeping personalities from collapse.

Prisoners pedalled bicycles wired to batteries. When they pedalled hard enough, one electric bulb glowed. Prisoners cranked drills into a stone wall. When they broke through my father filled the hole with concrete blocks and they started again.

Barrault was strapped to a cart. His head swung into walls as the guards careened him around corners. Barrault was put in the cold boiler, water poured in, and when he fainted Gruel dragged him out. Oberlander oiled the drop hinge of the old gallows, laid a rope around Barrault's neck. Barrault fell in a dark rush to gunny sacks.

My father made Barrault stand in the corner.

'Touch his hand, Jean.'

I touched Barrault.

'Now look at your hand!' my father exclaimed.

'It's black!'

One night my father sent Barrault into the yard naked. He watched Barrault haul buckets of wet, heavy sand into the shed. Blue mist circled Barrault's head.

'Father, it is cold,' I said. 'It even rains.'

'You see how he is, the Jamaican,' my father whispered. 'His balls.'

'Like walnuts.'

'Even in the rain – '

'Which is raining harder,' I said. 'And so very cold.'

'How he dangles!'

We walked home. My father rubbed his face. Darkness hung over the bluffs. Green-white alkali fell from the leaves under the lamplights. We passed through the Protestant district, the tiny French quarter, past the fields. The bluffs were a big black block above us. The wharf was audible in a light rain on the lake. He tousled my hair.

'Jean?' he asked. 'What do you make of *négritude?*'

With the change in light my father became restless. He spent more time at the Bon Garçon. He would rub his crotch, look out at the windows where the brown, yellow leaves rustled.

'Just a minute,' he'd mumble. 'I'll be right down.'

He went upstairs to Agnes Moosefield. Once I crept upstairs and peeked in. Agnes was a fat Ojibway with a skirt that buttoned up the side. She had turned against a pink fringed

22

lamp and her black hair hid her face but she leaned over him, his long legs in khaki trousers.

'Ha ha,' she laughed. 'I've caught him! Oh my – that little mouse!'

He kept doing that, all the autumn.

Our parents had their bedroom next to ours. We heard them.

'Like this – ' he grunted.

'Jesus – '

'Ha. Damn right.'

'*Jésu* – '

'Yes – like that – oh, Christ – '

'Unh – '

'Uh – huh – huh – HUH – *OHHHHHH*!'

'*JÉSU* – !'

'*Merde*. That was a good one! Look at me. I sweat like a pig!'

When the leaves blew our mother came down the stairs, brushed her hair, her eyes fluttered, and she fell. We drove her to Rutherford general hospital. Everywhere was white, blinking, white uniforms, windows. They put her in a white gown, like an angel. They slid her on to a steel table and into a big metal tube. At eleven o'clock that night she came out, unkempt, hanging on the doctor, sleepily.

'I'm cold,' she said.

We drove her home. The bungalow houses of St Croix were squat, cold, and the windows black. No one was around, just the tax inspector.

'So very cold.'

Our father cleaned the house, washed the dishes, and gave her tea in bed. Morning came. Six-thirty with fat salmon clouds. We knew it would be a hard winter.

'In fact, I'm frozen.'

She wandered into the living room and broke the dishes in the cabinet. She tripped over Pippi. She watched the morning star rise over the *cimetière*. She didn't quite know where she was. Dr Lacomb examined the brain scan. Our mother, our pretty mother, had epilepsy.

Later that week Father Ybert came to have lemon cakes.

'When you came to St Croix you were perhaps too young,' he said.

'Jack took advantage of me.'

'He came early and stole the baby.'

'Now he comes in me Wednesday, Sunday, Tuesday, Saturday, Monday and Friday. Like rain he comes and goes, comes and goes.'

'Perhaps God was dissatisfied with Ignace and Jean-Michel.'

'Morning, noon, evening. Like a rooster. Boom. When I least expect it. Boom. Comes and goes.'

'It gives you no pleasure.'

'None.'

'Well. That is something.'

Father Ybert reached to the lemon cakes. She moved the iced butter closer.

'Jack *is* a vigorous man,' Father Ybert conceded.

'He has the constitution of a goat.'

'A rooster. A rabbit.'

'He comes home from the prison, red-faced and breathing hard,' she said. 'I pray, *Jésu, Seigneur du Monde, mon Amour Divin, from the depths of my horror you cannot forget me, I, who grew up in your house.*'

'But Jesu never comes?'

'Only Jack comes.'

'Suppose Jesu were to come?'

'Big trouble.'

Father Ybert's eyebrows raised.

'Why big trouble?'

'Isn't Jesu also a man?'

The Galtieau Cement Works closed. Galtieau padlocked the fence. There were rumours of unemployment at the prison. My father eased his anxiety by going into *la forêt*. He built a sweat lodge and squatted hours by the steaming rocks. By accident I found him. He beckoned me and poked his teeth with the point of his hunting knife.

'The Jamaican Barrault has contracted pleurisy,' he said.

'I warned you.'

'Can black men die of pleurisy?' he asked me.

'Yes.'

'Even like white men?'

'The skin counts for nothing.'

Depressed, we canoed up the inland waterway. We tied up at a tangle of hickory and I carried my father's sleeping bag on the shore. We got drunk on cherry brandy. While I staked up our tent, my father carried his rifle into the maples, shot a rabbit, and we marinated it in what was left of the brandy. We added garlic, thyme and chilli sauce my father had brought in jars. Outside the ferns smelled wet, black spores in the wind over rotted logs in the lakes.

'To have power over a man, Jean, as I have over you,' my father said moodily, stirring the embers, 'is the source of an inflamed blood.'

'I have it, too.'

'There is a kind of lava in the brain.'

'Do you have it with women, too?' I asked.

'It is a matter of the hard and soft.'

When we were through with the cherry brandy and rabbit we broke up our chocolate squares. It became warm in the tent.

'Listen to me, Jean,' he said. 'If your mother loved me as she used to do, I'd build her a cathedral so goddamn high she could fly in an aeroplane down the nave.'

He lay against hickory branches, lazily rubbing his penis.

'But she has made me a producer of tears,' my father said. 'I leak sorrow.'

'Even Ignace.'

'That hairless albino.'

'She gives you no pleasure?'

'I work in one prison and sleep in another.'

He became nostalgic.

'Your mother was sweet-meat, Jean. Little bum. Skirt you could see up when she tied her convent shoes.'

He was drowsy. I brought a bottle of wine from the boat. The wind blew the tent flaps open. I threw out dead twigs and pinned the flaps shut.

'You know where I uncorked her?' he asked.

'Yes.'

'In the Portobello Hotel.'

'You went to the ballroom first,' I said.

He giggled. The echo carried to the pines on an island in the lake. A hoot owl answered, lonely and still in the moonlight, beyond our shore.

'Partially,' he admitted. 'I went to the Oddfellows Hall where she served the St Bonaventure fish fry. I slipped her red wine. I induced her to accompany me to the Portobello Hotel where I completed what I had begun, and with extreme – may I say, oceanic – satisfaction.'

He saw the disgust on my face.

'The Portobello Hotel was not so run-down then,' he said defensively. 'There was a garden with tea roses. There was white paint on the windowsills. Municipal workers, fisheries men, came for tea and dance. But of course when they let in the Verhaerens the place went downhill.'

He got drunker.

'I tell you she was tight as a pig's bladder and warm as sour milk.'

He opened a second bottle of wine and drank until the red juice ran down his grizzled chin.

'Squealed like a butchered pig.'

'Papa. You excite yourself.'

'Let me tell you, I stuck it in many women.'

'*Oui, Papa.*'

'But only women.'

He fell against the tent's centre pole. I laid him in his sleeping bag. I put his pack under his head for a pillow.

'I bruised that skin like lilies,' he said. 'I broke her teeth. I made her vulgar. Once I locked her in the closet and banged pots and pans against the door.'

'You *have* suffered, Papa.'

'That is why she is crazy now.'

'Life is a sad trick.'

'I even wanted to kill her.'

'But you believe in *le bon Dieu*?'

'I am a man. I believe, but . . .'

He chewed tobacco now. His teeth were gummy with it. When he spat, it dribbled down his shirt.

'Bah,' he mumbled. 'We'll be dead some day. Eh? Fancy that. No more Verhaerens.'

I turned out the lantern. I felt for the wine bottle. He groped and kissed me on the back of the neck.

'One has such desires, Jean,' he said. 'One can die of such desires.'

I pulled the sleeping bag tight around his shoulders. He slept. I put out the fire. Fish broke water around our boat. I drank wine.

I made boats of yellow maple leaves and sailed them on a black pond. Suddenly the leaves parted. On a thick branch was an Ojibway corpse, crumpled on its wood platform, surrounded by liquor bottles and a transistor radio.

'A *chibay*!' I said.

I crossed myself. The wind rustled through the corpse's long black hair. It grinned, because its teeth came through rotted lips.

Jean . . . What do you make of all this?

The Verhaerens went to mass.

Poles came in farm wagons. Germans came in business suits. The birds called, sleepy-wet. Beggars came out, our one-legged veterans of Korea. They leaned against St Bonaventure. Silhouettes flew into the skies, circled the French quarter, the unsatisfied dead, from near, from far, in big circles.

I fell in love with Antoinette Hartmann.

She lived in a yellow clapboard house by the railroad tracks on Stewart Avenue. Her hair was curly brown and her eyes were hazel but sometimes green. There was a crazy kind of confidence in her eyes. She was a champion ice skater. The *buveurs* followed her home one day. She walked faster and faster and so did we until finally everybody was running. She jumped up her porch, ran inside, and slammed the door.

'That would have been *some* rape!' Herman Pic laughed, catching his breath, bent over.

I craned my head back:

'Cock-a-doodle-doo!'

I followed Antoinette everywhere, stood at dawn outside her house. I saw her face on my stairs, in the Dybs' smoke, turning in the air. She existed in a special way. I explained this to Ignace.

'Makes no sense,' he said, scratching his head.

I called her the Marquise. I stalked her. I jumped out at her from the oaks, my thumbs in my ears.

'ANTOINETTE!'

One night I ate supper alone. Ignace was at a seminary class in Winnipeg. My father was on night duty. My mother was at St Bonaventure making cinnamon candles. Pippi trotted into the kitchen and when he bent down to eat I smashed him.

'That's what it is to suffer!'

My father unexpectedly stormed into the kitchen, grabbed me by the shoulder, and backed me against the door.

'Did you hit Pippi?' he demanded.

'No. I swear.'

'Who made *caca* on the floor?'

'It wasn't I!'

'You blame Pippi?'

'*It wasn't I!*'

'It could not have been Ignace. *It is not aromatic!*'

He yanked my ears, one for soiling the kitchen floor, the other for lying.

I invited Antoinette Hartmann to Uncle Artur's garden party.

Red peppers, wheat wreaths, red apples, a persimmon branch, apricots, little tricolours bobbed in the stiff breeze over his allotment on the bluffs. Berries flamed in *la forêt*. Maple leaves fell, groaned, and took root. Black vines on Artur's wall blossomed against the purple western clouds. Teal and redheads droned over the marshes. Red lights bobbed with the trawlers.

'Look at the *belles!*' my father said, using the feminine for Antoinette and me as we came into the patio holding our lemonades. '*Quelles jolies!*'

My father sang in a deep bass:

> '*Approche, donc, ma belle*
> *Approche-toi, mon bien*
> *Pour mon âme apaiser*
> *Donne-moi un baiser.*'

Antoinette blushed, put down her lemonade, and danced with him. He stumbled drunkenly and sat down abruptly on a folding chair. She ended up on his lap. He rubbed her flat belly.

'How much you pay for this, Emil?' he asked.

'A hundred dollars,' Emil said.

'Georges?'

'Two hundred dollars!'

'Two thousand!' I shouted.

My father became overheated with drink. He threw a crumpled wad of Canadian bills on the table.

'But only I *have* money, you shit!' he said, nostrils flared. 'Eh? What about it? *Jean?*'

My mother came from the kitchen. Antoinette went back to the lemonade bowl. Paul Hartmann spoke to Emil about a job. Georges sang. My father got out his red accordion. Antoinette and I danced.

'Do you like me, Antoinette?' I asked.

'You?'

'You find me amusing.'

She laughed.

'Well, you're so strange.'

'Antoinette – '

Somebody knocked over the lanterns. The dance was over. Herman Pic came with his date Edith Knobler. Danny Auban came with Sandy Gillickson. Strangers came, then relations of strangers. Gruel came, LeFèvre, Wils, Semml, Amboise, the French guards. The Zylches came, and Red Two Hats. Zena Courennes started throwing dishes, swearing. My mother sucked from the wrong watermelon and got dizzy with rum.

Pippi escaped and ran across the field. I brought Pippi back. Antoinette stumbled under the Chinese lanterns. Her weary, drunken, beautiful face grew transparent. Oak seeds twirled behind her transparent eyes. Everybody suddenly grew transparent.

'Antoinette!' I yelled.

I beat the snare drum like a maniac.

Rain, autumn, all over the French quarter. I went to visit Antoinette Hartmann.

I oiled my hair, stuck my jacket collar high, cleaned my boot cleats. A storm brewed. Leaves were flying all over the place. I could hardly see. A brassy light came from her house window and telephone wires shrieked. I crawled through the hedge and peeked inside. She stood on a red carpet which curved at the bottom of the stairwell. She straddled the banister.

She saw me peering in. Sweat ran down her neck. Her hands were white-knuckled. She pumped furiously.

'I can't help it!'

I backed away and tripped over a garden hose. Suddenly Antoinette's house divided. Rain poured in, glittery silver, on piano, portraits, wax fruit, oval mahogany dining table. Yet nothing got wet. The lights never even dimmed. Antoinette went upstairs. After a while she came out, zipping up her black and white jacket. I followed her up Stewart Avenue.

'I *saw* you in the storm,' I accused. 'The whole house divided.'

'You had no business peeping.'

'Your face was red, your eyes hollow.'

'I was in a compulsion.'

She walked fast under the maples. She was embarrassed to be with me. I double-stepped to keep up under the swinging streetlights.

'We were meant to be together,' I said.

'Us? Impossible.'

'Antoinette, you don't have to *do* anything – !'

She took out a steak sandwich, unwrapped it from wax paper, and shivered as she chewed, as though I had put a bad taste in her mouth.

'I'm not doing *anything* with *you*.'

THREE

I became a sailor.

I stole a ride on the *Deux Amours*. The freighter carried bleached cotton to Michigan. As I watched, St Croix receded through a porthole. The porch of the Hotel Portobello had crumbled in the storm and white water ran through its timbers. It was raining over HM Prison Swallowfield. The mines steamed in the dawn. Then Gilbertsonville and Heron Bay thinned to a hard grey line.

Lake Superior threw grey waves breaking. Pines whipsawed on dunes. The waters heaved. The dirty lake sprayed into the hold, over the cotton crates. The rain grew worse. I crouched in the dark *Deux Amours* and prayed on my St Christopher medal.

Deux Amours crossed Lake Superior, crossed the International Boundary, and came to Keweenaw Peninsula. We backed into Portage Lake canal and dropped anchor at Houghton. L'Anse Indians came from the grey wash in black oilslicks and carried drills and iced fish in flat containers into the holds. The freighter picked up smoked ham and slipped out the peninsula. It was night. I smelled stunted pines but saw nothing of the United States.

Because of high winds and waves the freighter was kept off at Marquette. Lights bobbed in the dark. About midnight the hatch opened, water poured in. A sailor came down, found me, and hauled me up.

'Who are you?' he asked, shaking me.

'Canadian.'

'Well, that's a hell of a place, Canada.'

He dumped me on a crate of bleached cotton. The captain came. Two mariners, then three more, stood around me below the light streaming down the hatch.

'*Pourquoi tu es caché chez le freighter?*' the captain put together in French. 'Why are you hiding here?'

'I'm running away.'

'Why?'

'Because the woman I love doesn't love me.'

'If you're looking for love – '

The captain rubbed his grizzled chin. I stopped rubbing my calf, which had cramped. I pulled my trouser leg down.

'There's a Czech circus,' a sailor said. 'It tours. It's at the train station.'

The captain blew his nose.

'Get out of here,' he said.

I picked up my duffel bag with its portrait of Pius XII, postcards of St Croix, underwear, my St Bonaventure scarf. I passed the customs and excise building. The rainwater was so bright that when I threw up it was in a hall of mirrors. There was a cinema with posters of a huge blonde, a lingerie store, a pornography shop. In a dark bungalow house married women sewed by a window lamp. High-school girls bent, going by, in the squall.

I went to the train station. The Czech circus was not there. I wandered back into town. People ducked into the spray. I was curious about the United States. I visited the police museum.

The building had been a dry cleaner's. Now the exhibits were framed and screwed on to metal folding tables. On a red cloth were mannikins of the Grayback twins, their necks broken. Behind them was a lacquered yellowed newspaper: *Death with a Crowbar in Negaunee*. There was a doll with nylon stockings around its neck: *Louise Flecks Strangled in Skanee*. A doll was slumped against a railroad tie: *Herman Dodd – Nail Pounded into Back of His Head*. Upstairs was Helen Leszke, barbed-wired to a chair: *Tied with Wire, Left to Die*.

In the chemicals room were forensic tools: awls, forceps, pipettes. There were signed photographs of the Marquette policemen playing baseball. I went to the buffet and stole a sandwich.

I went back to the station. Trains slid through steam, dissolving, trains coming in, waiting, going out. There was no Czech circus.

I wandered Marquette again. Spray lurched through the streets, parking lots, Americans jumping over flooded gutters, cars stalled. I went into a billiards hall and slept behind a Coke machine. All night a calendar of pornographic women fluttered over my head. In the morning the owner threw me into the alley. Canada was nowhere, a wall of rain in the north.

I went back to the station. The Czech circus had come. An American man opened the door of a rear compartment. I put my ear to the door.

'So, this is your first time?' a Czech girl asked.

'I am new to this.'

'To this, too?'

'I am so large!' he exclaimed.

'Every American's tool.'

'Like a telephone pole!'

'Now do like this – ' she said.

'Mama – yes, oh Mama – that's good. That's very good – '

'Oooooooo. He hurts me!'

'Do I? That excites me!'

'Uhhhhhh!'

'AHHHHHH!'

'OOOOOHHHH!'

'EEEEEHHHH!'

'Oh . . . my . . .'

'So that is what it is all about . . .' he said.

I walked to the head of the train where a Czech sat under an iron lamp. He had blue shade where he shaved. Behind him more Czechs rolled crates toward the freight cars. The Czech turned at a noise and yelled. One of the circus workers had dropped a heavy box. There were no animals, just crates and heavy boxes. He turned back to me, handed me a cigarette.

'I want to join the circus,' I said.

'You're Ojibway?' he asked.

'No.'

'Basque?'

'French.'

The Czech turned again and shouted at the circus handlers. He turned back to me.

'What can you do?' he asked.

'Anything.'

The Czech girl walked to our bench. She wore a white and black checked coat. She walked carefully, like she'd had an operation. Her slender lips were blue with cold. She sat down.

'This is Lilaine,' the Czech said.

Lilaine sat with her hands in her coat pockets, legs straight out in front of her, staring at her white boots. Her thin body was heavy. One had the impression of a great heaviness, though she was slender. She smelled of lilacs. She had a beautiful smile and speckles on her forehead. She had scars on her wrists.

'You like her, don't you?' the Czech asked.

'Yes.'

'Lilaine speaks English, German, French, Mexican, Basque and Romany.'

'Would she speak to me?'

'Lilaine will do anything you ask.'

'Anything at all?'

'Anything.'

'Extraordinary,' I said. 'How like a doll she is.'

I watched her face.

'Where do you come from, Lilaine?' I asked.

'Lübeck.'

Sheets of filthy water thundered on the glass roof. Grit sluiced down the girders. The concrete was cold and wet and we were chilled. A guard came down the concrete and the Czech looked away. When the guard passed the Czech looked at me again. Lilaine's silver eyes stared ahead, their pupils black, wet black.

'Lilaine,' I whispered. 'What is it like being a woman?'

'What a strange question,' she said.

'Are all women like you?'

'Of course.'

Her accent changed, more French.

'But aren't women different?' I asked.

'Different from men.'

'What is it like,' I asked, 'being you?'

She cleared her eyes by bringing her forefingers to the bridge of her nose. By now her accent was identical to mine.

'He is a strange boy,' she said.

'Tell me,' I begged.

She trembled, looked up at the rain. She sighed, but her breath did not come out evenly.

The Czech Girl

'I WAS AN ORPHAN.

'I grew up on a farm near Lübeck, Germany. It was after the war and many people had been killed and many were starving. I was sold to a Protestant sect that forbade speech on the Sabbath. Their dialect was hard to understand, even for the Germans.

'I had epilepsy. Like a winter wind that threw snow these blizzards blew across my brain. I forgot everything. Every morning the brethren taught me to feed the pigs, pluck the chickens, bake bread. Every night I forgot.

'After ritual bathing in the forest – even in winter – we read from the Bible. We made a special kind of cheese bread with pork in it and set it under the beds at night so nobody would have to cook on the Sabbath. On Sunday we took the *Betenbrot* to Bible meetings. Afterwards we came home over the snow and ice. There were crystals in my eyes. By Monday I had forgotten the Bible.

'My parents – all the brethren were my parents – taught me again the German script. They explained the meaning of *Himmelreich*, *Ewigkeit*, *Seele*. I was quick, and copied out the prophets' names: *Jeremiah*, *Isaiah*, and *Messiach*. They kissed me. They embraced me. We prayed together on the floor. But, of course, by afternoon, or the next morning, I had forgotten everything.

'They made me stand naked in the snow. My mothers hit me with a poker. But what could I do? It wasn't my fault. I forgot who these Germans were and why they had power over me.

'A stone wall separated the pigs from the kitchen. From them I caught a sickness that made my ears run red. I was afraid of the dark forest. Deer ran out into our farm. The brethren stunned them and killed them. They skinned the deer and sold the meat to the village. I was afraid of the boys that worked as itinerants. They were rough, and crude, and they snored. Every night I pushed my dresser in front of my door.

'The brethren took me to Lübeck. There was a medieval market with a fifteenth-century clock. At the hour the people stopped selling and watched. Two knights came out and jousted. The red knight fell dead. The black knight went forward into the clock. The merchants heard the bells all over Lübeck. The brethren sold me to the Lollingen family. I was eight. The Lollingens were well known in northern Germany. Gunther and Waldemar were the brothers. Fernand, Anton, Petrus and Klackus with the bowed legs were the cousins. The wives were Agatha, Elsbeth, Marie and Katrine. They spoke Romany, a strange language.

'I slept in Petrus's wagon. There was a red mannikin nailed to my bed named Malthusius. I was told Malthusius would stick briars in my eyes unless I did what Elsbeth told me to do. Elsbeth came in to stroke my hair.

'"*Cashty natty*," Elsbeth whispered. "Good night."

'My wagon creaked when we were moving. Malthusius grinned down at me. Straw flowers rubbed against the red paint. The moon came and went, came and went, through the wagon opening. There was a smell of cognac. But it couldn't mask a strange stink.

'Klackus named our horses dirty names in German:

'*Plackscheisser, Unflath, Nessler, Matzpompe, Misthammel, Gorsthammel, Kuh-Fladen.*

'Occasionally a drunkard peered in. Petrus or Klackus threw him back. The Lollingens performed magic tricks, gymnastics, and animal acts. I had a thin soprano and beat a snare drum. Petrus's wife twirled a red crêpe. A peasant bet his wife on a cock fight and after he lost Anton tried to collect. There was a fight with pitchforks and we moved to Kiel.

'The Lollingens lived in canvas tents that bent around a black pole. We slept on grey blankets sewn together, carpets with scarlet braid and scarlet pillows. The kettle hung over a fire. We boiled tea and dried Norwegian fish called *matjo*. We ate *balivar* and *goodloo*, bacon sugar. Petrus was a hunter and shot rabbits in the black forests. We travelled to Bavarian villages.

'They hung Sapeau the snake from a rafter in my wagon. They said Sapeau would bite me if I didn't obey.

'"*Rankny rackly*," Marie whispered, putting scarlet ribbons in my hair. "Pretty girl."

'They pierced my ears and hung gold hoops. They dyed my hair red. They put sparkle on my hands and forehead. Klackus was an expert *boshimengro*, a fiddler. Polkas were popular in the woods. They sent me in to dance with peasant men.

'She introduced me to a Bavarian peasant. But I didn't remember what happened next.

'"*Boro rye*," she said as he left, counting money. "A great gentleman."

'They called me dirty endearments in German:

'*Pritsche, Sackgen, Klunte, Hurenbag, Schandbalg.*

'By morning I always forgot everything. My wagon walls were luminescent with silver that sparkled down the rafters. A giant snail must have crawled through. The crescent moon shone through the earth's blue haze.

'Elsbeth sang a song in Basque:

> '"*Chorinac kaiolan*
> *Tristeric du caulatcen,*
> *Duelarican cer jan*
> *Cer edan,*
> *Campoa du desiratceu;*

38

Ceren, ceren
Libertutia hain eder den."

"Little bird in the cage
Sings sadly
What to eat
What to drink
He wants to be free
Because, because
Nothing is sweet but liberty."

'We went down the rutted roads of Bavaria. The maples swirled red. Klackus's long knives jangled in black holsters. Turquoise and silver hung from my canopy. *Spielverderber*, our mastiff, killed a rabbit. Petrus had a curious round stone around his neck which he made me touch.

'I went into the disappearing cabinet for Gunther's magic. Klackus twirled his *fjukei*, the bamboo cane, both ends loaded with lead, and beat up a policeman. We had to leave Bavaria. Elsbeth hung Tjun the knife over my bed. She told me Tjun would pry out my eyes if I did not obey.

'Petrus made up morality plays to suit the mentality of the Catholic villages. In those parables of Jesus, the Devil, and Pontius Pilate the Devil won every scene except the last. We performed along the frozen streams, in taverns, in warehouses. We crossed into Bohemia.

'Villages had been burned. Trains were still derailed. Tanks lay inside out in ditches and buildings had bloodstains on the walls. I saw a peasant woman give birth standing up. We stripped bodies and pried out the gold in their teeth. The Italian and Yugoslav borders closed so we slipped into lower Austria. The blue fog streaked in from the marshes, obscuring the white Austrian churches. We set up on the frozen plain of St Pölten. Petrus and Klackus slit a fox and threw the entrails to *Spielverderber*. Every night they dressed me in red fox fur.

'"*Juch he! Wer wollte traurig seyn?*" Klackus laughed, ringing the bell outside my wagon. "Who wants to be sad?"

'One night I escaped. The chains must have broken. Elsbeth

grabbed me but slipped and fell. I stumbled across the frozen marsh. As I crossed a frozen pond in the moonlight, iced cat-tails snapped and sprayed me with silver crystal. I went further and further, into the wide open, Austrian stars shining over the black forest. The moon turned upside down. The ponds suddenly chimed like glockenspiels.

'The Virgin Mary glided over the forest. She sat on a blue pillow. Starlight streamed up from her beautiful bare feet.

'"*Thou hast suffered,*" the Virgin told me, "*in the manner of women.*"

'"Dear Mother of God – " I prayed, kneeling in the snow.

'"*Therefore, thou art blessed.*"'

'Gunther caught me, dragged me back to the wagons, and made me drink horses' urine. They hung weights from my ankles. They burned my neck with hot gasoline rags. But I was not afraid.

'The Lollingens sold me to a Romanian who broke my arm and pulled out clumps of my red hair. The Romanian sold me to an Italian policeman who took me on his boat on Lake Constance. When he was through with me he sold me to a munitions dealer in Montreal. In Canada I was used for parties and he gave me to his partner who sold me to a cement manufacturer in Sudbury. Chinese merchants sold me to the Czechs and now I work the summer fairs.

'I remember when it rains.'

FOUR

My father belted me twelve times by the coal bin. I became delirious. My lungs filled with damp. My father made soup of sheep's brains and bathed me. Then he set me on clean sheets in the living room. My mother swept a broom over my chest, sweeping away the sickness.

> '*D'une feuille on fit son habit*
> *Mon Dieu! quel homme*
> *Quel petit homme!*
> *D'une feuille on fit son habit*
> *Mon Dieu! quel homme*
> *Qu'il est petit!*'

I laughed. Because like the little man who had a leaf for a coat I was small for my age.

> 'Of a leaf he makes his clothes
> Dear Lord! What a man!
> What a little man!
> Of a leaf he makes his clothes
> Dear Lord! What a man!
> So very small!'

I dreamed I chased Czech women. I woke in St Croix. I got to the linoleum, to my knees to pray in gratitude. But I must have been still dreaming because suddenly a gigantic hand, invisible and furious, grabbed me by the seat of my pants and threw me out the window, high over the Dybs' roof.

In spirals of black, dead trees I fell, fell, and woke up in St Bonaventure, taking an algebra exam.

Father Przybilski punished me for truancy. He made me turn the harmonium, a blue wooden post with a heavy crossbar in the courtyard. One walked it round and round until it squealed. But the rain had lubricated the post. I couldn't get a sound. Catholic boys watched from woodworking class, Catholic girls from the caged housewifery windows.

'There's no *music!*' the boys yelled.

I pushed until I drooled. The rain blew into my face. I prayed to St Martin to let me die. I saw two suns, one over the housewifery roof, the second, oblong and red, above the laundry room.

'There's no *music!*' the girls yelled.

I saw St Christopher at the gymnasium window.

'There's no *music!*' St Christopher yelled.

Every night at seven we listened to Cardinal Léger on the radio. We recited the rosary with him. Afterwards our mother turned on the brass lamp. She was illiterate, as I said, so Ignace read aloud the *Diocesan Newsletter* while I played my father's red accordion. The Dybs' house glowed into our house from the purple twilight. Brown leaves rattled at the gutters. Headlights swept down LeClerc, turning Ignace's face chalky.

'An eighteen-year-old girl crippled from birth decided to visit her former Mother Superior in Quebec,' Ignace read. 'She left St Croix at midnight and crawled east to Highway 17. She was seen by two labourers who raped her and left her in a ditch. The police arrived, by which time she had crawled a further quarter-mile east.

'The Poniatowskis took up a collection and drove her to the Greyhound station, where they bought her a ticket to Quebec. She prostrated herself before her Mother Superior, who recognized her, and cured her with a sprig of holly. The girl rode back to Gilbertsonville. The moon shape was gone from her face.'

We crossed ourselves.

'*Le bon Dieu soit béni!*' our mother whispered.

My father taught me to be a prison guard.

'When the vice-warden comes, step aside,' he said. 'Tilt from the chest and cock your head, like this – but when the warden comes, take two steps backward. You do not breathe. It is offensive to him. You make your eyes to him. By this incorporeal contact he knows you are his.'

'Yes, Papa.'

'But as for the other guards watch for the knife in the back. Remember: in prison friendships are provisional.'

'Yes.'

'And life itself is a prison.'

'It is clear to me.'

'Oh, Jean. What a future you have!'

Two prisoners jumped into Swallowfield's well. Guards shot into the well. My father pumped ammonia down the shaft. Later the guards found interlocked prisoners' hands on the banks of the Petit Croix. My father varnished them, and put them in his black museum.

'Nobody escapes Jack Verhaeren,' he muttered.

Red Two Hats, my father and I went hunting.

Shafts of sun poured into *la forêt*. Gold, brittle ferns carpeted the red maple leaves. Bark became moths and flew into the shadows. Toadstools spat spores as we trudged through. Red shot a small buck, strung it up outside his quonset hut in Ojibway Flats and boiled the brains.

'Jack,' Red said. 'I'll give you a haunch.'

'That's for you.'

'No. You take it. You got kids to feed.'

'Thanks, Red.'

Red brought a branch from the fire and lighted his cigar.

'What you give me in return?' Red asked.

My father rubbed the sweat from his face with his khaki sleeve.

'Oh hell. Take Jean.'

Jack DePré's penis died. We saw it in the locker room. It turned purple, fell in ribbons, hung in maroon threads and finally fell off. All that was left on him was a vertical scar.

The rain cleared. Blue skies arched over the bluffs. Loggers' dust churned white in *la forêt*. Freighters, barges, the moored pleasure boats, bobbed in calm shadows. Our twilights were touched with indigo. Mallards flew over the reeds in V-formation.

Etienne Bastide applied to join *les buveurs*. He was blond with a rosy complexion and blue eyes. We led him up the bluffs, blindfolded him, forced him to drink three pints of Lamont's Ale, twirled him around, and ripped off the blindfold. In this way he saw the falseness of St Croix. We asked his story.

'One day, last summer, I stole a chicken and my father's rowboat,' Etienne said, staring at his interlocked pink fingers. 'I rowed to the Galtieau Cement Works. By the time I came around Ojibway Flats I could see all of St Croix, brown houses with white stains like rooster shit. The chicken jumped from between my legs and drowned.

'A submarine surfaced. The captain came out of the hatch, a bearded man with pearl buttons. I got in, and we submerged. There was almost no light, only a dim red electric bulb in the ceiling. Shrimp eggs trailed up past the porthole. I could hardly breathe. Red mist came out of drains in the ceiling.

'In dark chambers naked men were covered in clay. By their sides were brass canisters which contained their names. They ate dirt from pewter plates and dust from lead goblets. I was frightened by the loose flabs of skin that folded down their chests. A mariner caught me watching and cuffed me behind the ears. I fought hard but he strapped a coffin on me.

'"Are we being taken to Nipigon?" I asked, "to work the fishing boats?"

'He didn't answer.

'"Are we being taken across Lake Erie," I asked, "to pick hops?"

'He didn't answer.

'"Are we going to Sudbury to work the steel mills?" I asked.

'"YOU'RE GOING TO DETROIT TO BE MALE PROS-TITUTES!" he screamed.

'The dead men turned away, ashamed. Suddenly there were depth charges. The submarine tilted, drifted, and then the propellers chewed grit. Stokers, completely naked in the heat, sweating by the red furnaces, were swept away in explosions of water. Religious icons bobbed around our feet. I escaped through a hatch, swam up and floated to St Croix.'

We blinked at Etienne Bastide. Nobody knew what to say. Etienne also looked embarrassed.

'Do I hallucinate?' he finally asked. 'I haven't even told Father Przybilski!'

I jumped up and pounded my fist on the table.

'Etienne Bastide is admitted,' I said, 'because he told us fiction *as though it was truth!*'

Etienne Bastide performed magic.

I visited him on LeClerc. Drawings of the St Lawrence Seaway hung on the stairwell. He had a beautiful sister named Katherine and the first time I saw her she came from the bathroom in a white terrycloth robe. She had eyes black as midnight.

'So,' she said, smiling strangely. 'Etienne's little friend.'

Etienne took me to his bedroom. The bedroom was wallpapered with designs of cowboys, his butterfly collection was on his dresser. He had a collection of blue clowns. He made two of them bounce on the bed, fast, then slow, turning slow somersaults, sparkling, rainbows.

He put a hand on my shoulder.

'I can make them do anything,' he told me.

There was an invasion of pond snails that autumn. Etienne and I collected them on the breakwater. The snails had a layered sac and genital ducts, blue mouths that led to the alimentary canal, which M. d'Aube called *invagination*. These shelled worms clogged the wharves, leaving slick trails.

'*Garde!*' Etienne said, pointing. 'They ejaculate into the air!'

'Why?'

'It is a compulsion.'

'Such a compulsion.'

Etienne nudged me.

'You, too,' he whispered. 'Soon. Very soon. Oh, soon.'

Etienne got a job at the Fleur de France bakery. He patted buns in a white cubicle behind blue ovens. He wore a white apron with a blue ribbon. I watched him pull the dough.

'This is the *levain de chef*,' Etienne said. 'This is the *levain de première*.'

Etienne adjusted his white paper cap. At that time he was not yet taller than I. His cheeks were flushed from the oven heat. His blue eyes, small and wet, watched me.

'Save me a *tarte*,' I said.

'For you. Here.'

Etienne gave me an almond *tarte*. It was hot and full. I bit into it. It was like biting into life itself.

'Jean,' he said, wiping my chin. 'You eat like a pig.'

'Could I have another?'

'Jean,' he said. 'Divine Jean-Michel of Canada.'

The nights were getting cold. I sat on the red divan, reading *Gasoline Alley*. My father came home, crossed the kitchen in giant steps and slapped me.

'How *dare* you be happy,' he hissed, 'when others suffer!'

I went to the boiler room of St Bonaventure. I threw a wire over the heating duct, tied it around my neck, and jumped into the coal-bin. Electricity exploded in my brain. It was Etienne Bastide. He was at the door. He had turned on the light.

'Jean – ' he blurted. 'I love you – '

★   ★   ★

46

Father Przybilski slapped me in his office.

'*On est bête, c'est pour longtemps,*' he said. 'Stupidity is for a long time.'

Father Przybilski twirled his sharp pencil. He didn't know what to do with me. The tall windows were filled with blue skies, tiny horsefeather clouds, wisps of cold. He adjusted his glasses.

'You like Etienne Bastide?' he asked.

'He is nice.'

'In fact, you are quite fond of him.'

'He is very nice.'

'You love him?'

'He is extremely nice.'

'Do you think he will love a suicide?'

'I don't want to be Catholic.'

'Well, it's too late *now*, Jean-Michel!'

I had to shovel coal after school for a week. Etienne watched from the chute hatch, his blue shirt neatly starched.

Etienne bombarded me with gifts: a glass paperweight of St Croix, a Sauk headdress, slippers, drawings of Katherine on blue paper with charcoal. I sucked his minted vapour drops. Etienne brought fudge. We ate sweets during the darkening days, Etienne and I.

We sat together in religion class.

'Luther was born in 1483 of Catholic parents,' Father Ybert lectured. 'He was instructed in the Roman Catholic faith and entered the order of the Eremites of St Augustine. He learned much but he became proud. He quarrelled with the monks. They refused him the office of prior so he left the monastery and became addicted to lascivious music. He went to brothels. He joined the nun Katherine von Bora in a God-robbing marriage.

'Luther perverted the true Gospel. He spread heresies. He split with Calvin and Melanchthon and died of the cholic in a drunken stupor in 1546. His corpse was carried from Eisleben to Wittenberg by an airborne devil.'

Etienne squeezed my hand.

'Luther was a doctor of Godlessness, a professor of villainy,

47

an apostate, a God-hating fornicator, and author of the *Augsburg Confession*. There are one thousand Lutherans in St Croix and they have all read the *Augsburg Confession*!'

Etienne was sweating.

I visited Uncle Bobo.

He worked in the fisheries for M. d'Aube, a low concrete building with dangling lights. Bobo had Reynaud's disease. His fingers were dead. He banged them on M. d'Aube's desk and soaked them in hot water but he felt nothing. Bobo's smock was smeared with fish eggs. He showed me the lampreys.

'They suck and suck,' Bobo told me. 'When they are through, they drop off.'

M. d'Aube hooked a lamprey and pried its mouth open. Circular teeth in double rows gleamed under the violet light. The urogenital canal flickered. Bobo took the eel in both hands to the laboratory desk. M. d'Aube smashed its head with a ballpeen hammer.

'There are men like this, too,' M. d'Aube warned.

'I am careful, Monsieur d'Aube,' I said.

'I must be blunt, Michel. You are not careful.'

He slit the eel's belly and dug out the egg sac with a gloved forefinger. He unwound the long intestine. He squeezed it down until white fluids oozed into his glass bowl.

'You think you walk a broad road,' he said. 'I tell you, it becomes thin as a razor.'

M. d'Aube poured the lamprey entrails into a pink solution. He washed his hands three times. He put a hand on my shoulder and offered me a Player's.

'*Tiens.*'

'*Merci.*'

Outside, red leaves lay wet and bright in the spray of the trout tanks.

'With respect, Michel,' he repeated, very softly, looking up at the blue sky. 'You are not careful.'

The September fête began.

St Croix's stores suddenly filled with religious emblems,

icons and corn-husk memorabilia. Brass chandeliers, *bijoux* of amber, hung in our doorways. Basques hung lakeshore moss. Germans roared in Gustave's Tavern. Suddenly a Roman candle appeared on the bluffs, visible from the middle of Lake Superior.

A Ferris wheel, five generators, a mystery house, and goldfish games rolled on to Swallowfield Meadows. Rockets went up at midnight. Romanians juggled knives. Catholic tents sold rosaries, coral crucifixes, folding leather prayer cards. Father Ybert heard confession under a white awning. My father patrolled *la forêt*. With a flashlight he found couples and doused them with a bucket of water.

'*Fas attention, monsieur!*' he warned. 'You'll get stuck!'

Ignace was Catholic Boy Bishop. He paraded the fair-grounds in a satin gown, reciting Latin, casting water with a pussy willow. He was nervous and had practised for hours at home in the afternoon.

'Saint Ignace!' Danny Auban shouted.

'No,' Ignace said modestly. 'I am but the Boy Bishop.'

By night the *buveurs* gathered around orange sparks flying high, a bonfire that burned horse manure. Black rivers of air twisted up to the stars. There was no Canadian flag then so we made our own, and flew it higher than the Polish double-headed and the German imperial eagle. Protestants burned an effigy of Pius so we crossed Isle of May Street and threw firecrackers at their punch parties.

Mormons sold *manna-cakes* of walnuts and honey. Jehovah's Witnesses fried *Kingdom fritters*. Austrian sausages sizzled. Yugoslavs carved a spitted beef. Smoke of kebabs rose into the moonlight and Poles hosed beer from barrels into glass mugs. We ate apples, *foie gras*, onions frying in butter. We Europeans threw up all over *la forêt*.

Etienne and I got drunk. Malt ales, lagers, rum, gin and whisky sloshed in cups on planks suspended between barrels at the Belgian tent. Etienne and I got really drunk. In the lights of HM Prison Swallowfield's black gothic gates, polka bands played. Flatulence rose like perfume, spiralling through the shafts of floodlights. One smelled sex in the cold wet grass. Couples danced on platforms. Etienne and I got piss drunk.

We danced under blue pennants, Etienne and I, and ended up in the white birches.

'Jean,' he said unsteadily.

'*Quoi?*'

'Well?'

Moonbeams twisted down the resinous oaks between the birches. Etienne trembled. I trembled a bit, too.

'Why not?' I asked.

I looked around. It was dark as a cow's belly. I couldn't see my hand in front of my face. We stumbled a few steps over rotted logs and groped toward the heat of each other's face.

'There's no one around,' he whispered.

'No one.'

'No one at all.'

I touched his chest.

'Etienne!' I said. 'You're going to have a heart attack!'

I leaned, he leaned. We missed. Suddenly he grabbed my face in both hands and jammed his lips into mine. I tasted new, red wine. He backed away. The moon came out. His blue eyes widened as though he had just learned something.

'I didn't hurt you, Jean?'

'You bit me.'

'Yes. I think I did. Here's my handkerchief.'

My arms felt so heavy I could hardly lift them.

'I can't.'

'Then let me, Jean.'

Etienne dabbed my lip. We walked back through the bracken to the dancing crowds. Faces of St Croix sweated. We were sweating, too.

'I'll go first,' Etienne whispered.

He walked into the crowd. I joined him later at the kielbasa counter. Everything was as it had been. And if it wasn't, whose business was it?

In the morning, there was frost.

I sang:

'De Bretagne sur l'eau
L'enfant arrive trop tôt
Son nom fut Jean-Michel
Un petit cochon-o

'Ah tra la la
Et la la la.

'From Brittany over the water
Came a baby much too soon
His name was Jean-Michel
A little pig-o.

'Ah tra la la
And la la la.'

It was dark on LeClerc Street. Sweat ran down our windows. My father sucked noodles and dumped red cayenne powder on to his potatoes. He gripped his fork convulsively, his skull visible under his red hair. The shrimp and noodles, bread and cayenne, came toward his mouth and he stared at them coming until he was cross-eyed. Our father was obsessed. With what was he obsessed? With Gregors Illuskvi, the Ukrainian guard who reported him for abusing Barrault.

Ignace smirked as he sucked his fingers. I smelled darkness like Swallowfield's drains.

'Etienne Bastide called for you,' Ignace said.

'Who?' I asked.

'Etienne Bastide.'

'When?'

'While you were out.'

'Are you friendly with the Bastide?' my father asked.

'I know him.'

'*Jean est amoureuse!*' Ignace hooted, using the feminine.

My father stopped chewing and stared at me, and his cheeks bulged with cayenne potatoes.

'Do you touch?' he asked.

'We do not touch.'

'*The higher climbs the monkey, the redder is its bottom,*' my mother giggled.

51

My mother put her delicate hand over her mouth. She raised a knowing eyebrow.

'*La p'tite Jean est amoureuse,*' she said, again in the feminine.

'Shut up,' I said. 'I am in a bad mood.'

Ignace lay on his bed in his white underpants, the only thing visible sometimes on those dark nights.

'Jean,' he said. 'I am afraid.'

'Of what are you afraid?'

'Of you.'

'Me?'

He turned over. Ignace had two navels. It embarrassed him. The pillow was pale. It blended with his shoulders.

'You and Etienne.'

'Meaning what?'

'Some day you will die, Jean. Then what?'

'I'm dead.'

Ignace believed in Satan. Bodiless, Satan grew trumpets for hair and French horns for shoulders. He lived in a walnut coffin fifteen feet long in *la forêt* and from the coffin a profane hurdy-gurdy shook the trees so down came the autumn leaves, regrets of the damned.

Ignace sang. I accompanied him on a concertina.

> '*Il fut, part un triste sort,*
> *Blessé d'une main cruelle*
> *On croit, puisqu'il en est mort*
> *Que la plaie était mortelle.*'

Ignace's voice was maudlin.

> 'He was by a sad fate
> Wounded by a cruel hand
> And is known to be dead
> For the wound was mortal.'

'The wound was mortal,' I reprised.

> *'Il mourut le vendredi*
> *Le dernier jour de son âge;*
> *S'il fut mort le samedi*
> *Il eut vécu d'avantage.'*

> 'He died on Friday
> The last day of his life
> If he had died on Saturday
> It would have been better.'

'It would have been better,' I reprised.

Then Ignace lay still, one forearm over his eyes, imagining his death, drowned in Georgian Bay.

'Am I lovely?' he asked after a while.

'You are white as a shroud.'

'Men are not lovely. But I believe in man, Jean. I believe man is capable of anything.'

'Under certain circumstances.'

Ignace became sad.

'Is it possible to speak with you spiritually?' he asked.

'No.'

'Lies, intrigues, slanders.'

'So? I find it difficult to be sincere.'

'Frankly, you are impossible.'

Etienne and I walked by the black canal. We went under the trestle bridge by Galtieau's yard. Branches and dead leaves floated by. A naphtha fire burned red behind the dry cleaner's. Etienne coughed, a long stringy filament. When I looked I saw that filaments hung from telephone wires all over town.

'Perhaps we shall go too far,' Etienne said. 'Our involvement.'

'Are you afraid?'

'I fear some things, Jean.'

'What?'

'Some things in particular.'

He spat green.

'Are you spitting because of me?' I asked.

'Against trouble, in general.'

My feelings for Etienne changed. It blew up one night at the Shell station where Paul Hartmann worked. The fluorescent lights sent a cold, flickering light over the *buveurs* who drank and played cards. It was grotesque. Our flesh looked decayed.

'Play, Jean,' Etienne said.

'I'm playing.'

'With whom?'

The card-playing stopped. All we heard was Paul's radio. I dropped my cards.

'Meaning what?'

'One hears – ' Etienne said.

'What?'

'You are still in love with Antoinette Hartmann.'

'One hears,' I said. '*One hears*. ONE HEARS. St Croix is full of ONE HEARS and never ONE KNOWS!'

I stood up. So did Etienne. The two chairs tumbled backwards on to the concrete. Paul Hartmann pulled us down to our chairs.

'*Buveurs*,' he said gently. 'Please. We are *buveurs*.'

Etienne and I shook hands. But if I had had a shotgun I would have blown his head off.

That night I couldn't sleep. I heard a noise and crept downstairs. Green mantises, six feet tall, stood upright in a cold green light and ate Etienne's gifts. They chewed his paperweight and Sauk headdress and spat them as sawdust on the floor.

Uncle Bobo died.

A freak accident – the petri dish broke in the fisheries incubator. He was infected through an open sore, lay down on his cot, went into convulsions, and died. We walked home after the funeral.

'Death had eyes,' Uncle Emil said, 'even for Bobo. And Bobo was a great man.'

The lights of St Croix went out, a power failure. We groped home.

'Touch a lamprey,' Uncle Georges said. 'Bang. One less Verhaeren.'

Bobo's widow washed our hands. M. d'Aube brought wine, my father Jack Daniels whisky, Emil peppers-in-rice, crayfish, beer bread and sausage. Georges brought sweet carrot soup and custards. A shriek suddenly shook the *cimetière*. Paralysed, we stared out of the window, our mouths full.

'Bobo – ' Georges gasped.

Bobo's soul was tangled in a tree, kicking to be free.

FIVE

I was an Ojibway.

I went north to Manitouwadge. The hills were maroon. Indian turnips grew in a lagoon, oldsquaw, and bitter onion. An old married couple picked radishes where the smoke gathered. Another man and his wife scraped bark. In a sod cabin two people stirred whisky mash. The sun fell low and smoky over the purple scrub when I reached the Pic where there was a settlement of Eastern Ojibway and, further north, the Crow Hill Indian orphanage.

In Crow Hill cracked posts supported the dock. A wood fishing house swayed over the lake and boats banged in the wind. Pools of dirty water rippled in mud alleys. A Dobermann with three legs chased a ptarmigan past a winch pulley. The ptarmigan turned into an alley and ran low to the lake shore.

I had lunch in the Manitouwadge Café. I had black coffee, chilli and soda crackers. Stuffed owls lined the yellow shelves. There was a moosehead over the door, a racoon rearing on the coffee machine. Posters of Montreal were festooned with strings of wild onion and garlic. An old Ojibway shuffled behind the stove in ratty slippers.

Red Two Hats, who sometimes worked for my Uncle Georges, chipped paint off a boat by the trading post. Maple leaves bobbed red in Lake Manitouwadge's slate grey waves.

'Nimiwanagocin,' Red said.

'Hello, Red.'

'How's Antoinette?' he asked.

'She's lovely.'

'Etienne?'

'Sulking.'

'Well, it's a hole, St Croix.'

'I want to be an Ojibway,' I said.

'What an ambition.'

Red introduced me to his cousin, Lawrence Woman.

'There's nothing to do in Crow Hill,' Lawrence warned.

There was nothing to do in Crow Hill. Ojibways carved carcases of elk and boated back and forth across Lake Manitouwadge with cases of beer. Smoke hung inside the quonset huts. Women wild-riced. Everywhere there was stink. The Ojibways suffered from tuberculosis, pneumonia, gonorrhoea, pleurisy, arthritis. The men, the women, were alcoholic. Children ran naked with the chickens and there was chicken shit and feathers even in the stunted pines. At welfare time Ojibways came to Crow Hill to pick up cheques. All night Ojibway men ran in and out of shacks, making new wives.

'Welcome to Crow Hill,' Red said. 'Fuck capital of Canada.'

I cleaned fish with Lawrence Woman. I worked with wild-ricing women. We kept the rice in blue canisters at the front of the canoe. We cooked rice and potatoes, plenty of pepper, and cranberries, with lots of fish. I moved into Lawrence Woman's fish house and slept on a rubber sheet under the fish lymph basin. I strung up red peppers and put a candle on the knife rack. Lawrence Woman came by and gave me a red blanket.

'My mother made it,' he told me.

One night I was awakened by shouts. I went to the fish-house window. Peter Jennings, Jim Mekoniwas, Joseph Five Ojibways and Lester Strange stood on the edge of the dock, their hair whipped by a frigid wind. Lanterns lined the shore. They worked their organs. It was hard work. They were so drunk three others had fallen in and even in the dark lake they worked. The Ojibways bet heavily.

'Hooray, Lester!'

'Shoot, Pete!'

'Come, Joseph, come!'

The pines suddenly swayed. Dogs howled on the bank. Henry stood on tiptoes, his eyes crossed.

'Oh – !'

Father Leszek canoed in and put boxes of old clothes, books and toys into the Crow Hill orphanage. He cleaned the chapel, held mass, and blessed the fish. When he left, fish that had dangled on the smoking wires flopped in the air, trying to fly.

Lawrence Woman gave me a turquoise bracelet.

'Blue is good luck,' Lawrence told me.

The next night Ojibways brought stray dogs, beaten and starved, and threw them two at a time into a sandpit. They bet heavily on dog fights, too. Afterwards they washed dog blood into the lake. Jim Mekoniwas called Peewee Peacon *dog soup*. Peewee ripped out his knife and cut off Jim Mekoniwas's left little finger and waggled it in Jim's face.

'Don't ever *dog soup* me!' Peewee said.

Ojibways grew restless. They came from as far as St Bérénice. They brought gifts of money, clothes, a transistor radio. Ojibway girls dropped out of St Bonaventure and came up to Crow Hill. All night the radios were loud, boys fought, dogs howled. Ojibways kept coming to Crow Hill. I had never seen so many Ojibways. They brought cases of whisky, venison, chicken, pig. Meat-roast smells floated through the alleys.

'You want to be a man?' Red asked.

'I do.'

'Hide in my pantry tonight. Keep your eyes open.'

Ojibways came to Red's house, put their totems on a shelf, and began eating: chicken, peppers, beer, oranges, wild rice, corn. Dogs ate off the floor and licked men's fingers. By midnight everybody was drunk. Red lighted a pipe. Everybody smoked it. Tommy Shanks came in. He was my friend from St Bonaventure, naked and rubbed with deer lymph.

Red Two Hats poured olive oil over Tommy's hands,

dunked them in gasoline and tossed a match. The Ojibways' dogs, walls, totems, chicken bones, suddenly everything glowed. Tommy panicked. He threw the fire back and forth like a spring coil. Red hit Tommy in the kidneys. Tommy peed. Flames dripped from his hands. Red stuck fish hooks in Tommy's chest and tied number five gauge wires to the hooks, picked up a hammer, and nailed the other ends of the wires to the house post.

'Run outside, Tommy,' Red said.

Tommy stared at him.

'I said, run.'

Tommy ran out the door. As he passed I heard the *rip rippity-rip-rip* of fish hooks popping through Tommy's pectorals. Veils of blood drifted on to the door jambs. Tommy chewed driftwood, beat his head, rolled in the sand in pain. When he came back his eyes were glazed. He ate but kept missing his mouth. Peewee threw him a loincloth. Tommy put it on, picked up his presents and went out.

I caught up to him by the fish house. Tommy's eyes were dilated. He didn't know where he was. He held up his hand.

'Don't touch me – !' he said. 'I am a *man*.'

There was a murder that October in Crow Hill. Robert Walking Shoes took Janko Petrzuski into a shack to see what it was like and beat him to death with a lead pipe.

The women and I gathered chestnuts above Crow Hill. The red tundra stretched unbroken among the pools and lagoons. I wore a bandolier of beer bottles, rodent skull and owl feathers. I called myself Johnny Hibou. The Arctic cold was coming through the forest, though there wasn't much snow yet, and geese gathered for the long flight to Louisiana.

Tommy Shanks came by with his black rifle.

'Go home,' he said.

'I am an Ojibway.'

'This Ojibway shit,' he sneered. 'You ought to be locked up.'

My fingers were white as a clam shell. I coughed a lot and when I sneezed I threw it on the fish-house walls. I shivered all night. Lawrence Woman came into the fish house. He stood in the doorway.

'Should I keep you warm, Jean-Michel?'

I was miserable. I hated Crow Hill. I packed up what I owned and went to say goodbye to Red Two Hats. He looked terrible. He was wrapped in an army blanket over his hunting jacket. Sparks from his bonfire fell on him, swirled around like a storm, and he didn't bother moving. His clothes smelled like cooked racoon.

'What's wrong, Jean?'

'I feel lonely.'

'Antoinette Hartmann?'

'I die for her.'

'Ojibways have woman trouble, too.'

'Do they? Even Ojibways?'

'Much worse.'

On Lake Manitouwadge dog bits floated on black water. A loon echoed on the far shore.

'*Animad pimadiziwin,*' Red sighed.

'Yes. Life is hard.'

We stared into the darkness.

'You know about women,' I said. 'Don't you?'

'I do.'

'And men?'

'Animals, too.'

'Tell me about Ojibway women,' I asked.

'Drunken animals.'

'What do they do to men?'

He passed me a flask of corn whisky. It was warm and tasted like burnt corn silk.

'Ojibways die many times before death and even death is not the end of their dying.'

'How does a man love a woman?'

'It is a very strong business.'

60

The Ojibway

'I WAS AN ORPHAN.

'My mother was Menominee. My father was Ojibway. My father died of tuberculosis. My mother drowned in Moose Lake. I grew up in an orphanage at Manitouwadge. It was not the Catholic orphanage in Crow Hill. It was a Lutheran orphanage.

'The lake froze by mid-November. Cat-tails and lake sedge became brittle. The Arctic winds blew right through the barracks. The Lutherans had us working on tractors, brick-making, laying pipe for the farmers. I carried hod, hauled bags of alkali. I fixed posts and chicken-wire fences, dug trenches. James Kenaukee, Bill Rice, Vernon Lacombe and Harold Sweet, my friends, died.

'My voice became rough. I was big for my age. I had the arms and shoulders of a man when I was only twelve. Though, like most Indians, I never grew hair on my chest.

'One day, when the red sun sank behind dwarf pines, I packed a canvas bag with food, a lantern, extra batteries, winter socks, and escaped up the inland waterway. I lived in the marshes. I ate snakes, robbed traplines, ate bark. I watched the purple clouds rise in the north like the shapes of women. I hung around the boat docks at Twisted Leg Lake, fought and got my fine Indian nose broken. I bought a Winchester 30–30.

'I stole from white men. I stole from Indians. I lived with a fat Slant-Eyed, Harriet Dark Arms, who rubbed bacon grease on her thighs so her dogs licked it off. But I was so hungry I had this terrible pain in my eyes. I could have torn off any white man's head.

'Illinois hunters hired me to take them around Grange Lake. We fished in St Lazare Lake and then portaged up to Bellefont's Rivière. They didn't seem to care if they shot anything or not. They were just shooting off their shotguns. They told me to take them up Otter Creek. I told them they were wasting their time. They said they would pay me $100 American. I took them, but even our fire looked sick. We slept on soggy beaches and in the daylight went looking for moose. But I could tell the moose were smarter than we were and had gone south.

'That evening I pissed off the boat against the sunset. Steam rose up from the circles of red water. The hunters watched me. That night I moved my sleeping bag further into the bracken but they pulled me out of the ferns and raped me. I went to the lake and washed myself. When they were asleep I brained one with an axe. The other two ran through the woods. I picked up a shotgun and blew both barrels into the dead man's head. Then I piled rocks over him and lit a fire. Parts of him came up bubbling.

'I walked across brown plains. I kept washing myself in the lagoons. The horizon was like steel through which the sun never broke. I ate moss. It was the worst famine I ever saw. Not a stick, not algae. I looked into dead lakes and saw nothing but stars. I ate half-rotted carcases in deer traps. I chewed one carcase and tasted flannel. A white man had fallen into a trap a long time ago and I had bitten into him.

'I saw Ojibway corpses, which we call *chibay*. We do not bury our *chibay* but put them on wooden platforms in trees. We give them gifts, like mocassins and watches, to travel the long road. I saw *chibay* ducking under pine branches, spraying snow, following me. I knew my time had come to die so I found a gulley to die in. Then I saw a white house with blue shutters on a granite hill. The blue shutters banged open and shut. I walked about twenty yards. The sun turned black and I fainted on the porch.

'I woke in the attic and saw a woman. Isabel Sobel was a half-breed, a widow. She was mute. She had black almond eyes, very French. I was afraid of those eyes. But where could I go? There was a thousand miles of famine and blizzards outside. So I stayed in the white house with the blue shutters.

'I hauled salt, filled the sheep pens, fixed the barn roof. I spliced copper wire to her mains. But it was a terrible winter. We had rumpless black Orpingtons, Wyandottes and little dumpies. Each morning we'd find hens pecked to death or blinded. I made a second floor for the brooder house and coated it with tar.

'One midnight Isabel came to my room. She lifted my nightshirt. I was so scared I couldn't move. She dropped the nightshirt, turned and left. I wanted to run away but the tundra had frozen, and a blizzard whistled through the dwarf pines all night. In the morning I dressed, went out the gate, but there was a wall of white. The real storms had begun, so I came back.

'There were *chibay* behind the barn. They were on platforms along a row of granite rocks, in ragged flannel shirts. Each time I came behind the barn the *chibay* were in different positions.

'Isabel stopped feeding me. I rummaged through the cupboards and ate dried soup, bacon grease, lard. All night I heard unnatural laughter. I peered into Isabel's room. The curtain was blowing heavily. Snow drifted on to the floor. Isabel lay under a *chibay*, her legs around its belly. The room stank of *chibay*.

'I went back to bed and locked my door. I was really afraid of her now. She watched me in the morning with those deep black, French eyes, distant as the frozen ponds. The wind shrieked over the house out of the blind, white tundra. I washed out the heifers. I chopped cow shit. A *chibay* was draped over the barbed wire. I put it on a sheet of plywood and nailed the plywood between two dwarf pines.

'I boiled a dead chicken in its own blood and ate it behind the coop, hardtack sopping up the stew.

'All night the *chibay* howled. I couldn't imagine anything more horrible than that sound. I went to get Isabel's shotgun to blow their heads off. But Isabel caught me. Suddenly *chibay* came in from the windows, tied weights to my hair, spun me around until I threw up in circles. They hauled me into the yard and rubbed me with barbed wire.

'In the morning I staggered across the drifts. There was a moonbow over the sheep trough. I wandered aimlessly and started crying. I couldn't take it no more. I took a crowbar from the truck and hammered a *chibay* apart. I caught a second behind the house and broke his back in two. I jumped a third and pried it apart. I went to the barn, got a can of kerosene, and started carrying it toward the house.

'Isabel came out with a rifle. She marched me to the smokehouse and hung me from meat hooks. The pain of the hooks was so bad I pulled on the hooks to die. The moon and stars burst in my head. I saw my Ojibway and Menominee ancestors carrying blankets, coffee and mocassins, my death shirt.

'But the roof broke and I fell. I put mud and snow in my wounds and slept in moss. The next evening I stole to Isabel's house. The low sun glowed blood-red across the pink snow. I dragged her upstairs and raped her. Our baby was born. It had no legs, no arms, just black ears and a grin. I hacked it apart at the sheep trough and buried it behind the chicken coop.

'In the spring I drifted down to Lake Superior. I worked the fishing boats. But I come back to Crow Hill and go north to Isabel Sobel when my need is on. She's white-haired now, but still strong as a diesel. She can lift a jeep right out of the road. We drink all day like maniacs and rut like animals, standing up. My vision turns me into a moose.

'Jean, know the art of woman's love.'

SIX

'*Le petit est malade,*' my mother whispered. '*Le petit va mourir.*'

I dreamed I rose on an ostrich of white plumes and wore a Chinese gown embroidered with my sins. The clouds parted and I flew into a corridor of pyramids and obelisks. I sailed over the Nile of death. At the base of the Sudan mountains altar boys swung censers billowing smoke. A bishop interrogated me. I refused contrition.

I fell. The air became dark, darker. I sank into St Croix.

'*Y va mourir!*'

My mother made *tarte à la farlouche.* I sucked molasses and raisins off my fingers. But she, my mother, went into the living room and beat her hands against the walls.

Father Ybert called me to his office. He wore bifocals now, but they weren't right. He kept taking them off and rubbing his eyelids. Sometimes he rolled his bloodshot eyes to the right.

'So,' he said. 'Jean-Michel goes on vacation.'

'I was in Crow Hill.'

'Who did you think you were, Louis Riel?'

'At least.'

'Did you like Crow Hill?'

'It was cold.'

'Perhaps, for you, the world is cold.'

'And getting colder.'

'Drop your trousers.'

Father Ybert warmed my buttocks.

'How is your father?' he asked, putting his ruler back in the drawer.

'He works.'

'It is so hard in an area like this, keeping a job. And his troubles with the Jamaican Barrault. How is Barrault?'

'He has pneumonia now.'

'We keep them both in our thoughts.'

'Thank you, Father Ybert.'

Ignace worked his diorama. Dromedaries, elephants, black archipelagos of lagoons and palms went by as he turned the handle. Dolphins leaped under a sacred heart. He turned the handle and Palestine passed. The Holy Family travelled in some kind of empty banana cart.

'You are really stupid, Jean,' Ignace said. '*Maudit niaiseux.* To have run away again.'

'Was I?'

'If you were killed – '

'So what?'

'You'd have gone straight to hell.'

News of Dienbienpheu filtered into St Croix. The disaster took hold. The British secretly smirked. We tried to make plans but we were under a *mauvais esprit*. Aggravated by paralysis, my father attended the city council. He demanded that fleas on the wharf be eradicated.

'But, *cher monsieur*,' said the city manager, 'we were discussing the street tax.'

'Well,' he said, sitting down. 'Now you know the French viewpoint.'

I became depressed. I spoke to St Bonaventure's nurse. I told her I wanted to commit suicide. I told her I had no belief in the Holy Roman Catholic Church. I said there was no afterlife, no heaven or hell. She sent me to Father Vigneau who beat me with a mop.

I had to wear a conical cap and blue fingerpaint on my nose. I wore a sign: '*I am a dumb pig. I wear this because I am corrupted. I am bad. This is a lesson to be learned. Stupid. Bad boy. Look. Laugh.*'

I walked home. Strangely, my house began to drift. I ran

down LeClerc but my house arched into the sky. I ran after, screaming, until I tripped. Something dragged me backward down Emilia Street by the heels and threw me against a warehouse door.

We took Ignace to Doctor Lacomb. I looked at Doctor Lacomb's collection of pipettes, awls, and stethoscopes in the foyer. I peeked into the inner room. Ignace lay on a high leather bed. The nurse swabbed his lower abdomen and gave him an injection. Dr Lacomb came in, washed his hands, and put on sheer rubber gloves. The nurse gave Ignace a second injection and his lips stopped fluttering.

Dr Lacomb made an incision across Ignace's belly, reached down, and fumbled.

'Damn it. Where are they?' he muttered.

After a while he found something, gave a jerk. He sutured the wound with a white nylon thread, the nurse swabbed the wound with brown liquid and Dr Lacomb took a drink of water. Dr Lacomb came into the lobby. My mother looked up from her magazine.

'He will breed like a pig,' Dr Lacomb said.

'Ignace is going to be a Jesuit,' she said.

'Oh. Well. At least he'll be normal.'

The nurse wheeled Ignace into a waiting chamber with a poster of Lake Van in Turkey. We went inside. The sun from the window came through his transparent red ears, over his white hair.

'How beautiful is sodium pentathol,' he mumbled, and fell asleep.

We drove Ignace home. As we drove up the driveway I saw the Dybs.

'Ignace got his balls!' I yelled.

We took him inside. He slept most of the afternoon, then came down for supper. My father bought champagne and toasted him.

'To Ignace Verhaeren,' he said. 'For on this day he achieved his testicles.'

★   ★   ★

My mother became nervous. She sliced her thumb at Kelly's and bled on the vegetables. She had a crying fit and had to sit on a folding chair by the brown curtains.

That October the patients complained of waiting for breakfast. Three elderly women said they lined naked to get their baths, and one fell and broke her hip. Residents were required to pay tips for afternoon tea. Then Amélie Ybert showed her bottom in contempt of the staff and they shoved puréed rutabaga in her ears. An elderly virgin, Natalie Mons, complained of the rude method of her bathing, and the orderly in shame burned his hands.

These were the rumours of Kelly's Nursing Home.

Our mother took the waters of St Lazare.

I carried her suitcase to the trunk-line station. It was midnight. A Polish soldier walked back and forth in the green rain, looking down the tracks into the darkness. She kissed my forehead.

'Don't torment Ignace,' she said.

'Who, me?'

She took the train past the bleaching factory, across Ontario to the Laurentian Mountains. St Lazare was near Quebec. She was shown her room, which had a bowl and basin, crucifix, folded white towels. In the morning she went to mass and then changed for the bathing pools. The smell of chlorine was kept away by pot-pourris of rose leaves. Arthritics stood with their heads like wine bottles in alignment devices. Steam rose, obscuring Quebec. Nuns served distilled water.

She toured Quebec. She visited Dufferin Terrace. She visited the Hôtel Frontenac. From the promenade she watched the St Lawrence surge around the island of Orleans. Lower Quebec was hung with lavender. She went to the Archbishop's Palace. It was closed. She left a bouquet of nasturtiums on the Plains of Abraham. She went to the panorama of Saint Anne de Beaupré and stayed three hours. She attended mass in Notre Dame des Victoires and heard the echoes of pilgrims. She knocked at the Ursuline convent. It was also closed.

On the way back she visited her old convent, Our Lady of Trois Pointes, on a bluff over the St Lawrence. Stone angels looked down with rain-ruined faces. She went to the administration.

'I am Yvonne Krems,' she said. 'I was noviced at this convent.'

'And you subsequently married?'

'I wish to re-enter.'

'Impossible.'

'I am unhappy. I work hard in a stupid town. My husband is cruel and my children are fools.'

'In every marriage there is regret.'

'You were my Mother Superior.'

'In every life, sadness.'

'I AM DYING.'

'You are not a sheet, Yvonne Krems, that can be sewn whole again.'

She went to the garden grotto. Partly screened by black iron bars and trailing moss, an impossibly old nun scrubbed rocks. My mother kissed her hem through the bars.

'O, there are children to be fed!' she cried. 'Things for them to do! And life is ugly!'

'Such was your decision.'

She went to the dining hall. Novices sat at long benches, one hand with the soup spoon, the other in the lap, under pewter candlesticks. She knelt in the chapel. Red and blue light from the stained glass fell on her black hair.

'Jesu,' she whispered. *I have lost everything.*

Our mother came home and dreamed of peonies growing from industrial waste. Each peony was a relative. The wind as it blew sang a lullaby from the cold Brittany shores.

> *'Savez-vous planter les choux*
> *A la mode, à la mode*
> *Savez-vous planter les choux*
> *A la mode de chez nous?'*

'Can you plant cabbages
In the way, in the way
Can you plant cabbages
In the way we do?'

And each peony grew until the tendrils tangled, and they
fell under a black sun into the ash and scattered seeds.

*'On les plante avec le doigt
A la mode, à la mode
On les plante avec le doigt
A la mode de chez nous.'*

'Plant them with the finger
In the way, in the way
Plant them with the finger
In the way we do.'

She woke with a start. I cooled her face with a cloth.
'Jean – I saw our dead – '
'So many Verhaerens,' I said. 'These Flemish names.'
'So many Kremses.'
I combed the little curls over her ears. Her little hands
covered mine.
'All crazy,' she said.

After work, before anybody came home, her hair in a paisley
kerchief, her housecoat with its little balls and strings of dust,
my mother sat in her red easy chair, sipped strong French
coffee, and listened to *Coffee with Bruce*. One day as it rained
she stood at the window looking out at the bare trees of
LeClerc.
'How I wish we could eat and fly, eat and fly,' she
whispered, 'like the blue-headed geese and die.'

I found a dead dog in the Petit Croix. I pulled it with a pole
but it floated away and sank.

★   ★   ★

I went up the stairs of the Bon Garçon.

Amber lamps lit a dirty Venus. Tattered pink carpets led past an armoire. Moose heads, racoon heads, muskrat heads, depending on the woman, stuck out over doors. On the doors were stencilled names. I heard groans. The further I climbed the longer the corridor grew. I crawled on my hands and knees under a low ceiling until I came to Agnes Moosefield.

'Jean-Michel,' Agnes said, 'your father is not here.'

'I am.'

'Ah?'

I dug into my pockets and held out four crumpled Canadian dollars. I went in and closed the door. On her wall was a picture of a woman bathing in a wooden tub with a man. An Indian headdress was nailed to a bedpost. I saw her health certificate over the dresser, and a bowl of almonds.

'Are you sure?' she asked.

'I will ride you like an alligator.'

'Let me wash you.'

She shuffled to the basin in pink slippers. She came forward and unzipped me.

'Look at you!'

'Is that me?'

I was hit with vertigo. I turned and slammed into the bedpost.

'Oh – '

'I'll get some paper towels,' she said.

Suddenly there was a movement at the door. Somebody had been spying. I hobbled to the door, holding my trousers. I ripped open the door and saw my father running away, giggling.

'Did you enjoy that?' I yelled. '*Did* you!'

Roger Vaucaire, a reform-school boy, caught *narcosis*. He came to St Bonaventure but couldn't concentrate. I saw Roger come down La Poudre Road. Roger wore a plaid green flannel shirt and black boots. Decayed wet stubble glistened in the dark fields. He thought he was alone. He danced down La Poudre Road. He jumped, twirled, slapped his boots and danced.

'Roger!' I called.

We smoked Chesterfields on a bench on the bluffs. Wheat freighters passed our harbour, going to Rutherford. Below the roofs were black with black wet wires. Rabbits lurched through the mud by our feet. Roger made finger pulls of invisible triggers. Suddenly Roger got *narcosis* again. He dropped his Chesterfield and leaned against my chest, delirious.

'I will make you, pretty baby,' he said, fingering my shirt. 'I will put my finger in your eye.'

'Poor Roger.'

'I will look babies in your eyes,' he said. 'I will pick silly corns out of your toes.'

'Poor Roger Vaucaire.'

'I will tear your door off its hinges.'

I had a strange dream that night: Roger Vaucaire in gossamer wings with a wand, stepping through gauze curtains.

Roger lived in a trailer by the quarry, an area we called the Arrondissement des Pauvres. His grandfather had emphysema. His sister Amy had a hole in her heart. Roger showed me his comic books and model railroad, moss islands with tunnels trimmed in stone, pine trees of lacquered needles. Roger had an extraordinary talent, the purpose of it as yet unknown. He had a black tumour above his right knee and rested his leg on a green footstool. I eased on his black slippers.

It grew dark. He turned on the light. Lamps he had painted with moose in wild rice lakes glowed. Tin angels revolved in heat. Gold foil twirled at the darkening windows.

'Roger – ' I said. 'You are an artist!'

Modestly, he waved his hand. He showed me his grandfather's bayonet, dented and rusted, and a piece of shrapnel. Roger collected anarchist posters. Rain started falling. The birches were whipsawing in *la forêt*. A big storm, something really big, bigger than with Antoinette, was coming. I learned later it was a hurricane – a freak. Roger's trailer wall divided the cold light outside from the warmth inside. I forgot St Croix.

Roger gave me a glass of *crème de menthe*.

'You are a master artist, Roger!' I said.

I put my hand on his shoulder. Suddenly my hand flamed.
I laughed.

'You are *king* of artists, Roger!'

Roger turned on the radio. The Alouettes were losing. He
turned it off. We drank more *crème de menthe*.

'*Y fait tellement noir, tout d'un coup*,' he said. 'It's so dark,
all of a sudden.'

'Night falls fast now.'

The storm beat against the quarry. We watched, drunk,
through Roger's window.

'*J'avais jamais rien vu de si beau*,' he whispered. 'I've never
seen anything so beautiful.'

'*Dieu que cé beau.* God, it's beautiful.'

He drunkenly touched my face. A cry came through the
rain. He pulled back his hand.

'What was that?' I asked.

'What?'

'I thought – somebody – yelled – '

Roger opened the window. Rain spattered on to his scarred
forehead.

'*Pitounes*,' he said, leaning out. 'Whores. In the Bon
Garçon.'

'So far away?'

'Women cry out to excite the men.'

'They do?'

'They cry out until they shake.'

There was a fly on the cold sill. Roger twirled a black
thread into a ball and the fly mated with it.

'See?' he said. 'The whole world. *Ficky-fick.*'

Roger showed me a contraband register of prostitutes. In it
were pictures, names, addresses, specialities, sketches, criminal
records and health certificates. He closed the book. We drank
more *crème de menthe*.

'One dives deep, Jean.'

'In women?'

'Astonishing what women do with men.'

'What do they do, Roger?'

'They move their bellies in the agony of love. Jean, I have

73

made women moan. They sweat on their bed, hair plastered to a pale forehead.'

'They sweat?'

'I tell her *it is only a momentary disgust*. She is intrigued. I enter her, slowly. Her eyes open wide: she has learned something. I ride her like a cowboy. She loses herself. She jerks at her crisis like a perch on the pier.'

'What technique!'

'Shut up. Listen. In a cheap tenement, the mother of one of our friends, even one whom you know, twists like a hanged man as I stroke her inside. Like a diesel stoker, up and down, until she loses all dignity in desire.'

'A master technician!'

'I am Ed Gien!'

Roger was sweating. He had reddish-brown hair on his upper lip. Now it was beaded with sweat. Hurricane Hazel swept the north shore, but we only heard about it later. We were inside a numbed cave. Roger poured even more *crème de menthe*.

'These Catholic women,' he confided, 'crack like almonds. They burn in fields of fire. They scream like scorched pigs. That is how they are. That is how they always will be.'

'Oh, my.'

'Don't you find it so?' he asked.

'I don't know.'

'You've never had a woman?'

'No.'

'I thought you buttered the bread on both sides.'

Milky gobs spurted into St Croix. It happened this way. Milkweed floated in clouds over the prison. A hydrant burst and sprayed water up the bluffs. Silky, milky gobs rotated down our streets, hung from telephone wires, dripped on cars. I saw Roger at the greengrocer. We turned away, blushing.

One night I sleep-walked out on to the roof. Roger caught me from the oak tree.

'You silly goose,' he said.

★   ★   ★

I walked down LeClerc and outside Etienne Bastide's house I watched Katherine dress. It must have been for a party, because she put a brooch on a full green dress. The lights in her room were warm and yellow. Her art project, a collage of leaves, stood beside her mirror. Suddenly a squirrel ran across the roof. She looked out and I backed away.

A heart beat on the sidewalk.

'Jean – watch what you're doing,' it said.

I slipped it into my coat, and carried it home.

Roger and I visited the museum of suicide.

It was in Heron Bay. We walked up the wooden steps and went into what had been a ropemakers' hall. Black cloth outlined the exhibits, mounted on enormous wooden spools. The first exhibit was Frantisek 'Frankie' Bremml. In a glass tank a doll sat in a steam boiler. Roger pressed a red button. Steam came out of a valve. Frankie turned black.

The second exhibit was Artur Dornbach. Dornbach lay in an aquarium with a *papier-mâché* rock around his neck. Roger pressed the red button. Inky water oozed into the tank. The third was Henry Silver Adams, whose doll sat in front of a painted barn. Roger pressed the red button. Adams tumbled into a tub of fertilizer.

The fourth exhibit was Ken Renquist. Renquist stood on the corner of Llewelyn Street and Georgetown in a miniaturized Heron Bay. Roger pressed a red button. Renquist's doll, red hair flying, fell under the wheels of a red bus. There was a diorama of Wolf Hazard. Wolf lay in a lacquered garden of real squash, hollyhocks, rosemary and marigold. Aspirin bottles littered the shadows. Roger pressed the red button. Wolf's torso fell apart.

In the foyer were news photographs of Emily Lanke, George Lipp and Gilles Scott, who burned himself in a bathtub of naphtha. Roger and I had cream tea, cakes in the buffet. We watched the shadows in the harbour.

'If only people died immediately,' he said.

'Carried straight from their mother's knees.'

'To *la cimetière*.'

'And were not,' I said.
'No. Never even were. To be not.'
'Not even to have been.'

The *buveurs* debated suicide.
'Dark rushes on the mind,' Herman Pic said.
'One does not even see dark,' Lawrence Otto objected.
'Not even dark,' Paul Hartmann agreed.
'Just that last little – flicker – ' Danny Auban said. ' –
perhaps bitterness – and – '
'Nothing,' Herman said.
'*Ploof,*' I said.
The *buveurs* passed a motion:
Ploof.

Many have said I was influenced by Etienne Bastide. Some
say my obsession with Antoinette Hartmann was the turning
point. In truth, all I ever was, all I ever could be, everything,
I owe to Roger Vaucaire.

I became addicted to *crème de menthe*. I was irritable without
it and couldn't sleep. Roger and I mixed *crème de menthe* and
coffee, vodka and sloe gin. We called it *The Pope's Demitasse*.
By sheer accident I found Roger one day lying on the railroad
tracks. He punched me in the face.
'Leave me alone!' he said. '*Lâche-moé donc*, you shit!'

Roger put on tight jeans like the Winnipeg Dew Droppers.
He slicked his hair back on both sides: a duck's ass. He was
very skinny. With his freckles, big ears, and a lopsided grin
he looked like a dangerous clown. Roger and I walked the
wharf at midnight. He taped a flashlight to the barrel of his
.22. A rat stood in Roger's beam, Roger blew its brains out.
New waterfowl had come to Lake Superior: the crested
northern egret, swan-tailed goose, birds we had never seen.
'Salt intrusion,' Roger spat. 'Eisenhower's engineers are
killing the St Lawrence.'
Roger and I drank *crème de menthe*. We toured the old

warehouses. There were trap doors, a discarded cane, pipes, welding flux, a sewing-machine wheel, ginseng jars, half an oboe, figurines of Bavarian peasants carrying faggots of twigs. We found a segmented goldfish with red glass eyes. When our mines had been working Chinese were ferried across the Great Lakes. Now, in October, the city electricity was low. Fog lit by the harbour crawled up the roofs. Roger's head was surrounded in a blaze, cradled in orange cloud.

'Kiss me, Jean.'

I kissed Roger.

'On the mouth.'

I did so.

The fog flickered with St Croix's neon downtown. Low clouds rolled on the harbour. A freighter churned to Rutherford.

'You have made me tremble,' he said.

'Yes.'

'With your little wolf teeth.'

'My hot tongue.'

Roger kissed me passionately. I lost my balance and slammed against the rough green door.

'Well, all right,' I said.

The lighthouse beam hit the warehouse roof and shot over the black water. I became light and flew where there is no Canada, no lampreys, no priests.

Father Ybert brought an engraving of John Calvin to religion class, *The Branded Sodomite*. I sat with Roger. Calvin stood naked in a bath with a married woman and her young son.

'Calvin ordered the murder of five hundred Catholic children,' Father Ybert lectured. 'He was an infamous lecher. He escaped into a monastery and infected thirteen nuns with venereal disease. He died under the lily, sign of the sodomist.'

Etienne Bastide sent me a present:

a lily.

I visited Uncle Artur.

Artur was a taxidermist at the Blue Gill Bait and Tackle

Shop on Long Sturgeon Street. Artur sat at his rack of knives and scissors. He had cutting pliers, flat-nosed pliers, camel-hair brushes and stuffing iron. Spools of black threads, arsenic soap, vials of potash bichromate, soda sulphate, burnt alum lay on his desk. His nails were black and brittle.

'You are drinking *crème de menthe*?' he asked.

'I am.'

'And running with Roger Vaucaire?'

'I am.'

'What does your mother think?'

'She cries.'

He took a dead St Mary hawk, cracked both wings close to the body and sliced each wing. He cut through and the skin separated. He skinned the stomach to the tail. The body fell off. Artur worked the eyes out and extracted the brains. He constructed a false body: wire pinned to the skin. He inserted cotton wadding, sewed up the hawk, and put in agate eyes.

'Stupid,' he finally said. '*Maudit niaiseux*. Really, dirty stupid.'

He stared at me.

'*O mon pauvre Jean*,' he said. '*Si tu savas tout le trouble pis toutes les larmes*. Eh? If you knew all the trouble and all the tears.'

Artur turned away. He took up the hawk, admired it, and set it on a resined branch. He splayed pine boughs under, put a stuffed mouse in the talons to make it fierce.

'Who will reassemble *you*?' he asked.

Gregors Illuskvi, the Ukrainian prison guard, committed a perversion on his blind son Peders.

My father cut two holes in a gunny sack, slipped it over his head, and made a torch of lilac roots and tar. Georges, Emil, Artur and he went to the Arrondissement des Pauvres. Freddie Granbouche came. Herman Hartmann brought a rifle. Gilbert Young, Hank Genycki and Marc Auberlin came from Isle of May Street. My father pounded on Illuskvi's trailer door.

'ILLUSKVI!'

My father broke Illuskvi's windows with a crowbar. Georges forced the lock. The Verhaerens yanked Illuskvi into the yard, stripped him, and tied the torch to his rear.

My mother, Zena Courennes, Old Woman Dyb, ran into the compound whirling noise-makers, wearing thick sweaters, pants under their skirts. Their faces were smeared black with coal.

> *'Sodomite, sodomite*
> *Voici voir le sodomite.'*

The Verhaerens dumped Illuskvi in a red wagon, lit the torch, and rumbled him down Emilia Street. Bits of burning lilac root dripped on to Illuskvi's bare rear.

'Jack – ' Illuskvi screamed. 'Don't kill me!'

'Snitch!'

'You didn't slap Barrault! You slapped nobody!'

'Damn right!'

Herman Hartmann shot his rifle. He poured flour on Illuskvi's back and Georges mixed it in with vegetable oil. They poured feathers on Illuskvi.

> *'Sodomite, sodomite*
> *Voici voir le sodomite.'*

They rumbled Illuskvi up Fourth Street, past the French quarter, back to his trailer. My father chased him inside and, when Illuskvi wouldn't come out, unblocked the trailer's wheels. It rolled down and crashed into the oaks.

Everybody went home. My father, still excited, sweated and breathed hard. He washed his face in the kitchen. He drank, cupping his palm under the stream.

'You were wonderful, Papa!' I shouted.

'Nothing. It was nothing.'

He bathed his squat, powerful arms with the kitchen sponge. He danced in glee.

'Illuskvi *pissed*!' he squealed. 'Did you see that? Squirted like a poodle!'

'Then he would have burned faster.'

'Eh?'

'Having less water in him!'

'Ha ha! A good one, that, Jean! Ha ha!'

My father uncapped two bottles of Export. My mother came into the kitchen, also sweating, still wearing her sweater and pants. She nuzzled his cheek. Suddenly she looked at me.

'Michel,' she said. 'Some day this will happen to you.'

On 24 November 1954, my dearest friend Roger Vaucaire fell into the Parsons turbine at the trunk-line rotating platform and was slashed to death. Ankles, thighs, forearms, shoulders, were chopped up.

I plucked roses for him at the *cimetière*. Suddenly thunder shook the tombs.

'*Jean* – !'

I looked up.

Rainbows of Roger arched over St Croix, bleeding through the season's first snow on to whitening fields.

SEVEN

St Croix froze.

Islands were lost in white and grey fog. The sun was gone. Vacant lots turned to Jutlands of ice. My mother practised her ice-skating. Red pom-poms, red skirt, swirled in the rink. In Swallowfield the prisoners huddled in their cells. Children on the bluffs fought the Plains of Abraham. Lake Superior turned to an angry mood: black water, arms of snow, vapour where ships disappeared.

Slowly the Arctic front moved in.

Nights fell like deep sleep. Badgers slept the narcosis of winter. A cow wandered La Poudre Road and died bewildered on its feet. It was the coldest Christmas on record. Antifreeze failed. DeSotos rusted and came apart on the lake. Father Leszek, Father Vigneau and Father Pic put on black Russian hats and rang bells for Crow Hill orphanage. When headlights moved through the snow, streets sparkled and black figures darted across the ice.

Snow fell in the schoolyard, on the trunk-line station, the Portobello Hotel, the vaults in the *cimetière*. Snow fell in the closed Galtieau yard. There was nowhere the snow did not fall, on Ojibway Flats, from the tundra to the islands.

Our faces were pink, mauve, green at store windows. Electric vacuum cleaners, radios and high-fidelity phonographs suddenly appeared in Prange's windows. It was Canadian Family Week. Mechanical dolls sang in front of posters of wives serving canapés to husbands. My mother bought sweaters, knives, a saucepan. *Chansonniers* came from Quebec.

Bad news: Emilia Dionne, the quintuplet, died in a Quebec convent.

The Edmonton Eskimos won the Grey Cup. The greatest team Montreal ever had, and yet they lost, 26 to 25. How do such things happen? Suddenly the Holy Father, Pius XII, collapsed. He recovered, but he was not the same. No, not the same man. We began to realize that not even Maurice Richard could save us now.

My father lost his job.

We moved to an abandoned motel on Abattoir Road. It was a low, grey building. The flag pole still rattled in the courtyard. The electric sign had been removed but the grey poles remained. An outdoor privy was connected to our room by a long corroded yellow ramp. I slept on a cot in the ramp.

My father became concerned about his bad luck. Periodically he stood on one foot, twisted his neck to the nearest window, and slowly clapped his hands three times, producing three slow, deep slaps.

'One reason I am unemployed,' he told me, 'why I am under suspicion, is that, simply, I have better ideas.'

He slumped on the edge of the bed. I went through a variety of postures, trying to cheer him, splaying my fingers over his head, jerking my knee toward his. It was no use.

'We are *au chômage*,' my father said, trying to smile. 'On the dole. Barrault's revenge.'

'It's bad,' I agreed.

'Maybe we should go to St Iglesias, Minnesota. Or Bunco, Louisiana. We have relations there.'

But he didn't believe it. The material world had failed us. He smiled bitterly.

'It is *mont-de-piété* for us,' he said. 'Bread of charity.'

'Father, you became a stone in the balls.'

My father became depressed and went hunting in *la forêt*. When he came back Herbert and Ronnie Krems, my mother's brothers, waited for him.

'Jack,' Herbert said. 'We are told you are jobless.'

'I have enemies.'

'Ignace labours at the seminary,' Herbert said.

'You have not lived up to your responsibilities,' Ronnie said.

'These are the lies they spread.'

'Ignace is peculiar. Jean-Michel is feminine.'

'*Le bon Dieu* made them that way.'

Herbert and Ronnie exhaled cigar smoke into my father's face. They backed him against the wall.

'It is now illegal to cause children to require psychiatric assistance,' Herbert said.

'It didn't use to be that way.'

Ronnie took him outside and slammed him against the motel's grey door.

'Hasn't Jean-Michel spoken of suicide?' he asked.

'He succeeds at nothing.'

Herbert pushed him to the edge of the porch.

'Ignace cries on the bus to Winnipeg. For no reason.'

'He has plenty reason.'

My mother sat by the fold-out couch. Light surrounded her pretty black hair, her golden bracelet that dangled. Pippi slept in her slipper. She painted by the numbers, a Bavarian chapel by a water wheel, gold, russet, dipping her brush into capsules of paint. Ronnie slapped my father outside.

'She mourns. She grieves. She works herself to the bone,' Ronnie said. 'While you take sweats in *la forêt*!'

'Is personal hygiene illegal?'

Herbert and Ronnie Krems threw my father off the porch. He lay there and they rubbed snow in his mouth.

'It is no laughing matter, Happy Jack.'

'I am not laughing.'

'You are in grave difficulties.'

'Yes. The grave. You're right.'

'You know what we can do to you.'

'Absolutely.'

'Be a man, Jack Verhaeren,' Ronnie said. 'Be good to your children. *Tuez-vous pour eux autres*. Kill yourself for them.'

'Yes. Kill.'

Ronnie and Herbert Krems trudged away. Their black galoshes made trails in the snow. Our father crept back in, scraped the dishes, took out the garbage, took Pippi out, shovelled the driveway. My mother went into the shower and sang sweetly until the hot water ran out.

Uncle Georges died.

It was a freak. He was stepping out of his trawler when a sudden swell pushed the gangplank and he pitched off. A dock post fell and struck his head. My father and I ran to his shack. Georges leaned against his Korean wife, Annie, who suckled him. Children and dogs ran around the bed.

'*Le bon Dieu* has struck my enemy,' my father said.

'I am not your enemy,' Georges wheezed.

'Why didn't you tell me my wife was crazy?'

Georges's face turned the colour of dirty underwear. My father put his head on Georges's chest. Georges suddenly hauled down the curtains in agony. My father threw him back on to the bed. I marched around banging pans.

'I ORDER YOU OUT!' my father yelled. 'OUT, *MAUVAIS DIEU!*'

Georges screamed. My father sweated terribly. Georges leaned over and vomited.

'Jesus, he's a tough fucker,' Georges muttered.

'*Y va mourir,*' Annie said, lighting her pipe. 'He's going to die.'

'*LE BON DIEU – SAVE THIS FRENCHMAN!*' my father screamed.

'*Yé en train de mourir,*' she said. 'He's dying.'

Georges stopped breathing. Annie knocked the ash from her pipe.

'*Yé mort,*' she said. 'He's dead.'

Annie covered him with a blanket. We crossed ourselves. My father and I stepped on to the porch. We were dizzy. St Croix was barely visible: three lights on the dark lake. Fog glided by. My father pulled me under his jacket and held my head.

'That's what it is to be human,' he said. 'Sadness. Lots of sadness. Just when you can't take it any more *le bon Dieu* gives you, for the hell of it, just a little more sadness.'

Gruel, Oberlander and Semml signed depositions that my father had stripped Barrault and sent him into the rain.

My father wore his black coat and went to his hearing. It was held in the second floor of the police building, an airless grey room. They read his dossier to him.

'*French-speaking. Sixth-grade graduate. Merchant Marine. Dismissed. Emotional instability. HM Prison Swallowfield probationary employment to June 1947. Prison guard third class to present. Works long hours. One count alcohol on duty, April 1950 –* '

'It was Tomczek's vodka,' my father said.

'Be quiet.'

'With pleasure, *mon supérieur.*'

'*Severe beating administered to prisoner Gillesfons, November 1951 –*'

'Never did a man deserve it so much.'

'Verhaeren.'

'Indeed, *monsieur.* I am quiet.'

'*Application for promotion denied December 1951.*'

'See?' my father said. 'A good dossier.'

The judge put the dossier on the varnished table.

'Verhaeren,' he said. 'This is not a good report. It is a veritable *cahier de doléance.*'

'Yes. It is abominable.'

'Gruel and Oberlander, for example, have three citations for exemplary duty.'

'Well, they know where to put their tongues.'

'Verhaeren?'

My father rose from his chair.

'This is a farce!' he said. 'I sent the Negro into the rain because he disobeyed me!'

'Yes, but – naked – ?'

'The Negro has dark skin. It keeps him warm.'

'Verhaeren. The man is nearly dead.'

'His skin failed.'

My father, red-faced, lit his pipe, but it sputtered. The judge leaned forward confidentially.

'I wouldn't be surprised if they hooked you up, Verhaeren,' the judge said.

'Hooked me up?'

The judge put a forefinger to his temple and crossed his eyes.

'*Pzzzzzt!*'

Prisoners were leased to the city as road crews. Poles, Yugoslavs and Germans stood in the frozen mud. They threw remnants of the Portobello Hotel's porch on to flatbed trucks. Albanians, Hungarians and Romanians cleared timbers from the banks of the Petit Croix. My father drove by and they threw frozen dog turds.

'Yah! Yah! Verhaeren!' they yelled.

Our lives were blind, instinctive, Catholic. We were miners with no lanterns. We danced in our city of the dead and thanked *le bon Dieu* for our graves.

I heard my parents.

'Yvonne!'

'Leave me alone.'

'I am under tension.'

'You thought I was an easy lay, a stupid girl from the convent!' she said.

'You *are* stupid. You *were* an easy lay.'

'*Maudit foureur,*' she said. 'Stupid fucker.'

'I refute that!'

'You do?'

'Yes!'

'How do you refute that?'

'Thus do I refute that!'

Our father stuck two fingers down his throat, leaned forward, and vomited.

In the morning Ignace played at the vomit. It had turned dry and satiny, like a rock crystal garden, with silver threads and golden speckles.

*   *   *

86

St Bonaventure rose pink at dawn. Black crows circled the town. Girls walked over the street grit. I heard Antoinette Hartmann and Claire Pic, echoes, ice breaking under their boots. They giggled far, far away . . .

Erland Szegy, the mortician's son, joined the *buveurs*. Erland was short, with brown deer's eyes. We blindfolded him by the prison, forced Lamonts down his throat, twirled him, and suddenly showed him the artifice of Canadian life. We asked his story.

'When people die,' Erland said, 'my father embalms them. Their corpses are taken to the cemetery, sure, but afterwards we dig them up and take them to the lake. The priests throw flowers, and a submarine takes the corpses past the lighthouse.'

'That is not the truth of the submarine,' Etienne objected.

I slapped the table.

'You do not have the Deadwood whip, Bastide. Silence. Continue, Szegy.'

Erland smiled prettily.

'The submarine dives,' Erland said. 'It sends the dead out in tiny *boîtes de cadavres*. Like torpedoes they shoot from the hatches. They tumble down in silver bubbles and crack in the weight of water. Souls exit, transparent as jellyfish, trailing sins and guilts. They hold their misshapen heads in agony, floating into deep canyons. A buoy's bell screams. Some fall in the mud and are consumed by lamprey eels. But a few, a very few, travel up. Breaking water they rise in globes of mercury. They ride silver shafts to heaven.'

'I don't believe you,' Etienne said.

Erland fumbled for a cigarette in the pack I tossed him.

'Ask those who fish the deep,' he said insolently.

I stood. I made my declaration.

'Erland Szegy, the mortician's son, is admitted,' I said, *'because he told the truth as though it were fiction!'*

I became muddle-headed. I actually got lost. I walked in circles. I ended up at the Szegy mortuary.

'What's wrong, Erland?' I asked.

'You don't know?'

He took me to his room. It had red curtains and a ceramic ballet dancer on a mantel. There was an armoire, a painting of Hungarian hussars. Fresh flowers grew in a maroon vase with painted carp swimming through orange reeds.

'You are in love,' Erland said.

'Me?'

'What is so strange about that?'

'With you?'

'Sure. I tell you, you arrogant bastard.'

Erland dug his boots into the carpet. The leather was worn, richly polished, with a reinforced steel toe.

'One can die of love, Jean.'

'One can die of the lack of it.'

He looked at me suddenly.

'Jean, without love, what is the good of living?'

I had no answer.

A funeral cortège below rumbled out of the mortuary. Erland went to the window. It must have been a big-shot. Men in top hats and long black coats followed the hearse in the snow.

'Well, all right,' I mumbled. 'Just don't *paw* me.'

On 18 December, the Night of Moving Shadows, we put on black hoods, knocked on Catholic doors and asked for papists. Catholics pretended to hide. We dragged them out, made them recite the catechism, and were rewarded with fruit cake made with cherries, icing of the purest butter.

All night silhouettes flew up the harbour, invaded downtown, went through Prange's men's underwear, roosted on black wires.

The Dybs' rooster escaped. Erland and I crawled out of our attic and chased him around the roof. I kicked the rooster over the lilacs. Norwegian freighters bellowed the low endless *beeeeeee-o* of the foghorns. The harbour lights flew on the wind. We tasted darkness that night, Erland and I.

★   ★   ★

I passed Etienne Bastide's house. Something kept drawing me there. There was a wood fire and sharp, stinging smoke lay low on the stiff hedges. Frost sparkled on the walks. I banged into an oak tree.

'Wake up, Jean,' the oak said.

In the morning I received a dozen long-stemmed red roses from Etienne,

'à ma belle fleur – '

Erland was terrified of the future. We snowshoed through *la forêt*, had hot chocolate at the Bon Sentiment Lodge above Rutherford. But nothing eased his anxiety.

We played blind man's bluff. I stumbled blindfold across Clark Street, past the dry cleaner's, and stumbled into a snowbank. Erland picked me up. He had turned into a deer. I became terrifically frightened. I ripped off my black bandana. Erland blinked shyly, snow in his delicate lashes, fur of the softest down.

'*Salut,*' he said.

Erland bought a roulette wheel. We gambled for Cokes, bubble-gum cards, American dollars. Whoever lost tied the other to the red chair. He got to do anything he liked. From downstairs I smelled formaldehyde, varnish, rubber tubing.

'The smells stimulate you,' Erland said. 'They signify death.'

'Pleasure is so close to pain,' I said. 'About an inch apart, sometimes.'

We swung in darkness, climbed endless ladders. Erland and I learned the art of slow love. We sweated in our ignorance. I tell you, we sweated those black nights on the steppes of Canada.

'Is it true?' I asked, bathing my face at his basin. 'The dead rise in bubbles?'

'No. I said that to snare you.'

At the Christmas pantomime Antoinette Hartmann played Aurore Gagnon in *La Petite Aurore*. We cried when she died. Antoinette ran backstage and reappeared in a *tableau vivant*: the

Madonna of the Rocks. When the violins ceased and the bells played, the Virgin miraculously lowered her head.

Erland sent me a note. I went up the fire escape, knocked at his door, and he opened it. His brown eyes brimmed. Hat boxes lay on his dresser, high heels, a muff. A coal fire burned in his grate. He had sprayed sparkle on his hair and looked awful. A Christmas fruit basket lay on his mantel.

'Why don't you see me any more?' he asked.

'*As-tu une cigoune?*'

He handed me a Gaulois.

'I'll put ginger in my hair,' he said. 'Pomade. Whatever you like.'

Erland lighted my Gaulois. Something must have hit the telephone wires outside because there was an electric racket, sparks, and shadows over Erland's face.

'It's Antoinette Hartmann,' he said. 'You still love her.'

'You're hysterical.'

'I am in love,' he said.

'Same thing.'

'I'll be feminine in public. But you – you pretend – it's Antoinette!'

'Well, it's a question of anatomies, isn't it?'

I stood up. Erland kicked a hat box. He looked strange. His hair was brushed straight up, like mine. Sometimes he imitated my speech impediment. The wind howled, the window rattled, and cold came in.

'Look at our firelight,' Erland pleaded. 'Our Hungarian posters, our red chair, the pot-pourri! Who is Antoinette to you?'

'You get on my nerves.'

'I'll kill myself.'

'*Awaye fort,*' I said. 'Suit yourself.'

'I *will*. I'll splatter my brains over Grange Street.'

'Oh, my little dictator,' I said. 'How you hate me.'

Erland's lips trembled. A rose blotch appeared on his cheek. I was also sweating.

'Jean, love – '

' – is a rubbing of flesh. Nothing more.'

I went to the door.

'Jean!' he squealed.

I ran down the stairs.

'Donkey!' he yelled.

'Egoist!'

'Pervert!'

On 21 December 1954, Erland Szegy, my dear friend, loaded his father's shotgun, went to the fire escape and blew his head off. The street crew steamed his ligaments off the parking meters. Manhole cover, hydrant, telephone pole, everything had to be steamed.

'*Le monde y meurt, le monde y meurt,*' I shrugged, telling the *buveurs*. 'If people die, they *die.*'

I went into St Bonaventure's boiler room, piled paper towels in a waste-basket and dropped in a lighted match. Smoke twirled up. I stepped on it, but it got too hot. I went outside, found Father Ybert and told him that the janitor must have dumped a cigarette in the waste-basket. Father Ybert ran in but the fire had jumped over the heating ducts. Father Ybert pulled the alarm, Sister Félice led girls down fire escapes, and St Bonaventure's old wing burned down.

In the morning the black iron staircase smouldered in mud. Heaps of charred gym uniforms lay in jumbles of red brick. Father Przybilski presented my dossier to juvenile court. My father signed papers. I was remanded to reform school at Espanola near Sudbury.

'Jean,' my father said. 'I taught you everything I know about prison. From now on you must teach yourself.'

I went home, depressed.

'I told you, asshole,' Ignace said.

Catholics crowded St Bonaventure Church. We went up past the frozen marsh, crossed through the ruins of St Bonaventure school. Ignace nudged me.

'Ha ha, Jean,' he said.

Catholics came from Crow Hill, Heron Bay, Gilbertsonville, the eastern regions. Father Leszek patrolled the pews. There was a mass for Estée, Bobo, Georges, Erland Szegy. Cradles had been brought in, trimmed in black ribbons. Yugoslavs carried *Salvator Mundi*, Hungarians brought bells, Poles their wreaths, from Czestochowicz. White tapers flickered in the Chapel des Enfants. There were maps with crosses where the children had drowned or been killed. The *ange des berceaux* was lighted. Orphans, all in blue, were herded in by their guardians.

Ignace led the procession.

'Ignace comes – !' my mother said.

Silver bells dangled from his surplice. His white hair glowed.

'Like an angel – !' my father said.

Father Ybert opened the winged mahogany doors of the triptych. People cried in the beauty of the Christmas vigil. We crawled on a red carpet. I must have gotten carried away because Father Leszek stuck ammonia salts in my face and hauled me back. I looked drowsily through the incense. Etienne Bastide waved. Antoinette Hartmann's brown hair was held back by silver ribbons. Silver ice still melted at her galoshes. She was very beautiful. Fragments of her hands, eyes, red candles, circulated around the church. I was ugly, yes, with a speech impediment, but I felt like a genius. My father, brooding over Barrault, hit me.

'Sit down!'

Father Przybilski came to the altar. Christmas mass began. The *kyrie* was sung.

'Save us,' I prayed.

Father Leszek's tenor filled the brick vaults.

'For the sake of your orphans.'

'*Deus, cui soli competit medicinam praestare post mortem –* '

'Save me from Espanola.'

'*– praestra quaesumus, ut animae famulorum famularunque tuarum terrenis exutae contagiis –* '

'Where the British lads will surely kill me.'

'*– in tuae redemptionis parte numerentur.* '

Suddenly Ynez Pic stood up. Father Elmo pushed her down. But Zena Courennes rose, fought him off and screamed, '*Le bon Dieu!*'

Old Woman Dyb shrieked.

'*LE BON DIEU!*'

Frédéric Ybert, foreman of the defunct Galtieau Cement Works, weaved up and down the aisles.

'*GRACE A DIEU! GRACE A DIEU!*'

Old Man Dyb banged into a pillar and fell through Hungarian bells.

'*MERCI AU BON DIEU!*'

'*LE BON DIEU!*' the congregation yelled.

'*LE BON DIEU!*'

Catholics trouped confusedly out of the church. Father Leszek and Father Elmo also stumbled into the street. Bill Aubourg, limping badly, whirled past the pine trees, sending snow flying.

'LE SEIGNEUR!' he shouted.

Father Przybilski led the cortège down La Belle Dormière Street, holding the Host high. The women of the decency crusade loped down La Belle Dormière Street.

'LE SEIGNEUR!' they shouted.

Ignace ran after them, skirt held high. Christmas lights trembled. Pine needles flew into town, green bullets through the black. Lutheran faces craned out their windows, impossibly extended, like balloons on sausages, all the way across La Belle Dormière Street. Our mother danced down the ice past Prange's and sang:

> '*Le bon Dieu vien, vien, vien*
> *Ce soir, à minuit, ce soir*
> *Voici'l vien, vien, vien.*'

> 'God comes, comes, comes
> This evening, at midnight.
> Look, he comes, comes, comes.'

We herded on to the wharf, under yellow sulphur lights, over black sloshing water. I looked for my father. He was by the warehouse, caught in the lighthouse beam. His hair blew up from his ears, white, blinded, a French caricature. My mother's head kept snapping back. Ignace and I carried her home. Once inside she walked around and around in dreamy half-steps. The Christmas cortège must have broken up, because we could see silhouettes going home over the black trestle bridge. I bathed her hands. Ignace massaged her neck.

We watched her for a while, Ignace and I.

'Maybe we should undress her,' he said.

'And Papa?'

'With luck he's fallen in the lake.'

I helped my mother upstairs and covered her in a pink quilt. It was cold. I closed the window. I got a blanket from the closet and covered her with that, too. Her pretty hand wavered up in the air, as though trying to touch something.

'Jean – '

'I am here, Mama.'

A few minutes later our father stumbled into the kitchen. I went downstairs.

'Where is she?'

'She sleeps, Papa,' I said.

'I want her.'

'Don't you want a drink?' I asked.

'Who has some? At this hour?'

'The Dybs. They make brandy.'

'The cocksuckers.'

Snow melted on his red hair. He must have fallen. There was snow on his coat, and on his knees. I went to the Dybs to get brandy. Old Woman Dyb sat heavily in her red chair. The windows rattled in the storm. Suddenly her legs shot out and her arms flew up over her head. I wrestled her back.

'Oh, he is tough,' Old Woman Dyb said.

'Who?'

'*Le bon Dieu.*'

I took the brandy home. My father slumped at our kitchen table mouthing the *kyrie*.

'I have seen death tonight,' he said. 'I have a nail in my forehead.'

'It was a lot of praying.'

'I need brandy.'

'You've drunk it.'

'I have?'

'Ignace came back hours ago,' I said. 'He sleeps.'

'My God. I don't remember a thing.'

'No.'

'And Yvonne?'

'You gave it to her like a donkey.'

'I did?'

'Why do you think she sleeps so hard?' I asked.

'Ha.'

'Even her feet curled.'

'Ha ha ha.'

He tried to rise.

'The glory of the French race,' he said.

He fell forward and his head crashed against the blue Formica of our table.

'How many will you kill?' he mumbled.

I went to my bedroom and brought back a blanket. He was already snoring.

'*Mon beau petit,*' my father said, sleeping. '*Ma belle petite.*'

I drank it all. I woke later. There were no lights on. Pippi had a cold. He snuffled on the kitchen floor. My father was sprawled on two chairs. I went upstairs to bed. I heard voices in my mother's bedroom.

'No, Mama. Jesu already came tonight!' Ignace said.

'Feel my heart – how it pounds!'

'Like a meadowlark!'

'So sweet – like wine – I am swept downriver – '

Pippi licked my face. I must have gone back downstairs. I found dog food, ate some, gave Pippi the rest, and drank cooking wine. Two hours later it was Christmas morning. Ignace and I found our presents, still unwrapped, in the pantry. He got a black locomotive. I got a breviary.

Old Woman Dyb invited us inside for cocoa. We swept her porch. Then we went down to the Petit Croix to look for hibernating turtles.

'What was she saying?' I asked Ignace.

'Nothing.'

'I don't hallucinate, Ignace.'

'Yes you do. You hallucinate all the time.'

I punched Ignace and shoved him against a birch tree.

'Swear on the Body and Wounds,' I said.

'Okay. She was hallucinating.'

Ignace started to cry, so we went back home. Our father woke and went to the state liquor store. He came back with two bottles of gin and spent the day in the basement. Our mother woke at noon and with black eyes that saw nothing on earth watched birds flying.

She pointed.

'Jean . . . Look . . .'

Over St Bonaventure's steeple, streams of brains and viscera trailed up after Erland Szegy, rising in silver sun-shafts to the skies.

EIGHT

I packed my black duffel bag. Mr Gregg, the discipline authority, talked to my parents. My father signed more papers and then took me aside.

'Jean,' he said. 'Make a knife of a pie plate. The British will leave you alone.'

Mr Gregg drove me toward Sudbury. The reform school, a grey building, was on the mud plain outside Espanola. It had neither barbed wire nor guards, but inside it looked like St Bonaventure. I lived in the south wing. The hard-liners lived in the north. Between the wings was the asphalt basketball court.

I looked out at the bleak British landscape. I wondered how anybody could bear it. Granite mounds, blotched with black lichen, fed no birds or trees. The British earth was uninhabitable. The smouldering ruins of St Bonaventure were far away.

We woke at six-thirty. The shower turned to scalding because of the broken boiler. We observed ourselves. So many were deformed: a club foot, a curved spine, hammer-toes, a claw thumb. We went to the cafeteria for breakfast of wheat porridge and bacon bits.

I learned to operate a book machine. I glued the backs on, forced the pages and cover into rounding rollers, and cut the threads. We stacked them in boxes and I carried the boxes on to pallets and rolled the pallets to the Espanola van. I bandworked with a shuttle needle until my right leg cramped from the pedal. These were instructional manuals for the army. We also made leather mailbags, electric cable, and machine parts.

In the twilight we played basketball. The night comes so

quickly in January. By three-thirty the air was black. Espanola seemed to float on a frozen granite plain. It was like playing on the moon.

We were in a death coma. We put pine boughs on the walls, pictures of hockey players, nude girls, but nothing worked. We lived in torpor, in a grey paralysis.

They sent us to farm houses to fix toilets and drainpipes. The houses were small with black tar-shingled roofs, vermilion wallpaper, clapboard houses with Elizabeth's coronation still on the doors, peeling from rain. Back at Espanola we listened to the radio. Sudbury lost a steel mill. The dredging of the St Lawrence Seaway continued. Lampreys still infested the Great Lakes. There was rock and roll. The north-shore town of St Croix had cracked open after a methane explosion. The bluffs were crumbling.

I worked out in the weight room. I could press my weight. I wore a black sweatshirt and black sweatpants and did sit-ups on the diagonal bench. I did one-armed pull-ups. I kept staring at the Union Jack on the wall and pulled but the numbness in my right leg grew worse. Mr Warner, the gymnasium technician, weighed me and measured me. He applied battery shocks and linaments to my right foot. It was no good. The nerve had died in my foot. My right leg had stopped growing.

We studied Canadian history, arithmetic, spelling and woodworking. There were lectures on the Canadian way of life. It was like the larva and the butterfly, they said. One day we would fly to distant mulberry bushes.

One night the British lads gathered at the windows staring out and whispered.

'There it goes – '

I turned.

'What?' I asked.

'Going – '

I rose to my feet, blinking.

'What's going?'

'*Going* – '

'What?'

'*Gone* – '

98

'*What?*'
'THE FRENCH EMPIRE!'

I dreamed. I walked to a house by a railroad track. It was midnight. I was looking for Roger, but he wasn't home. I went in and it suddenly rained inside. The light inside the house was extraordinary, like thousands of candles. Suddenly two Antoinette Hartmanns, both in navy blue dresses with crimson pockets, came down the stairs. I couldn't figure out which was the real one.

I woke. The odour of mud, horse blankets and sweat disgusted me. James Raley, a British boy, had caught *puritus* and was sleepless. I salved him and he took quinine but in his sheets he shuddered. He took me into his bunk.

'What did you do?' he asked.

'I burned down my school.'

'Why?'

'In memory of a friend.'

The dormitory guard came up the hall, casting shadows from moonlight.

'You better go,' James Raley said.

I received a letter from Etienne Bastide. I read it by the dustbins.

Jean –

Trouble follows us like dogs. Emilia Street exploded. Methane stinks all over town. Prisoners work but they say the town is in trouble.

A terrible thing has happened. Maurice Richard was pulled out of the line-up. Impossible? Nothing is impossible in hockey. Not in the present political climate. So. No scoring record for The Rocket. The French went wild. Riots dismantled half of Montreal. British have been hammered stupid. Here in St Croix your father beat up Albert Wilkins, the television repairman. But his (your father's) troubles do not end: James Barrault, the Jamaican, is dead. The court ordered him (your father) to stay in St Croix.

Antoinette grows prettier every day. She is dating a college boy from Rutherford.

Why don't you write? Aren't old friends, first friends, the best friends? I think so.

Je t'attend
Etienne

I got sick and spent the afternoons on the latrine. The guard Mr Harold read to me.

'You must bring my armoir into the bedroom,' Lady Hartnell said. 'I cannot lift it myself.'

'I should be glad to,' William Buck replied. 'But it has been devilish hot today and I have carried your armoire all the way from the quay. May I avail myself of clear water?'

'Certainly, there is wine on the desk,' Lady Hartnell said. 'You may also wash yourself with rosewater.'

William Buck did so. When he was refreshed he came back into the boudoir. He found that Lady Hartnell had loosened her laces. 'How now,' he said. 'Is it so warm for you as well?'

'I die of being overheated,' she said.

He approached her more closely, eyeing the swelling globes rising and falling like tides under the satin. 'One can die of being overheated,' he said. 'But you will not, I ween.'

'You yourself must prove it so,' she said.

He came still closer. He detected French perfume like the wines of Armagnac exuding off her white and heaving bosom, until his own trembled with desire. 'What does Madam wish of me?' he asked.

'I should test your workman's skills,' Lady Hartnell replied, 'and of what timber you are.'

'You will find me composed of the straightest and the stiffest, my lady.'

She lay back on the triple pillows and from the vantage of the canopied bed detected the tautness of his breeches which foresaw to her a pleasure of great power. She saw by his reddened face that she had well and truly embarked him on that journey from which no man returns unaided.

'I desire you therefore to work, and let your tools probe, and your aim be true,' Lady Hartnell commanded.

'I warn you, Lady Hartnell,' he said. 'That which will cure your present affliction will cause others. For my tool as you shall presently see is of no ordinary dimensions. Indeed, there are ladies, even of high degree, from Highgate to Kentish Town, who have been sorely caught short.'

'Let me see.'

William Buck the seaman and lost carpenter of the Atlantic unfastened his breeches. When he did so she bolted upright, crossed herself and exclaimed, 'Father of God, I would be ruined.'

William Buck came closer and in an excess of delirium stroked her ringleted hair, curled by the coiffeurs of Bournemouth, smelled its talcum perfume, made in Bristol, and toyed with her double gold earrings, handcrafted in Izmir.

'We must therefore find other means to abate our pressures,' he said, 'or we shall die.'

'What is it you would have me do?' replied the querulous aristocrat, her eyes fixed on the pulsating proof of his imminent intentions.

'Woman has other chambers than that which have heretofore contained your most private gifts.'

'Do I take it that you require of me to be used in the Turkish manner?'

'No. The Egyptian.'

'And should I not drown?' Lady Hartnell recoiled with panic.

'And that immediately, Lady Hartnell, for I am violent with desire.'

So saying he embraced her and exercised therein the explosive heat and wonderment which nature creates in man and woman. She too, primed to the very abyss of ecstasy by his skill and ardour, fainted in wave upon wave of gold light, soared, soared, like a wild hawk unleashed through golden meadows, to the far and uncharted shores of ecstasy.

'What happened?' Mr Harold asked.

'He came in her mouth,' I said.

'Why didn't it say so?'
'It's literature.'

We boxed.

Benches were drawn up around a grey tarpaulin on the gymnasium floor. Mr Harold put me in the ring with Danny Pacon, who was also French. We lost control and slipped into *French box*. *Savate* it was, foot-fighting, and kicks with the punches. I knocked his teeth in. He danced to his corner and shrieked. Mr Harold yanked out his mouthpiece in a drool of blood. I thought to myself, *I am the king of beasts*.

Colonel Canale, from the French Foreign Legion to recruit French boys, stayed to watch. Mr Fredericks, the governor, invited the Espanola Elks Club. High-school clubs came in to watch. I became intensely conscious of Colonel Canale.

Mr Fredericks put me in the ring with Brad Gillman. I bobbed and gave him kidney punches. He failed to get off his stool at the third round. Mr Fredericks put me in the ring with Harold Youngblood, a Menominee. My legs dragged like concrete. I couldn't raise my arms. I slapped him and accidentally struck him in the eye. So I beat him, too.

I fainted in the shower and Mr Fredericks wrapped me in a white sheet. Mr Harold took me back to the dressing bench. My eye was swollen shut. I must have broken my thumb because when I came to it was in a splint. I couldn't move. They could have done anything to me, anything at all. Suddenly Colonel Canale was looking down with a green glass eye.

'You must have put your head directly under the cold water,' he said. 'There's a hole in your skull. That's where the nerves are. The cold water hit the nerves and you passed out.'

'I never touched the water, sir. I was choking on mucus in the corner.'

Mr Warner, the infirmary technician, knelt at my bench. He looked into my eyes. He felt my pulse. He pressed my groin, felt my balls, gingerly bent and unbent my prick. He stretched both my legs, pressed for my liver in my red stomach.

'*Tu es de St Croix?*' Colonel Canale asked.

I couldn't even nod.

'A hard child,' Mr Fredericks said.

'Look when I poke his liver,' Mr Warner said. 'A localized convulsion.'

'Hmmmmmm. Interesting.'

They watched me looking up from my white sheets.

'Look how his facial expression keeps changing,' Mr Fredericks said.

'Milk in his diet might help.'

They let me sleep right there. Midnight I got up to pee, couldn't find the stalls, and pissed in the shower. I looked back at my wet sheet crumpled like a shroud. The dirty walls, the long corridor leading nowhere, into darkness, the pebble window in the door, made me so lonely I went back to the dormitory.

The British lads caught me and dragged me to the potato bin. They stuck a pillow case over my head and jammed a crucifix of crossed carrots in my fists.

'Do you have anything to say,' one asked, 'concerning free Quebec?'

'Fuck off, gits.'

'Oh ho. So small and so full of shit.'

'Eat the queen's shit.'

They fit a rope around my neck. Brad Wilkins lost his temper, ripped off the pillow case and with bulging forearms mashed me into the wall.

'You know, we tolerate you French, but our patience is growing short.'

Colonel Canale visited my room. He wore khaki and a red beret. His face was heavily lined and rugged. His glass eye was dead.

'You would like to join the Legion?' he asked.

'It is all I ever wanted.'

'You have strong legs,' he said.

'I am an ice skater.'

'You limp?' he asked.

'Not so bad.'

He had a blue-green good eye that examined my bare leg. To be possessed by him would be like falling into

103

the sun. He touched my foot, along the bottom of the tender sole.

'How is it for you here?' he asked.

'Tender.'

'And here?'

'Ticklish.'

He laughed and held my knee.

'I know it is difficult for you, Jean-Michel Verhaeren of St Croix.'

'But you have seen so much.'

'I have.'

'Have you tortured?'

'I have.'

'When?'

'As often as necessary.'

'Is that often?'

'In Madagascar it was not often. In Algeria it was required.'

'And the Vietminh?'

Colonel Canale let go of my leg.

'Exercise your leg,' he said. 'Or you will be stunted.'

Colonel Canale took me to the gymnasium. He showed me the stretching of the ankle tendons, the lengthening of the ligament. He left the gymnasium. It was around twilight. I sat on the sit-up bench and listened to Colonel Canale and Mr Fredericks discuss my dossier in the hall. Colonel Canale came back alone into the gymnasium. I stood, put his hand to my mouth, and kissed it.

'You may torture me,' I said.

He looked at me closely. He was troubled.

'Perhaps you had the wrong notion, Jean-Michel.'

'Had I?'

'Everything is in torment,' he told me. 'In the Empire, everywhere.'

'Is it?'

'And yet you want to join the Legion?' he asked.

'With you.'

'Well, it's a problem with your stunted leg.'

'Tell me. Tell me your adventures in the Legion.'

'If you insist.'

Colonel Canale lit a cigar and sat on the folded brown gym mat. We were deep in darkness. Nobody turned the lights on. His face was illumined only by his cigar.

'My first post was Madagascar in 1946,' he said. 'I was stationed among those who practised the cult of the dead. They built luxurious tomb-houses, part underground, with elaborate staircases and gates above ground. This was near Tananarive.

'Riots began. Two policemen had their throats slit. French farmers armed themselves and the French Catholic missionaries barricaded themselves in their churches. We conducted patrols. Refugees from forced labour leaped at us with machetes.'

It was now night. Colonel Canale looked to see if I was listening.

'*Continuez, mon colonel.*'

'Corpses floated in swamps. We threw the rebels to the courts and executed hundreds.

'Then, as I remember, I was sent to Algeria. The seasons had not been kind to that country. One saw mud huts, vacant fields, stones – that was all. We worked with the *Vigilance Africaine*, a vigilante group. At Philipville we dug graves open and found Europeans with their throats slit.'

Colonel Canale shivered.

'Bombs were thrown into cinemas,' he said. 'I was sent to the Aures Mountains. We burned farms. We shot their cows. Yes, we used the *manière forte*. We stuck them with electrodes, crushed their testicles. And it made a roaring in the blood. Perhaps you are familiar with it?'

'A little.'

'We shot *chaouia* tribesmen. *Bleus de chauffe* – Muslims – we shot down three at the Palais d'Eté itself. I woke informants from the *marchands de sommeil*, those tenements where they sleep in shifts, and beat them until their blood ran, but nobody knew anything. Where were the rebels? Where was Europe? Did anyone care?

'In the desert we heard the *melhoun*, in the cities, *rai*. To this day if I hear a *darbouka* I go mad.'

Colonel Canale fell silent. I watched the end of his

cigar. He did not speak for a long time. He had gone far, far away.

'I was sent to *Indochine*,' he finally said.

'*Oui, mon colonel.*'

'Ah. What can you know of *Indochine*?'

'Dienbienphu.'

'But what does one know? Eh? What does one really know?'

'What do you know, Colonel Canale?'

Colonel Canale's voice became hard.

'In Saigon, in French villas,' he said, 'Frenchwomen played cards, drank cognac and spoke beautiful French. Saigon suburbs were blown up, but did they care? A native girl might be raped but in the evening the Frenchwomen stepped over her and went to the *glacier*, to the *parfumerie*. Yellow sulphur lights came on, revealing corpses fallen from bicycles. Did they care? The Frenchwomen listened to *chansons* on French radio.

'The war became one vast aphrodisiac. Frenchwomen lay on ornate beds, in fluttering shadows, the mosquito netting calm. Suddenly the depot goes up. Sitting in its fiery glow, turning with quivering lips, she wakes her lover, touches him, strokes him, to a new vigour, a new position. And there are so many positions.'

' – You have seen so much, Colonel Canale – '

'I was sent to patrol the RC4 highway in the north. Before even Dienbienphu. From Caobang we could look into China. The Meos – born by the Great Holy Dog, the Xas – naked dwarfs who ate rotted earth, the Hunis – red-feathered long-haired horsemen – these were our allies. And Caodaists. Caodai was God, a man with ecstatic eyes and beautiful hands. Their emblem was a cogged wheel on a yellow flag. By night they rode on bicycles and speared the Vietminh.'

' – No Catholics – ?'

'*Au contraire.* Bishop Le Huu-tu's cathedral became a fortress. He recruited virgins and tortured the Vietminh. It was Catholic terror, confession against auto-criticism.'

' – *Continuez* – '

'We became obsessed with *la belle mort*. We had *panache*. We would defeat Communism by *élan*. We greased our bodies, slithered into the jungle, and committed atrocities. Executions brought laughter. We smoked opium. We ate *nuoc mam* – a sauce of rotted fish in little pots – and *durians* – lovely fruits that stank. The Vietminh circled Caobang. We guarded our roofs with machine-gun nests. But nothing stops the 308th Vietminh Division. No, one by one they brought heavy artillery. Yet we dined well, we Legionnaires. We had champagne, even caviar. I ruined many *congai*. Night after night, I shot hot French sperm into them.

'Finally we blew up Caobang. We pulled down the tricolour and marched south to Luong Phai pass. But our fort at Dongkhe had been annihilated. Our colonel shot himself. We panicked and ran off the road into the jungle, into a green prison. Clouds of mosquitoes sucked blood from our faces.

'Blindly crashing into Quangliet Valley we became caricatures. Moroccan Legionnaires were hacked to death. Suddenly we were a hysterical mob. I slid down lianas to the gorge. Legionnaires were blown apart with mortars jammed down their throats.

'I found a wounded Vietminh, tied him to a rubber tree, pushed my bayonet between his teeth. I pushed and pushed, with all my weight, until his brains came through his nose. I have never come with a woman like that.

'I got lost. I wandered deliriously. I said farewell to France, to the Empire. Bullets fell through the fronds. The vegetation smelled of wounds suppurating already. Suddenly in the phosphorous clouds I saw Napoleon's *caissons*, I saw the brave Zouaves circling Paris, machine guns on the Somme. Asia could never kill us.

'Twenty-three of us came back. Out of the whole garrison. I was insane, but my vision saved me.'

' – You were so frightened – '

'Such fear cannot be described.'

' – Even now it is difficult – '

'Yes. Especially after Dienbienphu.'

'And now?'

'Well.'

'Yes. Well.'

'You want to lean against me?'
' – No. You can lean against me.'
'Like this?'
' – Exactly.'
'You nearly dozed, Jean.'
' – Strange. I *had* fallen asleep. I dreamed I wore a black skirt and boots like a Parisienne. My ears were pierced and I wore long gold earrings. I heard nightingales.'
'Be quiet.'
' – Yes.'
'But enough. May I?'
' – *Mais tu m' tuera, monsieur.*'
'Not so. I kill you? How could you say so?'
'Ah – '
'Oh!'
' – Wait – '
'Agreed. I wait.'
' – Oh! – '
'It's okay?'
' – It hurt! – '
'JESUS CHRIST!'
' – Yes. – '
'Are you all right?'
' – You startled me a little. – '
'Just a little little.'
' – A little little – '
'But now?'
' – It's all right. – '
'Are you sleepy, Jean?'
' – I think so. In fact, I am sleepy.'
'Sleep. Jean, sleep. I had hoped it would be more tender, but, well – '
A bird fluttered high in the netting outside the windows. Its shadows scraped the walls as it struggled for the twilight.
' – You were very tender,' I said.

NINE

I was released by an intercession of Colonel Canale. I moved back to the motel on Abattoir Road. It was lonely without Erland Szegy or Roger Vaucaire. I painted birds on the walls. Mostly I walked around St Croix. I knocked on Antoinette Hartmann's door. She was in Winnipeg.

'Jean! JEAN!'

It was Etienne Bastide. He had grown a moustache. He was suddenly very tall. He put his hand on my head.

'*Le Gosse,*' he teased.

'Yeah, yeah. *The kid.*'

'So how is life in the motel?'

'Bleak.'

I must have changed. He looked away. Emilia Street had ruptured again. Freddie Granbouche's bakery had closed. The apartments in the Lacombe Building were empty. Caritas had boarded up. Etienne pulled a copy of *The Watchtower* from his parka.

'Have you been approached by Jehovah's Witnesses?' he asked.

'Who hasn't?'

'You don't like them?'

'They are losers.'

'And we are champions of the world?' he said.

'Quite frankly,' I said, 'De Plessis has the right idea.'

'You mean – ?'

'Exactly.'

I slid my finger across my throat.

★   ★   ★

I walked past our old house on LeClerc. Forgotten things were in the gutter: carpet, rose-pattern plates, paper lanterns, my crib with a sturgeon leaping through a rainbow, *roi de la mer* stencilled in blue. Our game of *Jardin de l'Oie*, a goose every ninth space, death's head to start again. Spiders crawled on our toys, even in January.

It was Twelfth Night. Children sledded down the bluffs. We put pine boughs, rabbit fur, the portrait of Catherine Labouré on the altar. The propane heater roared. It was so hot the windows misted. Pine needles had died brown and ruffled over the brown floor. My mother baked a fruit cake and we drank to the King of the Bean. Ignace, my father and I went under the table.

'*Le Roy boit!*' we screamed. '*Le Roy boit!*'

Our mother divided the cake.

'*Fabe Domini pour qui?*' she laughed.

'*Pour le bon Dieu!*'

My father's piece had the bean in it. We kissed him.

'So,' he said. 'Luck changes. Who knows?'

Someone knocked at the door. I opened the door but there was nobody there. We crossed ourselves and spat.

Kelly's Nursing Home shut down.

The patients were taken to Rutherford. All that was left were seven rooms in a low building, winter light on pieces of beds. My mother cleaned floors for Prange's. I gave her a gift of lacquered holly berries. At night our motel blinked with red, amber, candles but a dying animal looked at her from the mirror.

Uncle Emil died.

It was a freak accident. Fertilizers ate through his red chlorine sores. He had a seizure. Father DeVaux officiated. Emil's coffin jammed and my father wrestled it down to the wet clay. He climbed out, trousers black with mud, and lowered his head.

'May the angels wash thee,' he whispered.

★　　★　　★

My father dressed in black and went before the grand jury.

'You were the guard on duty in the E-wing on the night the Jamaican was sent into the rain?' the provincial investigator asked.

'I was.'

'Had he disobeyed you?'

'Yes.'

'How?'

'By not doing what I asked.'

'And therefore you stripped him naked?' the prosecutor asked.

'No.'

'No?'

'He stripped himself. I ordered him.'

'Is it common to be stripped naked in Her Majesty's prisons?'

'Of course. In the gang showers. Changing clothes. In the cells on hot summer nights. Nudity is a frequent occurrence.'

'Especially when you are on duty?'

'It occurs, as I say, frequently.'

'You sent the Negro into the rain?' the prosecutor persisted.

'There was work to be done.'

'But – *naked?*'

'We work hard.'

'Assiduously.'

'I am nobody's ass.'

'I meant, you are diligent.'

'I dream of prisoners.'

'Did you place hands on the *nègre?*'

'I did not.'

'Did you ever photograph him for your black museum,' the prosecutor asked, 'or cause him to be photographed by others, or make him stand in odd postures?'

'I no longer remember.'

'Did you cherish his skin?'

'He had smooth skin.'

'Or his eyes?'

'No. Not his eyes. Not so much.'

'And the genitals?'

'Excuse me?'

'Were you interested in his . . . organs . . .?'

'One is always curious about one's fellow man.'

'But the *nègre* . . .?'

'*Négritude* . . . *Monsieur l'avocat* . . . is a very difficult . . . concept to explain . . .'

Ignace stood by the motel window wearing a white scarf. His lips quivered. His wall was decorated with white paper-bag snowflakes.

'*Quelle tempête!*' Ignace said. 'What a storm!'

'Go back to bed, Ignace.'

'*Garde-là!*'

'I don't want to look.'

I closed my eyes. I was sick of Ignace.

'*Garde les étrangers-là!*' he said.

'What strangers?'

I cleared a space in the window frost. Over Poniatowski Fields men in black pushed wagons through the howling snow. They pulled themselves forward by grabbing white fence posts. Animals slid side to side in dark cages. Women in fur jackets shouldered the wheels.

'Are they the Czech circus?' Ignace asked.

'No. The Czechs are gone.'

'They are Doukhobours, naked and chained, marching to Ottawa!'

But they weren't Doukhobours. Ignace became excited.

'*Flagellants!*' he said.

But they weren't flagellants.

'I would like to join them, Ignace, whoever they are.'

'Why?'

'To die and live in a new way.'

'Go to sleep, Jean. You disgust me. What happened to you at Espanola anyway?'

The troupe grew smaller. They became hard, black as death

cards under the white sun disc. They went into a cloudy whorl. Down by the black cranes in the harbour, they were lost. Ignace rolled over. He dreamed of Ho Chi Minh, pieces of light, he was a bird-woman.

'Those women,' Ignace said, waking. 'They were beautiful.'

'Women are beautiful.'

'We will never know.'

Ignace lay with his forearm over his eyes. He imagined his death again: drowned in Georgian Bay.

'I believe that women are carnal,' he said. 'But the spiritual is in men.'

'*J'tu crois pas.* I don't believe you.'

'No?'

'Me, I want to explode.'

'Yes, I saw you rigid on the couch,' Ignace said.

'If I could explode – '

'You'd make a mess.'

'But I'll never explode.'

'So you won't make a mess.'

Ignace found the whole thing ridiculous.

'*Mais que cé qui t'enrage tout, Jean?* What makes you so mad?'

'Everything.'

'Egoist.'

'*Si tu savais.* If you only knew.'

Ignace became ethereal. I became sad.

'You'd think you were alone in the world.'

'*Finis ton rêve,*' I said. 'Finish your dream.'

Ignace slept. He woke.

'*Je l'ai finie mon rêve,*' he said. 'I've finished my dream.'

Ignace sighed.

'I should have been a *parfait*,' he said. 'I would give the *caretas*. I would fast to death.'

'And me?'

'You? You will wander the earth, a coffin on your back.'

'And you?'

'I will die some day, Jean.'

'What could death mean to such a one as Ignace Verhaeren?'
'It will be your fault.'
Ignace sat up. His eyes were red. He beat his little chest with an effeminate fist.
'And I – a heat of love – in a chaste body – !'

We sacrificed everything to Ignace. The best ham, my scarf, tea and rum in the afternoon, he had it all. We rubbed his feet in camphor. We stroked his hair. Ignace ate red apples. He became conceited and cruel. He told me there was a present for me. He said it was in the closet. But when I looked there was nothing. Ignace tricycled around the linoleum floor wearing a peaked cap, blowing a trumpet with a red tassel.
'*Soldats du Christ!*' he yelled.

He would come and sit on the edge of my bed.
'Things have been bad,' he said, 'but they'll improve now.'
'How?'
'You can work, with skills you learned at reform school. I can earn money through the Church.'
He laughed and punched me on the arm.
'You know,' he said. 'You're really nothing without me!'

We heard him in the bathroom by the short bursts of *peepee* he made. In the evenings we gathered at the toilet.
'He shit!' my father said.
'HE SHIT!' we shouted.
At night he shook in convulsions.
'Jean,' he whispered. 'What if I fail?'
'*We* failed.'
'It brought us to the basement of life.'
Ignace rose from bed, the blue-white street lamp making blue-white rivulets of sweat down his chest.
'I could die,' he said. 'Then what would happen to the Verhaerens?'
'We die.'

'But I speak of the spiritual life. Our failures brought us to the death of the spirit.'

Every night was the same.

'Hoooooooooohaaaaaaaahhhhh!' Ignace screamed. 'Hee-eeee*yaaahhh*!'

And then we went back to eating, smoking, shitting, whatever we were doing, waiting for something we desperately didn't want.

Ojibways dismantled the warehouses that had collapsed when the methane blew. Conveyor belts were removed to Rutherford. A barge with scrap metal crashed into the steps on Fourth Street. Tommy Shanks and I drank Lamont's ale at the hotel picture window. Beer mugs and photographs of royalty hung from rafters. British owners put up an old banner: '*Men Are But Gilded Loam*'.

A Portuguese freighter crashed through the breakwater. The lake submerged Fourth Street. Downtown between Fifth Street and Emilia Court was cordoned off. Raw sewage spilled into the trunk-line station and the lighthouse shut down. We stared into the dark for the first time since 1929 and crossed ourselves. St Croix lost its charter and was absorbed into Thunder Bay. People wandered the streets, calling for their children.

Our father was indicted for criminal negligence. Trial was set for March.

Red Two Hats ate lobster at the Fleur de Lis.

He walked to the Bon Garçon and had roast beef. He stopped at Lemke's Dairy and ate a gallon of vanilla ice cream. At Kelbo's Fish Restaurant he had crab. Red bought a litre of Jack Daniels, drank it, went to the Old Royal Café and had steak and potatoes. He bought a litre of Polish vodka, drank it and went to the broken wharf and hung himself by a black wire from a pulley.

Officer Zaruba found him dead, jerking, still throwing up.

Yes, there was a fatality against us. Ignace already knew it. My mother's epilepsy was proof of it. It had crushed my father. And I? I ate it for breakfast. The motel walls grew infinitely far away, and yet sometimes the boards flew up – smash – right in my face.

'Have you noticed?' Ignace said. 'The floors tilt against you, whichever way you walk.'

'Our French – our sacred *joual* – degrades.'

'Yet we sing in high French. Have you noticed?'

'What can it mean?'

'Jesu is pissed at us.'

My father salted roads. He carted rubble from Emilia Court. He vacuumed rooms for the Winnebago Motel and killed fleas in the cinema. He played the accordion for the prisoners.

'Hah! Verhaeren!'

I went to see Antoinette Hartmann. She was in Gilbertsonville.

'I dreamed last night,' Ignace said at breakfast.

'Of what?' I asked.

'I ran down Isle of May Street, chased by wolves. Vatican wolves. How do I know they were Vatican wolves? Because they had crucifixes on their chests. They chased me to a basilica on Ojibway Flats.'

'How bizarre.'

'I ran up the steps – I was in Rome now – into the corridors. There was a large fresco of Erland Szegy.'

'Erland?'

'Yes. Isn't it funny how these things work? Anyway, he was upside down like St Peter on a cross. In the next fresco was Red Two Hats.'

'Red?'

'Yes. He had been blinded and castrated. His viscera hung out on his knees.'

'No wonder you *peepeed* in your sleep.'

Ignace laughed.

'Did I? It's a pity you don't have visions, Jean. Instead of other people's.'

116

Ignace was excited. He brushed his hair to one side. His legs rocked under the table. My mother studiedly put butter on her roll. Ignace bored her. She looked out where the snow flew up the fields. It was fifteen degrees below. She sipped honey tea. Ignace filled another kaiser roll with strawberry jelly.

'Listen. I had a second dream.'

'What?'

'I was in an abattoir. In Chicago. Arteries shot blood in arcs. Men and beasts slipped in it. Heaving flesh – tons of flesh – all the flesh of this world – I caught the blood in a gold goblet.'

'Why?' our mother asked.

'I was the Holy Father. I was giving absolution.'

Our mother sat in a small shadow. She had creases across her forehead. Ignace pushed another roll into his mouth.

'I had a third dream,' he told me.

'Oh, shut up,' I said.'

'I was a *voyageur*. I transported corpses. Racoons splashed along the river reeds. You know how they look like they're praying? I saw their shadows on the black eddies. But I transported great treasure.'

'Dead men?'

'Yes. When I woke up my heart beat so hard I felt I was having a heart attack. I thought, *I am only fourteen. I cannot die.*'

Ignace studied patterns of light in the frosted window.

'What can it mean?' he asked. 'Who is it that creates these visions?'

Suddenly Ignace turned to me.

'Is it not a false identity imposed on me?' he whispered. 'Is not this the source of my difficulties?'

'I, too,' I said.

'You?'

'You don't think I *want* to be like this?'

'Well, *t'as mal au cul*, at Espanola. That's for sure. You got a sore ass.'

We drove to Georgian Bay to escape our troubles. White squalls obliterated Canada. It got whiter and whiter. Ice moved in clumps on the windshield and my mother wiped the fog. My father drank Polish vodka. We came to a Victorian hotel, the Windsor, and drove down a pink gravel driveway.

'*Le bon Dieu* has brought us to the Windsor!' he hooted.

A Union Jack whipped over the white breakfast nook. Chains rattled. We went into the Rivière Room, a red-carpeted dining room. We had *crêpes* with shrimp, white wine, tarragon. My father drank a bottle of white wine.

He sang:

> '*Ah! si mon moine voulait danser*
> *Ah! si mon moine voulait danser*
> *Un capuchon je lui donnerais*
> *Un capuchon je lui donnerais.*'

My mother winked at me.

'If a monk danced with Jean-Michel, he'd get more than a little cap,' she laughed.

Rain blew through the balcony. White deck chairs, metal tables and umbrellas flew in lake spray. Heavy grey water broke over the lawn. Somebody in black oilskin crossed by the garage. My father ordered the liquor menu. My mother took off her black galoshes and rubbed her cold stockinged feet.

'Why didn't she recognize me?' she asked.

'Who?' my father asked.

'My Mother Superior at Trois Pointes.'

'Ah. Her mind was old,' he said.

'How old is old?'

'One fades into darkness.'

'How sweet to fade like that,' she said.

'One slips into echoes.'

'One becomes memory,' Ignace said.

'One's existence ceases,' I said.

'It's black as an Ojibway's asshole, that's for sure,' my father said.

Lightning flashed. The stained-glass window, *Ich Dien*, glowed red where a white hart jumped. Pippi whined. I took him outside. The rain whirled around the rear stairwell. It was already night. Pippi pissed in their flowers, shook himself and trotted toward the garage. I yanked him back inside, wet footprints on their red carpet.

My father ordered a Windsor Royale: gin, egg white, crushed ice, grapefruit rind, a shot of *crème de cacao*. My mother had a Whisky Windsor: Jack Daniels with mint, pineapple, a cherry, cream and apricot juice. Ignace had the Sandringham dessert: strawberries in maple syrup. I had a *crème de menthe*. Misery grew like a forest around us.

'Let's fish,' my father said. 'Enough of this Barrault business.'

'In the rain?' I asked.

'Fish bite in the rain.'

'In January?'

'They have starved through December.'

'But it's dark.'

'There are floodlights.'

We rented four black fishing poles and walked to a white fence that arched over a sluice gate. We sat on the Windsor's white garden chairs in our raincoats, huddled in the warmth of our liquor. Georgian Bay was a vaguely perceived heaving of black, cold mass beyond the causeway. We fished. Our father went inside to buy gin. I told Ignace to be an Iroquois.

'No,' he said. 'It's dark.'

'Go down the bridge.'

'I'll fall in.'

'I'll punch you,' I warned.

'OW!'

'I'll do to you what Colonel Canale did to me!'

Ignace ran down the dark. I heard him on the slick rocks. Then I didn't hear him. I waited about two minutes and yelled the Iroquois cry.

'*Kaioueeeeeeeeee!*'

There was no answer.

'Jean!' my father asked, ducking back into the floodlights with two bottles of gin. 'Where the hell is Ignace?'

I didn't see him. My father came up the white bridge and slapped me.

'WHERE IS HE?'

'I don't know, Papa.'

My mother ran over the bridge, pointing into the luminescence.

'HIS SHOE!'

Ignace's shoe bobbed like a dead trout. My father punched me across the side of the head.

'You cow – you're supposed to watch him!'

The hotel ground crew thrashed into the reeds. Ignace's black fishing pole jerked up against the pylons.

'Ignace!' I yelled.

Boats lowered from the docks. Police launched into the bay. My mother found his white sock tangled in black fishing wire.

'*IGNACE!*' she screamed.

My father beat me up. With both fists he split my lip and knocked my right eye shut. He was so furious he went blind.

'IGNACE!' I yelled. 'IGNAAAAAAAAAACE!!!'

My father hit me so hard I fell unconscious. I woke on hands and knees in wet grass.

'*IGNAAAAAAAAACE!!!*'

Ignace drowned under a white boat that had capsized years ago. The bay patrol winched him up. Reeds fell out of his open mouth. Water poured from his sides. He glared at a black hole in the night clouds.

I was cheated.

TEN

I went insane.

It was early February and sleet howled off the lake. Fields were buried in darkness and crows flew over Poniatowski's farm, lighting on stubble. I walked past a retarded boy on a blue leash on La Poudre Road, Daniel Fenner, who drooled and swatted invisible flies. On the bluffs the prison was hung with icicles. *La forêt* was lost in heavy clouds.

Far away a freighter hung motionless, out of the United States, in a rain harsh and stinging.

A Polish alkaline worker gave me a ride. As he sang in Polish his rosary danced on the mirror. A picture of the Black Madonna flashed on his dashboard. The septum of his nose had been eaten away and he talked with a metal device against his throat. I could smell the inside of his face.

'Where you going?' he asked.

'Away.'

'Why?'

'To be cured.'

'Of what?'

'Of what, he asks.'

The Pole drove down to the lake. Pulp logs were covered in white-caps. Chains banged at the docks. The smoke of field fires stung our faces. We grew insular, the Pole and I, moody and silent. He adjusted his saints on his visor. It was a world unto ourselves, Catholic, overheated, damp. He let me out at Coldwell.

'*Oziękuje,*' I said.

'*Pederasta.*'

A man walked by, shouting at garbage in the snow.

The Slate Islands rose on my left. Fog covered a hospital, and shadows of owls flew by. On Hays Lake pines dripped with melting sleet. I walked to Pays Plat Bay. Ships dissolved in the frigid haze. I followed a path of ragged slag until night fell. Smokestacks were silhouetted in pink clouds. Frost sparkled on logs that bumped in black swells, pink reflections, ice, turning over like dead turtles. I sang:

> *'Madam, je reviens de guerre, tout doux*
> *Madam, je reviens de guerre, tout doux*
> *Qu'on m'apporte ici du vin blanc*
> *Que le marin boive en passant, tout doux.'*

But there was no white wine, no sweet sailor, passing by.

My throat was sore. I couldn't spit and a fever came. St Ignace Island rose to view, then Simpson Island and Simpson Channel. Factories rolled over, up from the lake. I reached Cooper Point and climbed into an abandoned DeSoto, but I couldn't sleep. I went into the Nipigon Café.

The Nipigon Café was decorated with posters of the salt pillars of Cappadocia. The owner was a hunchbacked woman who made grilled cheese sandwiches even when nobody ordered them. Factory workers held white mugs in knobby fists and squinted out the plate-glass window. Gulls hung over the factories where white smoke curved on the earth.

The waitress gave me coffee and eggs.

'But I didn't order – '

'Are you running away?' she asked.

'I'm going to be cured.'

'Of what?'

'Of certain . . . things . . .'

A man followed me outside. He chased me down Lake Street. I threw a beer bottle and it smashed against a brick wall. He picked shards, one by one, from his neck.

'Homosexual!' he yelled.

★   ★   ★

I visited the museum of orphans.

The museum was a two-storey building with a double wood staircase which had belonged to the Brethren of Superior, a commune of fishermen. Now the Salvation Army donated broken toys. The exhibits were dusty, under dim red lights. Nobody else was in the museum. Dioramas showed miniatures of orphans who picked hops in Ontario, girls who carried cigarette trays in Ottawa. Bellhops saluted in a Prince Edward Island villa. I put in a nickel in a slot. A panorama of Canada sang, arms moving.

> 'We are the orphans of Canada
> From the provinces we come
> To build the empire shore to shore
> Dawn to setting sun.
>
> 'O Canada, o Canada,
> Our hearts belong to thee.'

In the corner was a black metal box full of firespark wheels, Red Ryder ukuleles, a pink and green parasol, a chipped tea set, black rubber spiders, corn husk flowers, a Chinese lantern, peppermint hearts, a Beatrix Potter ceramic house, a sailor doll in navy blue. There were valentines, Mr Potato Head, flip-books, red crayons, broken linocuts, a turntable. By the stairs was a canister full of braces, crutches, shoulder alignment screws, finger splints, thumb-knuckle wires, elevated shoes, scissors, surgical trays, hearing-aid, orthopaedic straps.

Under the clock was a wooden box full of penny loafers, sandals, Mary Jane pumps, saddle shoes, ballet slippers, Dr Martin shoes, Oxfords, rubber shoes machine-punched to look like stitching, arch supports, black waders. There were spectacles on a shelf, astigmatic lenses, tortoise-shell frames, half-frames, chipped lenses, shimmering light. Penny-tossing machines lined the wall: the lion and the Christian, customer and Negro bootblack, woodsman and squirrel.

On raised plywood sheets upstairs were model orphanages made of white cardboard. There was an E-wing plan, linear, and a circular orphanage. There was also a plate of orphans' meals: lacquered oatmeal, potatoes, bread, coffee, and a collection of sports equipment: metal bar, black ball, rope. On the stairs was a photograph of twenty-one orphan couples married in one ceremony.

The white mist rubbed the Brethren's windows. I saw a finger scrawl:

I was cheated.

I crossed the Black Sturgeon and the 49th parallel. The United States smelled like stink cabbage. I was sick and felt hot and rubbery. The Kaministikwia Delta of Minnesota was half frozen, half flooded. The red sun and the clouds piled lavender over a flat-topped mountain that blocked the horizon. I collapsed in the delta and woke in an asylum.

'You slept a hell of a long time.'

A boy sat on the edge of my bed. He had a large face with blond down. His eyes glittered.

'An awful long time,' he said.

He stroked me with hands that were not hands but worm-like, boneless fingers growing straight out of his wrists. The fingers were soft and warm as pink rubber tubes. He curled and uncurled them. His blue eyes grew hard.

'What's the matter?' he asked. 'Don't like them?'

'Just startled, that's all.'

He crossed and twisted his fingers like soggy breadsticks. He kept staring at me.

'What's your name?' he asked.

'Jean-Michel Verhaeren.'

'Shit name.'

'I'm Canadian.'

'Me too,' he said. 'I'm from Canada.'

'Great country, Canada.'

'Well, you're not in Canada now.'

He looked around the room. A painting of a sea captain darkened in the purple of the corner sun. I heard adults crying, footsteps running.

'What kind of hospital is this?' I asked.

124

'Why did you come here?' he asked.

'To be cured.'

'Of what?'

'Of . . . things . . .'

'I'll bet you're homosexual,' he said.

I drew the covers over my head. He yanked the covers down.

'It's written all over your face,' he said.

'Leave me alone.'

'How old are you?' he asked.

'Twelve.'

'You ain't been crucified.'

'Crucified?'

He pulled down his trousers and pointed.

'I been crucified. See?'

He pulled up his pants and went to the window and leaned out. I smelled the sleet melting to rain, the black mud of the delta. He rolled a cigarette with that peculiar dexterity.

'That's what makes the difference,' he said. 'Being crucified.'

He wandered back to my bed.

'Spaghetti hands, they call me,' he said. 'They put my fingers in wooden boxes with copper wires. They take off the bindings at night but the blood never is right. The fingers are worse than ever. But I don't mind.'

He gave me his cigarette. He lighted it by snapping those fingers. The tobacco tasted sweet and dark.

'Truth is,' he said, 'I have strength in these fingers. Just because they look like nightcrawlers don't mean there's no strength. It's just that there ain't no bone. It's like the snakes that grow in the ponds. Or maybe there's a bitty skeleton inside. Want to feel?'

'No.'

'Sometimes I feel something leathery inside. Maybe it's the ligaments. I don't know a ligament from a tendon. Do you? But I can break a chicken's neck same as any man.'

'Why are you here?' I asked.

'As if you didn't know.'

'I don't know.'

The cripple smoked a long time. He laughed. He squinted because of the heat of the smoke.

'I'll bet you killed somebody,' he said. 'Or will.'

'It was an accident.'

'It has to do with bodies,' he said.

'What? Whose? What are you talking about?'

'Bodies.'

'But they're different,' I said.

'Are they?'

I waited. The cripple stared out the window.

'I once left my body,' he said.

The Cripple

'I was an orphan.

'I grew up in Queen City, Saskatchewan. I lived in public housing behind a tavern, with an old woman who cleaned the baths and toilets. I slept in the coal-bin and stayed in the public housing even when the old woman died and the flat was empty.

'I had no clothes. I wore the dresses of the old woman. I slept on her rotted mattress during the day and at night scavenged Queen City. It was a gateway to Saskatchewan and plenty of hunters left lots of bottles. All night there were fights, and even gunshots. I collected rags and rats. One day a hunter told me that my mother was alive in Minnesota. I got men's clothes and left Queen City.

'I walked by night. I would sit on the cold marshes with a nail and pick out the snails and eat them. I carried pepper in my pocket and I lived on that, too. I caught frogs and ate the soft parts and the bark of fallen logs. I was skin and bones. The earth started coming to me like a broken cinema with parts missing. Suddenly I would be in the lumber stacks, or by a river, or in a field, and I didn't remember getting there.

'I lived in the woods and came into town to steal. There was a turkey farm and I ate the cast-offs. I hated it. I couldn't digest anything. I used to get a penny's worth of cow udder from a farmer and it was dreadful, like a piece of sponge that wouldn't break apart in my mouth.

'There was a terrible flood that spring. Gas stoves and refrigerators floated past overturned garages. The funeral parlours were packed. The water was so cold my fingers got wriggly. That's where it happened, in the United States, in Minnesota, on the Kaministikwia Delta. For miles the shore was bright with trails of jelly fish popping on the mud. Cartilege lay on the ponds. I ate it, too. Buckthorn with berries washed into the pools. I sucked it. A skate sparkled in the moonlight. I chewed it.

'One night I heard a lake perch as it sucked air on the mud:

'"Where is *your mother?*"

'You see, I was very sick. I heard animals talk. Even now, I hear you, but see a donkey. I found some crow garlic and ate it. I ate stink cabbage. I couldn't keep anything down. After a while I threw up whether I ate or not. I camped for a week by a charred log deep in the delta. One night I suddenly woke. A tramp squatted by my log. He had made his dinner, and now he unrolled his bedroll near me. He lay down and began snoring, so I went to sleep, too. I woke a little later. He was up, staring at my hands.

'"What's the matter?" I asked.

'"Who put worms on your hands?"

'I tucked my hands inside my coat.

'"Nothing's wrong with my hands."

'He came over, jerked my hands out of my pockets. He spit on them and finally went back to his bedroll. Later I woke again. He had crawled out of his bedroll and was looking at my hands again. I sat up.

'"Don't be frightened," he said breathing hard.

'I crabbed backward.

'"Why are you frightened?" he asked.

'"Shut up."

'"You're alone."

'"Leave me alone."

'I went backward but I banged against the log. His face was deep red. I never seen a man's face so red, like a turkey's wattle. He slipped a hand under my overcoat.

'"Please – "

'I ran out into the delta. He chased me over the mud.

'"I need love – " he bawled.

'I hit him with my sand shovel. He sagged. He began to mess with my hair. I hit him again. He tried to mouth me, but he lost consciousness. I hit him harder and harder. I hit him in the bloody face until it went soft. He grabbed me around the knees.

'" – love – !"

'I hit him again with the shovel. I cleaned his brains off. Somewhere far away a freight train echoed over the delta, the most lonesome sound on earth. I saw the black creeping out from behind the body, the black that wraps us all.

'I woke in this asylum, same as you. Orderlies cut my hair, bathed me. The orderlies rubbed my fingers. They used steel pipettes to suck synovial fluid, but the bone never grew back. You're beginning to understand, aren't you, to learn the meaning of loss?

'Dr Robinson put a hand on my shoulder. Light glowed around his face. He had the most handsome face I ever seen, the only man I ever let touch me. We walked down a corridor and he showed me the ward. Pairs of eyes glistened from beds, like rabbits, just been born. I became frightened so he took me outside. Old men were silhouetted by the walls, slow-moving, humpbacked. I cried and they took me to Dr Robinson's room to sleep.

'"My poor schizophrenic," he said.

'An hour later a slit opened in the wall. Two boys in nightshirts ran in, giggling and limping. They saw me, stopped, and pointed at my hands.

'"FINGERS!"

'They ran back into the darkness. The wall closed. Orphans danced in the corridor. Their legs were twisted up. Some had no arms. Their teeth stuck out like white stones. Men in wheelchairs carried pigs' bladders. Nobody could stop the hallucinations. Dr Robinson tried all kinds of drugs. But I knew nobody would get out of the delta. Not you, not me, not Dr Robinson.

'Sometimes the walls sparkled with a strange beauty. Look! A red flare! Somebody must be dying.

'Mount McKay blocks the stars. I once saw a black fox run by, on fire, its head backward. Labourers, grown men, real men, the kind of man I could have been, watched from the balcony.

> '"*Ach mein Orphelin, wo bleibst du am Abend?*
> *Wie kannst du schlaf', wie kannst du schlaf'*
> *Wenn ich so kranke bin?*"

'No. How *could* I sleep, so sick?

'One night I went deeper into the clinic. It's the world's longest asylum, you know. It goes from Queen City to Minneapolis. The air became hot. I could hardly breathe. I passed orderlies with walkie-talkies and patients unreeling balls of string to find their way back. Overhead the ceiling dripped.

'"Mamma . . .?"

'I took a flashlight off a shelf and went looking. I was so frustrated I punched a hole into a room. Dolls sang on balconies. I was very, very sick.

'"Mamma . . .?"

'I went into the operating theatre.

'"Mamma . . .?"

'I went past the stirrups, straps and surgical curtains. I walked and walked. I must have walked thirteen miles.

'"*Mamma!*"

'"I'm here – "

'I recognized her voice. I ran into the next chamber. I saw wrecks bandaged and oozing fluids, all the diseased of this foul earth. My heart pounded so hard I nearly blacked out. I pushed the last curtain. I didn't see nothing. Just cotton sheets folded on shelves.

129

'"Don't you recognize your mother?"

'I turned. In the centre of the floor was a pedestal and on it was a mound of flesh with a hole in it.

'"I am your mother."

'"No!"

'She told me my name.

'"NO!" I yelled.

'I floated toward her. My feet never touched the tiles. I couldn't believe how repulsive she was.

'"*DR ROBINSON!*" I screamed.

'The hallucination snapped out.

'Dr Robinson ran in. He swept me up in his arms. Was it a hallucination? Then what are you? And what can sickness do to me, against that power? You already know what I'm talking about, Jean: when the sickness comes we hold tight, don't we? We hold tight. Your hard times are just beginning, but already you know one thing:

'Truth is power.'

ELEVEN

I went to St Iglesias, Minnesota.

Finns, Norwegians, Germans and Dutch lived on the Nemadji River. The Indians were Menominee and Sauk. The highway ran to the docks and became River Road where burial mounds lined the maple woods. The Grgic and Vilamowych farms started at the Five Star Laundry on Little Oslo Street. It was as pretty as St Croix. There was even a birch copse by Buechle's Shell and St Vincent de Paul's mission. That's where my parents lived now, at St Vincent de Paul, because my father jumped bail.

My father had tattooed his forearm with penknife and ink: *Sauve qui peut.*

'I'm sick and I want to come home,' I said.

Nobody answered.

The red divan and brass floor lamp were jammed between the sink and stove. A brown propane stove was in the middle of the floor. My father's black museum was by the windowsill and my mother's altar under a food shelf. I sat on a spare bed. My father knocked me to the floor.

'That's Ignace's bed!'

My mother wore a black armband and listened incessantly to *The Little Drummer Boy* on our red portable record player. I gave her an ivory cameo from the museum of orphans.

'*Môman. Pardonne-moé,*' I said. 'Forgive me.'

She threw the cameo out of the window. Logging trucks rumbled up Little Oslo Street, throwing snow. I took pieces of glass and tied them to the window. I twirled them.

'Look, Mama,' I said. '*Chimes.*'

★   ★   ★

I slept on the pink shag carpet. Pippi was my pillow. Christmas bulbs blinked around the altar and my mother's perfume was sweet. Headlights turned on Little Oslo Street, flashed and burned my right eye. The cracked linoleum shifted as the building creaked. Stains, wild cowboys and desperate calves, ran over the peeled brown wallpaper. One smelled the frigid Nemadji. In the frosted windows were portraits of anxiety: Antoinette Hartmann, Erland Szegy, Father Przybilski in a drugged stupor.

'*Chus chez nous, à c't'heure, ici,*' my father said, asleep. 'From now on, this is home.'

My mother cried at the edge of her bed. I touched her gently on the cheek.

'Poor Mama,' I said.

She opened her eyes. She didn't know where she was.

'*Cé juste un rêve, Môman,*' I said. 'It's only a dream.'

She looked around the room. It was a chamber of corpses.

'You lied,' she said.

We were primitives, she and I, crippled by bad memories. I made her barley soup. I cooked potatoes, cut tomatoes and served them with oil and vinegar. I rendered a duck to crisp strips. I went shopping and bought the best fish roe, which I made into an omelette.

I heard her voice:

I was cheated.

She developed multiple voices, sing-song:

> '*Le sacrifice est consommé*
> *Ignace est massacré*
> *Nous avon, Jésu, contemplé*
> *Ta puissance et ta bonté.*'

> 'The sacrifice is consummated
> Ignace is massacred

We have seen, Jesu,
Thy power and thy generosity.'

I made her lemon tea and tea of sassafras. I created throat
lozenges out of lollipops, honey and menthol. She ate bread
with crosses of egg. I bought a prayer card of Ste Dymphna,
but her shadow didn't move, even when the sun shifted.

Every night at dinner she set places for Ignace: the meatballs
he loved, the buttered noodles, *piquant* sauce, barbecued ribs.
She cooked him perch with marmalade marinade. My father
finally sent for Father De Vaux and Father Naukkonen.

'What troubles you, Yvonne Krems?' Father De Vaux
asked. 'The little peasant girl from Trois Pointes?'

'Destined to be a saint,' Father Naukkonen said, smiling.

'Or the mother of a saint,' Father De Vaux said.

'Now I envy Protestant houses,' my mother said.

'It is not for us to question God's will.'

'Bring Ignace back.'

Father De Vaux swallowed hard and coughed.

'It is not possible.'

'Then God is not God,' she said.

My mother took all our cash from the ceramic pumpkin. She
went to the Menominee. Without even a kerchief she walked
to Vernon Street and asked Fred Black Shoes to bring back
Ignace. Fred Black Shoes told her to bring pepper from a house
that death had never seen. She ran down Vernon Street. She
knocked on a door. Ildefonse Hammerfest opened the door.
He wore a purple bathrobe and maroon slippers. His eyes were
bloodshot.

'Pepper . . .' she begged.

'Please,' he said. 'My wife has passed away.'

She ran to Fjornberg's Hardware. Dick Fjornberg leaned
out the window.

'Pepper . . .'

'Please,' he said. 'Our son is dying.'

She woke Gary Lauk the trading post gas pump operator.

'Pepper . . .'

'Please,' he said. 'My brother has died in his sleep.'

She ran over the boulders. Menominee passed by in an outboard. The moon wasn't up, only a red mist on the shores. It was a funeral party, going down to the St Croix River, Wisconsin.

'Pepper – '

Three dead Menominee, still wrapped in braided rawhide and coloured burlap, sat up.

'Death is King,' they said.

She cleaned houses for Protestants. She left early with a black bucket, red rubber gloves and housecoat. In the evening she sat on the red divan, propped the *St Iglesias Journal* on her lap, put on spectacles and turned on the lamp. But, of course, she was illiterate.

Hungry for news, she listened to Ontario radio. Eisenhower's engineers had dredged the New York locks. Sea bass had been caught in Lake Erie. Mary Evans would swim Lake Huron. My mother sewed by the lighted portrait of Catherine Labouré, by artificial flowers and wax oranges, listening to *Les histoires des pays d'en-haut*, or singing along with La Bolduc.

My mother wore red gloves to handle our laundry. *We are repulsive to her*, I observed. I played French-Canadian reels on the red accordion. *She wipes what we touch. Observe her grimace.*

One midnight I opened a jar of preserves. I sucked out half-fermented apricots. I saw my father doing the same. Sweet, heavy syrup dripped to the floor. My father and I avoided each other, sliding around the room, back to back. We were starving.

'You saw Ignace,' I said. 'Or you heard him.'

'I saw nothing. Heard nothing.'

'He's here.'

'Not.'

'Is.'

Yes, we were inarticulate. We communicated by gesture, gaps, senseless winks. Our life was artificial, half-remembered, while all about us was decomposition. They had cut out my tongue, but I had the power to destroy the earth.

'I'm lonesome,' I said.

'Barrault deserved it,' my father said.

'Nobody listens to me.'

'They want to poison me. Though, from far away, I suppose I don't look like a criminal.'

'I scream because nobody listens to me.'

'Bah. We'll all get our throats cut, anyway.'

'As though I was dead.'

My father turned angrily.

'*T'es pas assez importante pour qu'on passe notre temps a t'espionner, t'sais,*' my father said. 'You're not so important we spend our time spying on you, you know.'

I grew silent.

'Jean,' my father asked. 'Do you confess?'

'Frequently.'

'And what do you confess?'

'That I have evil thoughts.'

'That you touch yourself in an impure manner?'

'That, too.'

'And that others have made you female?'

'I have.'

'But of Ignace, nothing?'

I confessed to Ignace's death. But my mother slipped into insanity.

I shined shoes at the Blue Mound Bowl-a-Dome. A Menominee corpse stuck his stinking black leather sandals on my stand. I looked up. His broken teeth were yellow, the corrupted flesh black. There was a foul wind out of its mouth.

'*What are you living for, Jean?*'

The black Nemadji threw timbers flying. In those days of purgatory I saw red antler-headed animals on the streets of St Iglesias. Wires to our apartment whipped in frenzy. My father used me as a footstool and wiped his hands on my hair.

My father worried about losing his tools. He hid them under the bed. He inspected them at night. He counted them.

He cleaned them. He recounted them. He had brought knives, hatchets, axes, hoes, spades, files, nails, scale and weights, cloth, a shroud, braided mat, baskets, his Swallowfield uniform and badge, clipboard and summer hat. St Vincent de Paul became his museum.

To amuse him I bleached my hair, wore a black shirt and polished my shoes red.

'Ah, you little schemer,' he laughed, '. . . so terribly naughty . . . you little schemer . . .'

I wiped the sweat from my face.

'This St Iglesias,' my father confided, 'is my tomb.'

'It is bleak.'

'This country is banal.'

'Nothing is as it was.'

No, of course not. My nose was crooked where he had broken it. Ignace was drowned. It was an alien red sun caught in bare trees. We were bloated and disfigured, our skin hung from the elbows. My father and I searched the apartment for ourselves.

'I am not *originaire* here,' he whispered on his hands and knees. 'I want to be shipped back to St Croix.'

'When you're dead?'

'Like a sack of shit. Where the *Métis* are respected. Where there are no Barraults, no extraditions. Carried up Abattoir Road on an embroidered mat to the *cimetière*. The priests blowing incense and the girls with white lilies.'

'Lilies?'

'The virgins. They'll all be there. Agnes Victoria and her sister Adelaide, Phyllis Suze and Rachel Patrice. The Indian Mary Willow Water, that fat slob. No, not just virgins. Antoinette Hartmann. Antoinette will be there, too.'

'Did you seduce Antoinette?'

'Wouldn't you like to know?'

'Yes.'

'You always liked her,' he said. 'Didn't you?'

'She was special.'

'Antoinette has such' – he struck his chest twice – '*vitality!*'

'Her eyes.'

136

'Her eyes!'
'Even her hands,' I said.
'Well, and what about her fine hair?'
'Her lovely throat!'
'Her sweet voice!'
'Papa!'
'What?'
'*DID YOU?*'

My father stayed inside during the day and walked St Iglesias at night. He kept looking for the FBI. We visited Del Badaude's brewery. The mashing screw turned in the ooze, Del raked it, and the whole basement stank. Del brought out dark bottles of ale.

'Money is the goal,' my father said.

'Damn right,' Del said.

'If an asshole became a millionaire Eisenhower would lick him.'

'Women would spread their legs.'

'Money,' my father said. 'That is what I have devoted my life to.'

My father sang.

> 'Money, money, I love to call you honey
> You're my bunny, money, my honey
> Who stole my money?'

'We ought to sell our wives,' my father said.

'Would you?' Del asked.

'Sure.'

'How much?'

'Two hundred dollars American.'

'It's not legal.'

'You can if she has a halter around her neck,' my father said.

Del wiped his lips.

'How much?'

'One hundred ninety dollars.'

137

'Well – '

'She's crazy, you know. She prays. Day and night. A goddamn vigil.'

'I like crazy women.'

'Do you?'

'They come like rag dolls with – frenzies – '

My father shuffled the cards.

'Three hundred dollars,' my father said.

Del whistled.

'That's quite a bit, Jack.'

'She's a woman, after all.'

'I know, but – '

'Still moist.'

'Is she?'

'Oh. Yes. Certainly. She drips with love.'

'Well. Maybe two hundred. If she drips.'

'Five hundred.'

'I'm not going to argue with you, Jack.'

'Enough haggling. Play.'

My father and I visited the Finns' tavern. It had once been a garage over the waterfront. There were dioramas of fjords, miniature skiers through pines. A reindeer antler was over the door, carvings of hamlets in Norwegian pine. The Brotherhood of Hammerfest came in on snowshoes.

'We should have been Finns,' my father said.

Bitter black seeds streaked the windows like coal dust in the rain.

'Did you taste them?' my mother asked. 'They're good.'

Nothing helped.

Pippi saw the wind and howled all night. Coal smoke filled the air. Coal dust blew right across the floor and voices came from the black pipes. An insane celestina played downstairs.

I made gestures of propitiation: rubbed doors with interlocked thumbs, right angles against the axis of walking. I distended my mouth. I polished her cornelian amulets. I washed our cupboard of emptiness. I dressed like a Finn. Nothing worked.

My mother slipped between the cracks.

I called the last meeting of *les buveurs*.

Etienne Bastide, Herman Pic and Paul Hartmann came down from St Croix. We gathered in a switching shanty and burned the Deadwood death cards. We buried the Deadwood whip. We each took fragments of the *Quai des Brumes* poster and lit candles for Erland Szegy, for Ignace Verhaeren. It rained. Rivulets ran through the shanty.

Paul Hartmann gave me a photograph of Antoinette. She wore a blue party dress with a white corsage. Her hair was darker. Her dress had cleavage.

'Thank you,' I said.

Danny Auban told me Colonel Canale had been killed in an automobile accident in Sudbury.

'Thank you,' I said.

Etienne stood with me under the eaves. I got plastered in the rain. As it rained I walked out. Etienne walked after me.

'*Oh, buveurs désolés*,' I cried. 'Our lives are so bleak!'

Paul Hartmann started to cry.

'All our misery,' he said, 'came to nothing.'

So, after five years and countless adventures, *billisme* broke up and died for ever in a railroad shanty outside St Iglesias, Minnesota, 3 March 1955.

My crippled foot got worse. I went to Dr Bernard, who fitted me with a thick-soled heavy rubber black boot. Sometimes I sat outside the park and watched young boys build forts of green budding branches.

My father earned money with card tricks on Fourth Street and Bakewell. He shovelled walks, begged and worked as a clown for the public school. He played the kazoo and snare drum on Little Oslo Street.

One day he put on his black suit, grabbed me by the hand, and took me to Toynbee Hall. Toynbee Hall was an orphanage.

The window panes were fitted with sharp metal strips and there were cages on the roofs so nobody could commit suicide. The diet was potatoes and stir-about. There was a laundry room. The boys worked at Nemadji Motors. There was no fire alarm. Girls scrubbed floors. Many were retarded. They were easily seduced. Babies lived in a dormitory on the third floor. In 1942 a fire had killed thirteen.

Mr Victor explained.

'The truth has to be told. These boys and girls are ineducable. No amount of schooling is going to make them intelligent citizens. They represent a level very, very common among Indians and Negroes. The dullness appears to be hereditary. The fact that there are so many like this suggests that the concept of racial mentality will have to be investigated.'

My father ground out his Chesterfield.

'I don't think we can support him much longer,' my father said. 'Or want to.'

A scream came through the caged vent. Mr Victor looked away, startled, then winked at my father. My father signed papers. Another scream came through the vents.

'What do you think, Jean?' my father asked. 'Could you handle this? Could you succeed at being an orphan?'

I went home, took my father's rifle and stuck the barrel in my mouth. I counted to ten. Darkness squeezed. I felt veins like steel bands tightening.

'. . . eight . . . nine . . . t — '

Suddenly the door flew open. Ignace stood there stupidly, blinking, his galoshes dripping. He held his books the way girls do, against his chest. His ear muffs dangled, the strap hanging down.

'Jean! What are you *doing*?'

'Goodbye, Ignace – '

Ignace ran across the room, knocked the rifle against the window, and slapped my face three times.

'You'll get blood all over Mama's *floor*!'

Buds opened suddenly on my mother's altar. A rock crystal garden blossomed in pink. Our window chimes, which I painted with green flowers, tinkled untouched in the wet air. My mother stared out the window, far, far away.

'Mama,' I whispered. 'Do you have a presentiment?'

She nodded.

'Is *le bon Dieu* coming?' I asked.

'Somebody is.'

On 7 March 1955, after a week of restless fevers, my mother saw St Martin of Tours standing in the door.

'Yvonne Krems,' St Martin said, 'who flies above boundaries.'

'Yes?'

'Fly with me.'

'Where?'

'To Ignace.'

'Will it be cold?' she asked.

'In a strange way.'

'Will I be lonely?'

'Excruciatingly.'

'And my virginity?'

'You will be whole.'

'Again?'

'Medically, everything.'

'Yet espoused fully?' she asked.

'*Le bon Dieu*, Jesu, everybody is moved by your suffering.'

St Martin went to the window and wrote his name on the wet wood. Rain dissolved in headlights that turned on Engel Street. He jumped into the bright droplets and was gone.

'When . . .?' she whispered.

Came the echo.

'Sooner than you think . . .'

On 13 March 1955, my pretty mother combed her hair on her bed, then collapsed in a fever. St Christopher walked into the room. He wore a burlap pad where Christ had sat. St Christopher smiled.

'Yvonne Krems,' he said. 'Whose boat glides downriver.'

'Yes?'

141

'Follow me to Ignace.'

'Where is he?' she asked.

'It is difficult to explain . . .'

Suddenly his flames burned green. The oil portrait of Catherine Labouré glowed. The Palestine sand of Ignace's diorama burst into flame. St Christopher went to the window, under the photographs of our dead relatives, and jumped.

'St Christopher . . .?'

My mother threw her wedding ring into the Nemadji, burned her marriage certificate, her *permission de marriage*, virginity certificate, and scissored my father's uniform into ribbons. She busted up his black museum. Ed Gien lampshade, lead pipe, everything she threw into the dustbin outside. She scrubbed the floor, even the ceilings of his smell.

'Oh, Jean, my heart beats like a jackhammer!'

There was a light. The door opened. Catherine Labouré came in. She walked stiffly, as though in pain. Light came from her face. The apartment filled with sweet clouds. Catherine Labouré wore a grey dress with no pockets, a penitent.

'Yvonne Krems,' she said, 'who flies in a golden sun.'

My mother prostrated herself.

'I come to interrupt your sleep, Yvonne Krems,' she said.

'I was not asleep.'

'But now you are awake.'

'You will shoot arrows into my flesh,' my mother said.

'No one will shoot anything into you.'

My mother sank lower. The atmosphere congealed. I became invisible in the dark and reflective windows.

'Is it necessary to die?' my mother asked. 'To see Ignace?'

'In a strange way.'

'When?'

'Soon.'

'Very soon?'

'So very soon . . .'

Catherine Labouré touched my mother at the back of the neck. Then she jumped into the air and was gone.

* * *

'*Le bon Dieu* . . .' my mother whispered, her hair damp, her cheeks flushed. The lamplight fell across her face. She looked seventeen. She hadn't moved in fifteen minutes.

'I clutched a living bird . . .' she finally said.

I kissed her under the ear.

'Poor Mama.'

'I was a shadow under her wings . . .'

'I love you.'

'She took me far, far away . . .'

'I believed in you.'

'Jean! Her sleeve drifted on my skin.'

'I loved you.'

'Jean . . .'

'But you never knew it – '

She was asleep. I kissed her again and covered her in a blanket. I stepped back. She danced in chains down the long Verhaeren prison. These were the visions of our poor mother Yvonne Krems, between 7 March and 17 March 1955, which I also witnessed.

Our mother entered Fork Rivers Clinic.

They undressed her. They tested the electro-galvanicity of her nerves. She was moved to a muslin-covered cot in a soundproofed room. I peeked in and smelled head jelly. Straps bound her arms crossways. Her fine black hair was mussed. Her toes twitched and they wheeled her to a machine.

'*Y sonnent les cloches, fort . . . fort . . .*' she said. 'Those bells ring so loud . . .'

A grey rag was inserted in her mouth. Delusions fled down the asylum halls.

'Mother – forgiv – '

Suddenly a thousand mandibles clacked in a flash of light. *Pzzzzt.*

'IGNACE!' she yelled. 'I SEE IGNACE!'

My father jumped on to a chair and crashed into the wall. He clawed the air and hissed.

'They've destroyed her mind!'

★   ★   ★

My father dragged me to Toynbee Hall, threw me in, and slammed the doors.

I carried my pyjamas up the corridor past the linen shelves, communal bathroom, gang showers. Outside, beyond long meshed wires covering the windows, down in the courtyard, was a shed of mechanic's equipment, vises, chains. Across the basketball court was a laundry room. A red light was on over a tractor.

There was a wood dresser, mirror and a basin in my room. Diagonal slats of moonlight crept up my stone wall. I smelled the Nemadji, the wet woods, ferns, sap, berries, small birds, dripping snow in the birches of St Iglesias, Minnesota.

'Jean . . .'

I looked out. Etienne Bastide stood on a burial mound. I thought he'd gone back to St Croix. He wore his St Bonaventure jacket. A wolf howled beyond the rapids and warm spray moved across the black mud. He showed me a bandaged hand.

'I cut my wrist for you . . .'

I crept back into my orphanage room.

'Jean . . .!'

I looked again. Etienne was still there. In the graveyard buds were opening. He held out a towel in both hands. It must have been an old towel because it had a gold cross on it and fringe. On it was the razor.

'. . . I . . .' he said, smiling. 'It is I, Etienne Bastide, who loves you . . .'

He unwrapped his bandage and raised his red wound.

'. . . for ever . . .'

TWELVE

I was a hobo.

I travelled west to Sainte Rose du Lac. It was mid-April and the rain was falling. Everywhere I went rain fell in the pines, the fir, the trash timber, on flooded ponds, in logging camps. After a while I couldn't see a thing. I carried my duffel bag full of oranges, my father's flashlight, a photograph of Antoinette Hartmann, and slept in cranberry bogs by the peat pots. Black clouds piled over the lakes. Birds screamed from the black clouds:

I was cheated.

I salved my nose with Vaseline.

I dreamed. I climbed black boulders where Antoinette Hartmann was mauled by a bear, but as fast as I climbed I couldn't get there in time.

I crossed the bogs but the bogs expanded. Everywhere were cranberries, smoke pots and twisted pines. At Little Fork I moved into an empty cabin owned by the Albion Brotherhood. I moved to a better shack that belonged to the Sons of Shiloh. I fell in with Oneida Bible Communists, who fed me hot bread and cranberry soup. I left them for a trailer of Jerusalem evangelists.

Farmers slaughtered cattle because of sickness. I limped through bone piles and slept in them, too. At dawn, at noon, at evening, the sky was blank. I went to Dr Fitzimmons, an ophthalmologist who treated the poor in Bemidji.

'What is your difficulty, Mr Verhaeren?'

'I see only blank.'

'When you look at Bemidji, what do you see?'

'A vague white.'

The nurse, Marjorie Kims, came in. She was a young woman with orange hair, white stockings. She stuck a hypodermic needle into a bottle, drew off fifty ml, held it against the light, and tapped out the air. She injected me. Miss Kims had a lovely freckle on her wrist. I touched her elbow while she plunged the needle. She paused. She had extraordinary black eyes.

'Did I hurt you?' she asked.

'No. Not at all.'

She went to the door.

'NOT IN THE LEAST LITTLE BIT,' I shouted.

She retreated out the door in little phases, such that she was slightly transparent. She raised an eyebrow and smiled knowingly.

'. . . Are you . . . *sure* . . .?'

The injection worked. I threw up three times between Dr Fitzimmons's office and the river, but when I stopped the streets were cluttered with dark shapes: Protestants, nursing old wounds.

I went to the White River Diner. It was decorated with lacquered fish on wood ovals and gold chains. Behind the counter a one-armed man made sandwiches. Men bent out of the swirling rain and stomped their feet on the welcome mat. Suddenly there was a brightness. I ran out. A bird was electrocuted on a telephone wire, trapped.

I went to Woolworth's. Suddenly I saw something in a bright light. I wanted it more than anything in the world, but when I bent down to look the shelf was empty.

I visited the museum of religion.

It was in a tenement on Brick Street behind a shelter run by the Presbyterian mission. Hobos begged outside. It was dark inside, very quiet. I was the only one in the museum. Brown carpets absorbed light from the windows. The foyer had bowls of rose petals. Paintings of Jerusalem lined the wall: Kidron, Siloam, the Mount of Olives.

The Catholic exhibit was in a brass case. Inside, against black velvet, brass keys hung on thread over gold brocade fragments. There was a portrait of Pius XII and a dwarf palm tree, and a silver reliquary with a finger in the shadows. Incense smoked around the reliquary. A black iron lion turned on a gold pole.

The Mormon exhibit was in an aluminium case. Joseph Smith knelt on black velvet in miniature white birches. In plastic ferns, between red berries and mugwort, in a shaft of white light, the *Book of Moroni* opened. Deer watched as the light from the *Book of Moroni* bathed Joseph Smith.

The atheism exhibit was a sundial with no numbers. Broken white columns rose from an empty, cracked pool. Silver milk pods splayed from white vases and silver seeds lay in milk-white ceramics. A white moth moved its wings back and forth. Around everything was black velvet, the deepest black.

The Pentecostal exhibit was in a tin case lined with black silk. Old men and women, dolls with shaggy hair, were on cogs. I pressed a red button. A *papier-mâché* dove descended and in a fiery light of aluminium reflections the elders danced.

The Jewish exhibit was in a copper case. There was a Polish village in a deep black forest. Jews in gaberdine stood in a circle wearing black hats, black coats, beards, black shoes. By the well a baby lay in a wicker cradle. I pressed a red button. Smokestack plumes rose behind the forest.

The Calvinist exhibit was in a black velvet-lined wood box. There was a Swiss chalet where Calvinists stirred an enormous kettle. Hands went around inside the brew. Ears were nailed along a fence rail. Calvinists came from the mountain path with Catholic heads on pikes. Catholics were chained to a millwheel, crosses jammed into their fists. I pressed a red button. The millwheel ground the Catholics.

The Methodist exhibit was in a black lead box. A lantern projected into smoke the vision of the Drummer of Tedworth. Behind that were field preachers: John Elias, Christmas Evans, Praying Johnny, Lorenzo Dow. John Wesley clung to the London Wall, his hair wildly flying.

I went outside. Rain fell from black skies. Beggars followed.

'I'm sick – in a terrible way – '

'Save me.'

'I need grace.'

I was out of money. I slept on Fitzwater Street. The dosshouse was crowded. Snow blew in from the broken windows. Men groped drunkenly in the dark. The toilet was broken. A watchman sat on a high wooden stool. Men cried in their sleep.

'Jennifer . . .'

'Marie . . .'

'*Antoinette* . . .'

A bum stroked my neck. I hit him. He left me alone. He went toward the toilet, collapsed like a piece of rubber, bounced down the stairs, crashed into the garbage cans outside. He picked himself up as though nothing had happened, groped back up the stairs and re-registered. In the morning rainwater ran down the streets. A different hobo climbed out of a florist truck.

'I've gone blind,' he said. 'In a terrible way.'

I heard there was a hobo camp at Tenstrike so I left Bemidji and followed the rails.

The camp was in a railroad embankment where a trestle bridge faded in the fog. Dead trees turned on a deep, sluggish black river. Chains banged against submerged logs. Hobos stirred a kettle on a fire, flames reflected on their coarse faces. I went down and a tramp gave me soup.

In the curve of the railroad two men turned from the dark, bodies sewn together.

'We work in festivals and fairgrounds,' one head said. 'All over America.'

'What do you do?' I asked.

'You know.'

'No. I don't.'

'Sure you do. You were born that way. It's written on your face.'

'Show me.'

The men twisted. One sodomized the other. The other never stopped smoking.

'You owe us two dollars,' they said.

'What for?'

'The show.'

'I ain't got two dollars.'

'You want to be next? With both of us?'

I threw my watch in their laps and walked away. A passenger train went by. When the tramps saw the people eating, served by Negroes, they raised their hats and peed. I walked back to Bemidji. An Albanian named Kurt Flood followed me. He wore a khaki duffel coat with insignia from the Korean War.

Kurt and I drove trucks, shovelled walks, carried bricks. It rained almost every day.

Kurt and I got jobs with the municipal park. I went into the toilets and spread disinfectant. We hauled rotted grass in gunny sacks and dumped it on the edge of town.

We lived in a railroad shack. Locomotive headlights swept through at night over the chair, table, and broke into a raving cinema on the wall. Pine resin oozed from the rafters. Kurt showed me photographs of what the Turks had done to his people. From him I learned the force of racial hatred. Sometimes he got the coughs so bad his whole body shook. Then I would go out behind the shack with a lantern so he thought there was a train coming, and he would calm down.

'Bless you, Johnny,' he whispered.

During the day we robbed children. They came into the park, Kurt would throw them into the pines, and I rummaged their pockets for change. We survived, but the handwriting was on the wall.

We ate breakfast at the Roadside Café, on Blackwater Street. The café was decorated with photographs of railroad men. Kurt held his hands over the napkin dispenser. It turned into a tureen, full of steaming pea soup.

'I can do that any time,' he said.

I asked him about the Kaministikwia Delta.

'There's no asylum in the Kaministikwia Delta,' he said.

'There isn't?'

'Hell no. I've been there a hundred times. You must've had an episode.'

'Something. That's for sure.'

Suddenly I banged my head on the table.

'I can't stand it any more,' I said. 'What is the meaning of my suffering?'

'Beats me.'

'I am a living statue, Kurt,' I said. 'I don't *feel* any more.'

'Who said that?' Kurt Flood suddenly said, eyes sharp.

'I did, Kurt.'

'Oh. I thought . . . somebody outside us . . . women's voices . . .'

'We've become blind,' I said. 'In some horrible way.'

We were disgusted with Bemidji. We decided to go to Brainerd. Kurt Flood coughed, shook his head, waved his hands and when he was through coughing said, 'But the cripple was right, Jean. You can leave the body.'

'I never told you about the cripple.'

'Shut up. Listen.'

The Veteran

'I was an orphan.

'I grew up in Sault Sainte Marie. The orphanage was run by Arminians, Advanced Agents. Charles and John Wesley's portraits hung over my bunkbed. Camp Meeting Methodists, the Connexion, Bible Christians, Independent Methodists, Primitive Methodists, I knew the history of my people. I became an exhorter by the age of eight. We used to drive to Brimlet to have watch nights. We rode to Bay Mills where we sang John Wesley's hymns by firelight. John Wesley came to me in dreams, out of the grave carrying a lantern.

'I had weak lungs and was sent to a sanitarium in Bryces Hill. I met Albanians who taught me the tragedy of my people, the falseness of my name. I worked at the age of nine carrying trash at the Father Marquette grave in St Ignace. I cut hay in Paw Paw. I cleaned gutters in Schoolcraft. I had an affinity for the railroads because of the people who lived along them. I sensed they understood my rootlessness, my sense of racial tragedy. I followed the big lines to Chicago.

'You don't know anything until you go to Chicago. Chicago is the centre of the world. You always fall back to Chicago. Chicago is full of Balkans, French, Germans, Poles. Chicago just has this stink. It's the stink of humanity. We all stink, see?

'Thousands of us passed through Chicago. I moved with socialists, anarchists and bolsheviks. You couldn't walk on the sidewalk without stepping on moochers. Those were the days. I beat up mush fakers. Pinkerton agents patrolled the railroad yards. They beat us up, but what the hell, we beat them up, too.

'So this society of wingies, blinkies, and sticks, this was my society. I graduated with them. I got a degree in cheap wine. Our language was different. I didn't invent it. But it was my life. You're born that way. It's funny how it works. I knew the minute I came to Chicago. But there was this element: stew bums and jungle buzzards, stinking bits of running sores and scabs. I had to be protected. See, I was good-looking. Understand, Jean? Understand what I'm saying, Jean? I became a kid, a road kid.

'His name was William Brick. He was a bad man. He abused me. He threw me to the wolves until I was covered in spunk. But I was under his protection. Nobody touched me without his say-so. And he fed me regular. He was a bad man, William Brick. Toughs came from as far as Cicero to beat him with planks. Vigilantes came and then the Chicago police beat the shit out of William Brick.

'William Brick and I travelled down the small lines to Missouri. We set up a tent. Men came after work. They wore flannel shirts and denim trousers stained red and everybody smelled like pig turd. We laid tarpaulin on floorboards. William

151

Brick and I performed a play: *The Love of Jenny Logan*. When the men saw me in a dress they got restless. William Brick sang a dirty song. Night came on. We served beer. William Brick and I did the dirty dance. He invited the men into the back of the tent. That was where I made our money. Sometimes I couldn't walk for weeks afterward. William Brick counted his money all night. He was very cruel.

'One morning I strangled him with barbed wire. I shoved his body inside a burlap bag and dumped him where no train could stop in time.

'I went back to Chicago. There were more missions than before. Something was changing. Methodists, Jehovah's Witnesses, Seventh Day Adventists, Church of God, proselytizing. The Methodists fed me and put me on a train to South Dakota. We were going to Camp Bethesda, their farm on the Belle Fourche. The train waited two days and two nights. Pinkertons argued with the Methodists. Methodists fought with private detectives. There were a hundred drifters in the car with me, and many working men who had never been on the rails before. Finally we pulled out into the suburbs and the open country.

'We heard that the Ohio National Guard had chased tramps into the desert. Vigilantes caught a tramp and nailed his tongue to the roof of his mouth. In Elkhart, Indiana, tramps had cut wheat and those who died had their mouths and assholes packed with fish and were buried between the rows as fertilizer. In Indian Creek, Oklahoma, firemen beat tramps with hose nozzles and those who fought back were hammered with crowbars.

'The Pinkertons set a wire on the ties with a spike on the end. The cars ahead bent the wire down and when it whipped up at sixty miles an hour it tore a hot rodder's head off. That grizzled head bounced like a cantaloupe into the brush. A mush head slept in the coal car. The train took a hard curve and in the morning the Methodists shovelled what was left into the furnace with the coal.

'Methodist guards lived in the rear car. We ate soup, bread, carrots, onions, and barley cake. Men slept in tarpaulin, using broken shovels for frying pans. We peed out the doors. We passed through rail yards but only at night. The Methodists told us our bodies were ruined. They said our windows were broken, our mansions blighted.

'The train seemed to go on and on. I never rode a train that knew less where it was going. We rode all over the North American continent. Overhead the Kansas stars twirled senselessly. We passed steel factories, black trestle bridges, silver silos. And the rails, those curving rails, blue-bright at noon, red at sunset, snaked back to the same factories and bridges. A tramp killed himself jumping on to the rails. There was a woman – Mary Topeka – tattooed herself with iodine and a penknife. Some drank paraffin, or rolled cigarettes in kerosene. We strained lighter fluid through kerchieves, drank it, and went blind.

'The Methodists came on board and held covenant. Some of us converted and we saw them later, wearing black coats, carrying rifles.

'We lost all restraint. We had orgies in the sandstorms. Jockers fought jockers for wives. Men bent over other men. Twenty of us, thirty, three dozen in the car, kneeling on slats, while the yellow dust whistled through the freight cars. The homosexuals rode like thunder through the storms, the rain and hail. Stones kicked up by the train shot into the mêlée. All night, all day, it continued, in the moonlight, up the Black Mountains.

'We got to the Belle Fourche. We got to Camp Bethesda. It was just a burned warehouse on concrete foundations. The Methodists became dispirited. They let us walk off into the washes. I was starving. I heard meadowlarks singing the New Connexion. Barbed wire bloomed. Silver Bibles rained over the buttes.

'But Methodism is terrible. Listen. I enlisted. In bootcamp I ran twelve miles, cleaned and disassembled rifles. But at night my blood was sick with cheap wine and Methodist fever.

'I went to Korea with the First Cavalry Division, to Unsan. The Chinese attacked over the cliffs, burning jeeps, lobbing grenades. I was hit by shrapnel. The Chinese bundled me to a POW camp at Huichon. I was thrown in with prisoners from the Second Division, and from the Fifth Marine Division, and Turks. Canadians, too. The Chinese turned us over to North Koreans. I lived on rice and dirty water. I got dysentery and became a human skeleton. North Koreans passed down the rows and shot two of us. Trucks brought more Americans. The North Koreans shot two more.

'United Nations jets strafed the roads and American artillery destroyed the road, but the Koreans only became more insane. They killed Private Jim Flowers with a shovel and garrotted Corporal Perry with a leather strap. They dragged Privates Sam Lepke and Jim Jakes with a jeep until their teeth were driven up their gums. They snapped off Corporal Esparto's legs with a snowplough and hauled Sergeant Prester into the snow and shoved him into the earth-turning tractor screws.

'They hauled me into the administration annex. Now here's the unbelievable miracle. They knew all about William Brick. They told me every detail of the corruption of the gospel train. They asked if I was saved by grace or by faith. I said I didn't know. They hit me and carved Christ's name in my thighs. I showed them my Methodist papers, but they didn't believe them. They ripped up my certificates and beat me with lead pipes.

'Suddenly an American shell hit the annex. The pain was so awful I jerked right out of my body and turned in a circle of fire. Stars rose with me through green veils, like the northern lights. Have you seen the northern lights?'

' – I've seen the northern lights.'

'Below me were screaming men, everywhere men were screaming. Pure as dark light I floated. I was attached to my body by a long segmented silver cord. How I prayed the cord would break! But the American jets pounded the camp below and I suddenly rushed down and snapped back. The camp was liberated. The Red Cross brought me tea, porridge. I sat on a bench with an army blanket over my head. A psychiatrist interviewed me. I never said a word. A mortar fragment had lodged in my arm, but what did I care? I had learned the grace of Wesley, which lets me endure the wretchedness of my degraded existence. I will survive. I am not afraid. You've heard it before, in a different way, now hear it again.

'Eternity's ends justify the means.'

THIRTEEN

I was a derelict.

I went to Chicago. Newspapers blew down the sidewalks. It was May but very cold. Negroes rode buses and yelled from cars. Department store windows were full of Negro mannikins. Chicago was the capital of Negroes. Billboards rose over telephone wires, advertising skin-whitener. I circled to Division Street, and slept under a fire escape behind a Negro hairdresser on Clark Street.

I changed my name to Michael Jordan and worked as a cook's assistant. I was a grocery boy. I lived by stealing. Ruined people lay in doorways. There were ruined people everywhere. We all drank. A Negro chased me with a knife down an alley.

'Come here, white boy!'

It stayed very cold. Chicago smelled like cattle shit and petroleum. Buildings were lost in rain. I lost my photograph of Antoinette Hartmann and coughed all day. I walked under the El to the stockyards. By night I slept under fire escapes.

A Negro stopped me on Clark Street.

'What's your name?'

'Michael Jordan.'

'You need a job?' he asked.

'Yes.'

'Be here same place. Tomorrow. I'll get you a job.'

I killed time by riding the buses. Rain slid down the windows. Negro women climbed on with huge packages. I went back to Clark Street. I woke in a parking lot. I ripped

156

my trousers, which had stuck to the asphalt. I went back to Clark Street. My Negro never came.

I walked along the North Branch Canal. Concrete was dark and dirty under the warehouses. The wind whistled up the railroads. Suddenly the Negro grabbed me.

'Do you still want that job?'

'Sure.'

'You be right here six sharp. In the morning.'

I couldn't sleep that night. *Crème de menthe* had ruined my stomach. I got up at dawn, drank, and limped over the trestle bridge. Light shattered against the dirty canal like a broken chandelier. My Negro never came.

I visited the museum of love.

It was a white building with columns, established by a disciple of Elizabeth Cade Stanton. It had once been a Christian Science church. There were derelicts outside. Inside, on the newel post, was a copy of the Declaration of Sentiments and a portrait of Sojourner Truth. Broken exhibits from the natural history museum were jumbled in the upstairs hall, where tilted mirrors reflected the viewer.

In a six-foot-high diorama Indian women wild-riced. The moon was bright, silver crossed by flying silhouettes. Owls, badgers and muskrats peered from bracken. A moose foraged in shallows. A bigger moose with antlers mounted the first.

In the second diorama a midnight hawk flew through the north woods. Below were a winding river, moonlit lakes, a tavern. I put a nickel in the slot. A chrome ball rolled down a forest road and dropped through a hole, came out below, rolled between miniature pine trees and dropped into a darker hole, which triggered a light in the tavern: plump and pink, a woman knelt on pillows.

In a glass panorama two sailors kissed on a pitching deck in a rain of silver beads. I pressed a red button. Far away a raft became visible. On it was a shipwrecked sailor.

There was a cage of tomatoes. I put a nickel in the slot. A mechanical spider crawled down the ramp, feeling its way. Suddenly a needle slapped up and pinned it to the roof. Below the cage was a dish of honey. There must have been poison in it because cockroaches lay dead in radiating lines.

In the darkest part of the museum the exhibits were locked. A creature of rodent bones and antlers, dressed in feminine rags, was luminescent, and she sat on a four-legged cabinet. A flood light hit her out of the dark. She opened her antler arms.

Jean-Michel.

I knelt and crossed myself.

It is I.

'Oh,' I whispered. 'Love . . .'

Down the row were exhibits. Decomposed pigs wore uniforms, pipes stuck in their mouths, trotters rigid, and a two-headed owl with a crucifix around its neck. Beyond that was a three-legged calf, its liver protruding from its belly, a grin of red lips leering. In a velvet robe a baby horse, a hoof sticking through its forehead, fluttered its tongue.

I went even further. In a glass case was a silver canoe resting on razor blades in the ferns. Behind it were two dolls joined at the waist. Over their heads was a stuffed owl leaking feathers.

I came out of the darkness and there was a white church in the wilderness. White bonnets hung on wooden pegs. Eiderdown floated from the rafters. I put a nickel in the slot. Mechanical men banged a drum. Bald women, naked and hairless, glided into a dance. One caught an imaginary ball. A second poured invisible tea. A third petted a dog that was not there.

A history of fashion concluded the exhibits. Women's large-brimmed hats, lace blouses, gold bracelets and a case of perfumes. I bought postcards of deformed women, photographs from New Orleans.

Beggars followed me.

'A little love?'

'Please – love – '

'I need love – '

I left the museum of love.

I lost track of days. The wind was dry but fierce. My

coat turned to rags. Crossing Union Street I ran into my Negro.

'You still want that job, Michael Jordan?' he asked.

'Where've you been?'

'Meet me right here, tomorrow, corner of Union.'

I waited on Union Street. My Negro came. He wore baggy blue trousers and a wool hat. He said his name was Roost.

'My grandmother say, trouble come to roost.'

We went down a concrete ramp. I followed Roost and we came out on a mezzanine. Cattle, thousands of cattle, moaned under filthy skylights. A hammer smashed their foreheads. Their knees buckled, hooks on rails yanked them up, Negroes slit their throats. Blood poured into troughs. Negroes ripped out fistfuls of intestines. By the time the cows reached the packing room they were hairy skeletons.

'How old are you?' a white man asked me.

'Sixteen, Mr Kobacki,' Roost said.

'He don't look sixteen.'

'He worked two years for Armour Star.'

'Put disinfectant on him.'

Roost gave me galoshes. I worked in the calves' section. Negro boys jumped at hanging calves with long knives and shot hot water into cadavers. I pushed brain fragments and viscera into a canal using a squeegee pole. Flayed ligament waved like anemones. I felt cow hair tickling my throat. I scraped a carcase.

I stepped out of the canal.

'I'm going to be sick, Roost.'

I bent at a standpipe and vomited. A whistle blew. We took off our gloves. Negroes ate lunch.

'See? Like women,' a Negro said. 'Folds of flesh, hair. Tongue.'

I leaned over again.

'Oh, they've made him ill,' a Negro said.

Roost tore his sandwich in half and gave it to me. It smelled like the calves.

I hosed viscera all afternoon. We quit. We gang-showered. I bent over to rub my bad foot and Roost winked at me. I got into my stinking shirt and trousers. Roost and I went into the twilight. Neon lights were on, women were carried along in the rush of evening. Roost gave me two American dollars.

'Eat, Michael Jordan.'

'I don't sleep with men, Roost.'

'Didn't say you did.'

'Just so we understand.'

'I understand.'

'I'm glad you understand,' I said.

'I'm glad I understand.'

'I mean, I used to, but I don't any more.'

'Me neither.'

We separated at Clark and Division. I bought a bottle of Seagram's and a bottle of Southern Comfort and when I woke I was in a cheap hotel room. I don't know how I got there. Roost was at the foot of the bed, leaning over me. An aureole of light speared outward from the back of his head.

'Today's Friday,' he said. 'Yesterday was Thursday. You wasn't to work yesterday.'

'Who put me here?'

'I did. I found you in the middle of Clark Street. I brought you here or they'd've taken you to General Hospital. You don't never want to go to General Hospital.'

'How much you pay for this room?'

'Eighty-five cents.'

'Take it from my pay,' I said.

'What pay? You got seventy-five cents times seven hours. That's five dollars and twenty-five cents. But I got you the job. The money's mine. In fact, you owe me two dollars that I gave you on the North Branch trestle bridge.'

'Did they fire me?' I asked.

'Yes.'

I sank back against the pillow.

'Also,' Roost said, 'you owe me eighty-five cents each day you stay in this hotel.'

'I got no money.'

'What you planning to do?'

'We can work something out.'

Roost walked around the room. He urinated into a blue and white pitcher. At the top of a wall partition was a draughty gap.

'They subdivided the room,' he said. 'There's another room across the partition.'

Suddenly he turned to me. He leaned so close I saw the pores of his skin.

'You ever see Negro lips this close?' he asked.

He vibrated his lips.

'Bbbbbrrrr – '

'Go away.'

'You don't see *that* every day,' he said.

The draught blew harder from the dark gap above the partition. An old man coughed. Roost looked up.

'Somebody's dying in the next room,' he said.

The dark gap began to undulate.

'I'm hallucinating, Roost.'

'You got the blood sickness.'

'My dead friends – blood – heaving and rolling – '

Roost sat on the edge of the bed. He shook me by the shoulder. I snapped awake.

'I don't care about your goddamned friends,' he said. 'Or your women problems.'

'Get off my bed.'

'Do you want to know the kind of things go on in Chicago?'

'Get off.'

The old man in the next half of the room coughed long and hard. Roost got up and banged on the partition.

'He *is* dying,' Roost said. 'I'll bet he's got a wallet.'

'Is his door open?'

'I'll go see.'

Roost went out the door and peered into the room. I got up. The floorboards shot up and hit me in the face.

'You okay?'

'I think so.'

'Well, this guy's just lying there dying.'

The next room was even smaller. An elderly man with

wavy white hair lay on his bed, staring at the ceiling. He wore tan slacks and a white shirt, a black string tie with a turquoise clasp. From time to time he worked his Adam's apple. We went inside.

'We was wondering if you was all right,' Roost said. 'We heard you coughing.'

'Quite all right,' he said. 'Thank you.'

We came closer. The old man's baby blue eyes were enlarged by thick spectacles. His forearms were so thin the wrist knobs protruded. Suddenly Roost tore the old man's watch off. I pushed the old man over and searched his pockets. There were two pieces of turquoise.

'Take them to the pawn shop,' I told Roost. 'See what you get.'

Roost hit the old man hard on the spine and ran from the room.

'What are you going to do to me?' the old man quavered.

'I'm not sure,' I said. 'What would you like us to do?'

I turned the old man over and slapped him in the face. I yanked out his dentures. He started to bleed. I made him rinse his gums.

'Why do you hurt me?' he asked, trembling.

'Shut up.'

I didn't know what to do with the old man. I made him lie down.

'You look like you're ready to leave the body,' I snorted.

'I already have.'

'Tell me.'

The Rosicrucian

'I WAS AN ORPHAN.

'I worked on a farm near Anadarko, Oklahoma. I drove the tractor, picked cotton, and built sheep pens. I was sent to work

162

around Verden, Apache and Fort Cobb. I tried to run away but they caught me, tied me to a tractor wheel and beat me with a cattle stick.

'I married when I was fifteen. She was one-quarter Cherokee. We had a little boy. The farms began to fail. Our boss, Mr Dilworth, said there wasn't but room for one hand now. I would have to contest it with a Mexican boy. We didn't have much food and the baby was sick, so I really needed that job. The contest started on Thursday morning at six. I picked down one row, the Mexican down another. It was hot, but we never stopped. At seven-thirty in the evening I had picked ninety-eight pounds of cotton and he had picked ninety-nine. So he got the job.

'I met up with him in the woods. I pulled a knife. I told him I needed the job. He went back to his truck and he got his knife. He told me in Spanish that I had to leave Anadarko. He said I'd been beaten fair. He said Mr Dilworth had had coffee with him and had hired him.

'This Mexican boy was a tough fighter but this time I was tougher. He cut my forearms but I cut his leg. He got so scared of the big artery opening that he tied his shirt around it. He had real smooth skin like the finest Swiss milk chocolate. I had my way with him and afterward I got my wife and boy and we left Anadarko.

'We lived in Cordell, Clinton and Foss. My wife died of sceptic poisoning. I took my boy to Woodward and worked in a mail order firm. My boy was killed crossing the highway. I moved to Alva on the Salt Fork. I made money killing dogs for the county.

'I searched for the meaning of life, the cause of my suffering. I attended field gospel meetings. I handled snakes in Bartlesville. Nothing lighted the darkness inside. I went north to Kansas City. There I heard the Rosicrucian Elias D. White. After one of his lectures I went up and told him I figured he had as good a handle on things as anybody.

'I was proud of being a Rosicrucian. I wore the red ribbon crossways on my shoulder. I was rebaptized in Elias D. White's home. I was wrapped in a clean YMCA towel and anointed with

163

herbs. Handel's *Messiah* played on his phonograph. I underwent lavation. He showed me the Codex. We collected snakes and I became the bridegroom. I was taught the Cibation. Henceforth I was known as Delius.

'There was an attempt on White's life and I became his personal bodyguard.

'White taught me physical metamorphosis. We went into his garden and cast my male seed into the nasturtiums. He gave me a green lion with a red star. I recited the Ode of the First Material and was given the key of Basilius.

'It was the 1940s. We exposed many lodges, fake resurrections. We were attacked from New York and Missouri. There were warrants, suits and perjury trials. We fought the Shriners, the Masons and the Light of Egypt, both the American Mahatma and the Grand Maitre of the USA. The Great White Lodge of Tibet sent proclamations to Kansas City. In the end, a bomb crippled Elias D. White.

'I was burdened everywhere by the collapse of man. It seemed to me the United States was a wasteland of sterility and greed.'

'So I left my body.

'Fox, geese and owls ate anti-tumescent plants. Flames blew out of our bellies and turned lust to sweet generosity. Rainwater washed me clean. I became sweet. We walked arm in arm, the crippled and the holy, into savannahs shrouded with birds of paradise rising over rumbling volcanoes. Eagle feathers fell golden and twirling into the sun-shafts.

'It was the garden of God. There were no soldiers. There were no slaughterhouse workers. There were no felons, homosexuals or blasphemers. Johann Comenius was there, Ezechiel Foxcraft, Solomon Trismosin, and Heinrich Khunrath. I saw Marcus Aurelias. Elias Ashmole was there. Pilgrims pulled themselves out of deep wells. Soldiers held shields. Scribes wrote in silver light. Men crawled out of dungeons waving pennants on which was written *IHS*. That was how they spent their days: in allegory.

'We grew *helleborus niger*, *symphytum tuberosum*, aconite

for friendship, willow wort against enmities. Christ Himself watered clematis under the pergola.

'We became androgynes and danced between the crocus and lilac, through the graveyards of delusions. Exquisite clocks ticked. Nights we heard the Divine monochord. I wrapped myself in wings like an upright bat and slept standing on the lake shore.

'One day we found a perfect-cursed-blessed man in the woods.

'"Look," he whispered. "In the skies . . ."

'People were being taken up into the clouds. We said of such a one that he *was not, for God took him* or she *slipped away and became light.* As at a train station now I wait. I wait for the angels in handcarts to ride me to the skies. O, so many have already gone up in streams of silver light!

'You have a crippled body. Some day you will kill somebody. But let me tell you something. We're trying to get it across to you. You've heard it before. I'll tell you again:

'*Search for the fruit if you want to, but remember the gender of the root.*'

FOURTEEN

I was a Negro.

I enrolled in a book-keeping course in Wilbur, Nebraska, at the firm of Fitzroy and McKimmon. It was a yellow brick building on the corner of Fifth and Jackson behind the mortuary. It was late May. White blossoms were in the cherry trees. Birds chirped on the funeral hall. It was warm and there was pollen in the lilacs. Our instructor was white and severe. We studied double column, percentage reckoning, carry-over and incremental accounts. There was Adrian Greenberg, who had cancer, Mary St Cloud, Genevieve Kiek and Harrison Bond, all Negroes.

'Jack,' Harrison said to me. 'You're a very nice person. Strange. But nice.'

Unable to commit suicide, I became a clown.

I moved to south Indiana, wearing tomatoes in my hair. I stole watches and wore them on my shoulder. I perfected card tricks. I lived in an abandoned railroad shack in Paoli and made potato beer. Two white railroad guards fought with knives. I heard them bawling but I saw nothing, just the water tank. I carved the incident on the walls.

I dreamed that a black flood covered Indiana but, fast as I rowed, I couldn't save Antoinette.

I crossed into Kentucky. The road, now white, now black, curved into the hickory hills. I came across a white skin stretched between birch trees and a mattress rotted in the rain. My mother passed by, sparks in her hair.

Pzzzzt.

★   ★   ★

I worked my way through Kentucky. I skinned geese, loaded radishes. I wore my puerility like a badge. The heat paralysed me. The old plantations, the weatherbeaten shacks, sizzled in waves. There were quick white clouds overhead, but slow black rivers below. I told people my father was a Negro who had been killed by a white prison guard.

At night lightning sizzled over the hills. Ignace led a horde of dead children down Tea Rose Street.

Pzzzzt.

I moved to Wingo. White developers were moving cemeteries and Negroes were hired to probe the funeral fields for corpses. They hauled up rotted caskets and sometimes bodies fell out. Brass pins opened, the shrouds unknotted at the head, bones tumbled to the ground. Then there was a field fire. A white couple burned to death in a yellow Ford. They turned black as Negroes, embracing. Then the creek flooded, swept through a graveyard, uprooted coffins. Corpses jumped up stone walls, climbed hickory trees.

'Jean, Jean, the jailer's son,' they sang.

I darkened my face with shoe polish. I stiffened my hair with resin. I perfected my limp.

I joined the Zion Church of God. I lived in a bus behind a rectory in Louisville. On Saturday I washed the church steps. Negro derelicts came for ham sandwiches. I served non-alcoholic mint drinks at the Louisville Negro Men's Club. They sang:

'O Death, spare me over one more day.'

I visited the museum of Negroes.

It was a tenant farmer's shack now owned by the Committee of Negro Educators. It was warm, very dark. Sunlight streamed through a hot open door. In the foyer a Negro mannikin hanged by the neck from a cypress branch.

There was a curved painting of the Atlantic, full of storms. A white sailing ship glided past black clouds. I pressed a red button. The anchor chain rattled out of a porthole, and on each link was a Negro.

By the stairs was a table of mechanical Negro girls. I turned the crank. The Negro children danced.

Upstairs was a Negro skull. Arrows showed the cranial tilt, the brain capacity. On a steel tray inside a glass cabinet was a patch of Negro skin. Glass flasks held black pigment. Collections of knotted hair, with name tags, were pinned inside white boxes on beds of purest cotton.

A table was laid with a Negro dinner: yam, asafoetida, green beans, catfish. On a mahogany dresser was a display of catgut, hair oil, a stuffed Negro dream bird. A Yoruba necklace dangled over a cracked mirror. There was a ticket to a Louis Armstrong concert, and photographs of famous Negro criminals lined the wall. I bought *Negroes of Cincinnati* by Phelps T. Edwards. I went into the courtyard. A pomegranate tree, broken by red-orange fruit, burst into flame.

I moved north to Michigan.

I cleaned cars in Sturgis, hauled dirt in Union City, and cleared brush for Frederick Newcombe in South Haven. I learned dialects. I studied variety, disguise. I studied *négritude*.

I went north along Highway 131 and went by the name Jimmy Verhaeren. I cooked eggs for William McKee, who made a steel bar for my right shoe. I moved to Pando and worked for Manning Evans, who made propeller toys. At the mouth of the Père Marquette at Ludington I sold fishing bait with Peter Baldwyn. A locomotive went by, transferring caskets to the north. The corpses sang:

'Death is a hard man to know.'

I woke up in the Mackinac Café. I must have fainted. The owner, Reynolds Kayran, a blue-black man from Surinam with a bent spine, gave me a room upstairs overlooking his rusted cars by the lake. The yellow walls were soaked in sun. Outside I smelled warm juniperberries, blueberries, black raspberries on the dusty road. There was a hot smell downstairs, too, a smell

168

of endless days. I stood hours at the window.

'You were in bad shape,' Reynolds said.

'I was in a bad way.'

'But you can rest here, with us.'

'Already I feel better.'

Reynolds put a hand on my shoulder. He put a string of garlic around my neck. I bowed my head and tapped my iron bar three times. Reynolds shook his head.

'Poor, poor Jimmy Verhaeren.'

I mopped Reynolds's floors, delivered his hot sandwiches, and bathed his legs, which were cruelly scarred. It embarrassed him, so I didn't ask. Reynolds had worked the assembly line in Flint and he taught me to work bumper grilles into sculpture. We charmed each other. Each night I closed the shutters while he shivered, and covered him with an army blanket while the lake rustled beyond the pines.

Reynolds's friends came by on Saturdays when huge pots of beef bubbled on Reynolds's stove. They wore grey jackets, and with slumped shoulders, heads down, gathered on the porch with harmonicas and guitars.

Reynolds and I took a week off and lived in a cabin on Burt Lake. We fished in the rain and ate filleted perch, eggs with chillies, onions and cinnamon bread. Reynolds drank each day almost a litre of black coffee through his busted yellow teeth. But his chills got worse. I slept with my arm over his shoulder.

'B–b–bless you, J–J–Jimmy,' he stuttered.

I stole from motels. A motel owner saw me.

'Hey you – !'

I butted him in the belly. He was a soft man, and lay trembling in the ragweed. I threw stones at his head.

'White man!'

Reynolds and I hunted in southern Illinois. It was white property so we crawled through tree stumps and thorns in a charred forest. We became slimy with fatigue. Reynolds couldn't breathe. I put down my rifle and grilled a racoon. Reynolds made soup of the bones. Slowly he felt better. A blood-bag of a sun sank into the hot blooming lily pads. There was a hydra. The more I knifed it the uglier it got.

'This obsession will kill you,' he said. 'Being a Negro.'

'Why?'

'The Negro is a prisoner.'

'My father is a prison guard.'

Reynolds spat into the brown water.

'You have a limited concept of prison. Didn't Colonel Canale teach you anything?'

'I never told you about Colonel Canale.'

Reynolds showed me his camera. I was amazed by its bellows, its chrome trigger, its tiny wire.

White foremen were severe. Negroes hauled logs, laid wire, dragged granite from the quarry. It was hot and humid, even at night. River Negroes spitted a baby alligator and their children sat on the backs of pick-up trucks and ate it. Negroes bathed under a lantern. Black knees, black shoulders, dripped, red palms, white teeth, in the hiss of the lantern. By torchlight we staggered down the country roads. I got drunk and fell in the creek to my knees.

'Dry your hands, Jimmy,' Reynolds said, 'on my white woolly hair.'

'No, Reynolds. That is one thing I will not do.'

Reynolds whistled, cooking squirrel brains. Blue vapour circled the lily pads. By midnight the whole forest choked in blue fog. Fireflies winked in blue waves around tree stumps and fish in skillets gleamed blue. The blue-misted shore dripped with *négritude*. Negroes danced like drugged bears. Reynolds tapped his foot. But he was not American. No, he put his red kerchief on his peeling forehead and kept to himself.

'The *métissage*,' Reynolds said irritably. 'The bloodlines are confused.'

'France has failed.'

'Life is a living horror,' Reynolds said.

'A nightmare.'

'Yet living has sweet things.'

'What?' I asked.

'Women.'

'Women? Hazel eyes, houses that divide in the rain? But who pays the price? Tell me that. *Who pays the price?*'

'Simmer down,' Reynolds said.

'Women! Make me crazy!'

'You're the craziest person I ever met.'

'Who said that?' I suddenly asked, looking behind at the dark, moving forest.

'I did. I said that.'

'Oh. I thought . . . somebody . . . women . . . were eavesdropping . . .'

We drove back to Michigan. It was July and the fields were yellow. Reynolds's room was like a grotto, dark with blue blankets on the walls, one bed, a pot-bellied stove, some tools he had stolen from the assembly line. Over his bed was a pig's foetus in a tin can. He showed me his fetishes, tree boles stuck with parrot feathers.

'You feel okay, Jimmy?'

'Much better.'

'You were a little . . . depressed, I think . . . in Illinois.'

'I felt nervous. I don't know why.'

He unwrapped his votive painting. It was three feet square, dated New Albina, 1934. In it, a Negro prisoner struck a soldier with a rifle butt. From the soldier's mouth came a green balloon.

'What's the balloon?' I asked.

'His soul.'

'Soul?'

'When it leaves the body, you die.'

Under the soldier was an inscription:

> '*Sa-a di'm lipet*
> *Conn'n fe abi min*
> *L'ap mouricamem.*'

'What does it mean, Reynolds?'

'*So you'll die like everybody else.*'

'What happened, Reynolds? Why are your legs scarred?'

Reynolds took a degraded Camel from his plaid shirt. He said nothing. He looked old as a bear. I put the cigarette in my mouth, lit it, and put it between his lips.

'Why did my brother die?' I asked.

He shrugged.

'Why is my mother insane, my father unemployed?'

He shrugged.

'Why can't I be a Negro?'

Reynolds stared at the glowing end of the Camel and dropped ash on the cold, cracked floor. He got a tin cup and scooped the ashes into it.

'Why does life hurt?' he asked.

The Maroon

'I WAS AN ORPHAN.

'I grew up in the outskirts of Popakai, Surinam, in an orphanage run by Catholic missionaries. Father Reynolds taught me to read and gave me his name. I ran away, lived with the Indians, then with the Bush Negroes. When I was fourteen I followed a coloured girl home from missionary school and raped her. After that I lived alone.

'I lived on stealing pigs and manioc. I got drunk on manioc beer and raped an Indian woman. I moved away from Popakai and drifted downriver toward the Atlantic surf. I earned money stripping bark. I raped a white woman and was sent to prison camp at New Albina.

'New Albina was a mile up the Maroni River from Albina, full of *kunu*, souls of murdered prisoners. Prisoners cut timber, stripped the bark, boiled resin, and stacked planks. The camp had prisoners' huts, Governor DeGroot's house, and outlying buildings for the guards. There was a saw mill, planking house, and a river dock.

'We worked from five-thirty in the morning when it was

cold and foggy. By noon the camp steamed with heat and we got mash and water. We lay in the shadows until two-thirty and worked until sunset. Electric lights came on and we worked to nine at night. Men fainted from the heat. Many broke out in boils. Flies clung to them. We bathed only in low tide when no sharks came up the river.

'The Dutch gave us *bugnee*. What is *bugnee*? Gifts. For example, *bonne-bouche*, mutton balls roasted with ground nuts. They gave us rum, cheap rum, and cordials, bitters, and roast pig, bananas and manioc, sweet gum. These orgies lasted days. But we were enslaved by them. They gave us white towels and these towels were very beautiful. Men wiped their sweat with flourishes. They worked very hard for towels. The Dutch gave us brass rings for the women's arms, which the women prized.

'We had *soirées dansantes*. What were they? On Saturday night, to amuse the Dutch, we danced to Radio Maracaibo. DeGroot put a radio on a stump, the Dutch got drunker and drunker. They picked the best females and took them to the basement of DeGroot's house.

'The Negro women the whites so badly wanted. DeGroot put on a three-day *colungee*. *Colungee* is a bridal party. They picked a good-looking woman and dressed her and took her into the governor's house where white men stripped, chewed hallucinogenic leaves mashed in *nicou* and *cacheiry*. After the bridal *colungee* DeGroot opened the men prisoners' huts and threw her in.

'You understand these things, Jimmy? *Nous sommes frères?*'

' – *frères* – '

'We weren't prisoners, we were *esclaves*. The most powerful enslaver was Egbo. When we heard Egbo's drums we hid. Egbo wore a black jaguar skirt and a fur cape. He came through the huts and fucked anybody, anything, he wanted. Man, woman, pig. Anybody objected, he cut off their hands. Egbo ordered:

'"*Obey DeGroot. I have given him power over you.*"

'One morning Helmstad vander Zandt was stabbed. His son, Kirk vander Zandt, lined us up and tapped each and every

173

one of us, asking, "*Who killed the white man?*" A prisoner named Wilson Gairie flinched. Vander Zandt had an iron pumpbolt riveted into his mouth. Gairie worked after that like a mule with a bit through his cheeks, swallowing his own blood.

'Vander Zandt and Demoullines whipped us. One man got gangrene. He stank so bad that Demoullines fed him laudanum and killed him. We got the heavy melancholy. The Negro goes into a shadow world. And many died from that. Some escaped. They caught one and clubbed him with gun barrels. The ravines were full of logs that had leaped the rapids, vines and orchids, and there they threw him to be eaten by the wild hogs and ants. The ravines filled with blue vapour.

'Cholera swept through New Albina. I was on corpse detail. We threw them in the Maroni too. Negro, Indian, they went into the rapids. A brother and sister died. We chopped them apart and buried them in the sand.

'I was put in the *cachot*, the dungeon. Demoullines lowered oatmeal in a bucket full of flies. They put a *fleur de lis* on me. Look. Like a cow. I got leg ulcers from the iron ring. I became a shadow. Blue vapour left me, heavy, dripping, my *négritude*.

'The cook, a Negress, Amelia Maurice, killed the infant Samuels DeGroot with a hat pin to the brain. They tied her to a tree, and had starved dogs eat her.

'That night we broke out of the sheds, caught a white guard, cut off his head, and made the other guards kiss it. Then we caught Anthony vander Zandt, poured resin on him and set him on fire. We found Demoullines, roped him to a log and sent him down the saw slide where he blew apart into the Maroni. DeGroot ran out of his house, shot two of us on the porch, then ran upstairs into the bathroom and shot himself. We caught the white guard Willems, swung him by the feet and clubbed him on to tree stumps.'

' – liberty – '

'For the next three days we dressed in DeGroot's top hats and military ribbons. We danced in European finery. We chewed *coca*. We smoked tobacco. We took collaborators one by one to the big logs and brained them. We found DeGroot's wife and raped her until she went insane. Then we hacked her apart and threw her into the choked ravine. This went on in drunken liberty.'

' – sweet liberty – '

'We danced the *balancez*, *avant-deux*, hornpipe, double shuffle and egret dance. I had taken a round through the tendon of my left leg. It never healed. See this twisted flesh? That's why I limp. You limp too, don't you, *mon petit*? But I danced. One dances in liberty.'

' – oh, liberty – '

'Rangers set up machine guns across the Maroni. Suddenly bullets punched our huts, splintered piled logs, ricocheted off saw blades. Many were killed. I swam the Maroni, but my friends Henry Lemoine and Joshua Fremml drowned when a ranger cannon blew off their legs. The rest of us ran into the forest and buried sharp sticks smeared with our shit in the path. Two rangers cut their legs and died of infection. We crept back to the Maroni at night and strangled two more rangers by their gunboats.

'During the day the boats shelled the jungle. Shrapnel hit our manioc and blew open the torso of my friend Ramissey. I killed him and threw him in the gorge so the ranger dogs wouldn't smell him.

'We raided farms for white hostages. We caught Peter de Havelaan, his aunt Sarah, Henryk van Siemens, and Demoullines's grandfather, Ezekiel, a babbling idiot. We hacked them apart. Only one survived, Fernanda vander Zandt, aged eleven. I forced her mouth open and pushed fish down her throat. I caught a monkey, skinned it, and made soup full of ground nuts, olive oil, sweet yams. But when the monkey skull came up she fainted.

'I rubbed sap into her lips. She tore at my eyes. I frizzed her hair with clay and put bark plugs in her nostrils. I did everything I could to make her understand she was my honoured guest, that Egbo would not hurt her, she was my wife. I would sell her for a passport to the Antilles. I was frightened by how wide her eyes grew. After a few nights I sold her for salt to the Bush Negroes, she was so worthless.

'I lived alone on freshwater fish: *patoyayes*, *yaya blancs*, *oeils rouges*, *brobro* and *coulans*. Low, broken clouds rolled on the green Atlantic that threw rotted logs on the beach. I was disoriented with the pain and horror I had seen. I walked into the cold surf to die. Suddenly gazelles jumped out of the waves. A circle of huts appeared behind a reef. My relatives smoked beef in the sunshine. *Orisas* – African ancients – threw spears from the rainbows. I wanted to go back to Africa so bad, I tied logs together with vines and paddled into the sea.'

' – oh, Africa!'

'I was captured by Venezuelans. They sold me to Cubans. I worked two years in the sugar cane, then went with a fisherman to Florida where I cleaned fish five years. I lived in Louisiana, was arrested, worked my way up the Mississippi River and came to Michigan. I worked in the motor car plants. I started a café. Like you, I looked for a place where there is no *Code Noir*, no *négritude*.

'But, of course, there is no such place.'

FIFTEEN

My parents moved to Vincent, Missouri.

I went up and down the Mississippi River. There was a Vincent in Wisconsin, a Vincent in Iowa, and a Vincent in Kentucky. I found many Vincents, but none was the true Vincent. A riverboatman told me there was a Vincent on the Mississippi in Missouri near Quincy so I followed the bank and found Vincent, an old slave town with a prison, a Catholic church, French quarter and birch woods.

On the edge of the woods stood four burned black cypresses. Our Chevrolet was rusted, on blocks in a horse paddock. Someone was writing in a window of a trailer. I went closer and smelled strong coffee. It was my mother. She was practising her letters.

Her hair was white.

'Mama – '

'Just a minute.'

She dipped the end of the pencil on her tongue. She bent over and wrote a large *U*. She looked at me.

'You're dirty.'

'It's dirty out there, Mama.'

'Your hair is stiff.'

'It's the resin.'

'And your face – '

'Shoe polish.'

'You can shower by filling the metal bucket and setting it on the top of the trailer. No sense being shy.'

I showered. The trailer had the red divan, the altar, a crucifix above the bed, Ignace's religious theatre, my ice skates and tea

177

cups hanging on brass hooks. Brilliant sunshine came in oblongs on the braided rug. Over the bed was the portrait of Catherine Labouré. Even the dust smelled clean. The bathroom was a ditch covered with boards.

Ignace's books, prize ribbons, St Bonaventure jacket, death certificate, *Catholic Encyclopedia* filled the trunk of the Chevrolet. I tossed my duffel bag into the Chevrolet.

'I *wondered* where that was,' she said.

My father was very thin. His red hair was fluff. He wore khaki trousers baggy around his skinny knees, tied with rubber bands.

My mother washed the curtains.

'Where were you?'

'Michigan.'

'What did you find?'

'*Négritude.*'

'What a clown.'

One day I came around the paddock and saw Death in a red flannel shirt. He tried to rip my father's throat. My father hit him in the crotch. Death bit him on the neck. They fought over the hay bales and around the Chevrolet.

'Papa!'

'Jean!'

Death punched my father in the balls. I picked up a shovel, ran in, and beat Death on the head.

'*Vous – vous –* FUCKER!' I screamed.

Death melted back into the birches. Crows circled the trailer.

'It was a good thing you came by just then,' my father said.

Death came to the Belle Rivière Hotel. He played poker with my father. Death sat by a red tasselled lamp perched on a black television, badly lighted. They bet on numbers, suits, wild trays, red hearts, black tens.

'Who is this guy?' my father asked. 'He's damn good!'

My father went upstairs to Georgia Berenson. She yanked his limp dink.

'Nobody home?' she laughed.

*   *   *

My father went to fix his watch at LeMoin Jeweller's. Skeletons stood in black leather jackets and motorcycle caps in the doorway lights. He backed away and went to the Big Muddy Tavern. After two lagers the bartender wiped the bar with a bloody rag.

'What the hell is that?' my father asked. 'A menstrual cloth?'

'It's the cloth the Jamaican, Barrault, spit into as he lay dying.'

My father ran to the edge of town. Stumbling into the public housing projects, he got tangled up in laundry hanging from the lines. He crawled to the swings and heard:

'*It is so cold, mon capitaine –* '

'Who said that?'

'*The rain –* '

'WHO'S SPEAKING?'

My father tumbled backward into a cart full of carrots.

'*I am so very cold.*'

My father went home and ordered me to carve his tombstone. It would be three feet above ground, one foot below, rounded, of red granite with black letters. It would read, '*Jack Verhaeren. 1914–1955. Prison guard, HM Prison Swallowfield. Vive la France.*' I found granite in a slag heap. I stole a chisel and *click-clicked* until my hands were raw and white with granite dust. It was no good. The letters were crooked. The stone cracked. I pasted over the mistakes with clay and glue. My father admired it.

'The one good thing you ever did,' he said.

My father could no longer dance. He bumped and ground to the radio. His face discoloured. His abdomen bulged like a grasshopper's. His knees jerked in spasms. He sank into the Verhaeren melancholy.

'I am but a pair of legs,' he said, 'carrying future Verhaerens. A germinal sac, through this world.'

He dreamed of prisoners turned to swallows in the fields. In the morning my mother laid a noose at the trailer door

179

to ensnare Death. She smeared chicken blood on the window, Pippi's excrement to disgust Death. I burned Death's effigy.

On the dirt my father scrawled:

Sauve qui peut.

Living became odious to him. He hated Kiwanis, Oddfellows, Optimists, Rotary, Junior Chamber of Commerce, all the congregations of the living. He moved in wind-shadows and watched impotently as houses on the Mississippi collapsed. A chain gang drove in pylons. A warden cradled a shotgun over Negroes.

My father murmured:

'Negroes . . . and a *shotgun* . . .!'

The heat grew bad that August. Dogs hung over the edge of the canal, tongues out, baking in red shadows. Stink bugs swollen with blood crawled the wharf. A huge catfish, the largest ever seen in the county, died in the posts. It had come up from the Gulf. I dragged it home and my mother cooked it with garlic and basil.

I was very depressed having to live in the United States. The people were tedious, the food banal.

Old Frenchtown grew hazy in the heat, but at night – oh God – Boulevard d'Horloge, La Vache Street, Oignon Street, Boulevard des Martyrs d'Amérique Nord – red lanterns hung in black streets. Negroes danced, men with men, smoking, bloodshot eyes glazed with vodka. Men cursed in every *patois*. We danced, a bassoonist blew the blues.

I met René Yville there, from Portage des Sioux, also Gene Phipps from New Madrid, and Tyrone Montoie from Carthage. We forgot everything in the vodka, the sweat and foul breath of miners, railroad men, mechanics, boiler-makers.

It was a hell of a summer.

Relations and friends of relations came down from Canada for the summer fair.

'Paul Hartmann!' I yelled.

'God! Do you look awful! Your hair!'

'It's the resin!'

'Etienne Bastide wants to see you!'

'Who is that girl?'

'You don't recognize her? That's Antoinette Hartmann!'

Antoinette Hartmann wore a rust-red dress with white pockets. She was assistant sales manager at Kreske in Rutherford. She was tall, full-grown, with small breasts and intelligent eyes, but she still had a few freckles. When she smiled the sun exploded in the trees.

'Jean,' Antoinette asked. 'Why are your teeth so bad?'

I went home and filed my teeth into points.

Verhaerens stayed in Quincy. Nightly they drove over to party. I hardly recognized my female cousins. Groups of two and three roamed the wharf under the lights. They tossed fish boxes into the Mississippi. They danced. Their backs and legs became sore. They could not stop dancing. They fell dead and jumped up again. They danced under the moonlight. They danced, female with female, in the stiff spiked grass around the oaks.

The priests of Holy Sacrament Church patrolled the birches and pried them apart.

'How lovely – ' Antoinette Hartmann whispered, her legs wet with sweat.

The August fair began. Headlights appeared across the Mississippi. The river was golden in streaks as cars crossed the bridge. Gnats hung in clusters over Vincent. Rain fell far away. Everything was suspended. A great delirium was ours. We moved downward in darkness, selling what we had left to Americans.

'Hey, American,' Antoinette called, 'buy French lemonade?'

'*Would* I? Shit, yes!'

St Croix women sold breads, sausages, mustards, seafood, beer, garlics and onions at the fair. They stirred stews, played cards, rolled dice and told smutty stories about homosexuals.

Country music boomed through fairground speakers down the Mississippi River. St Croix dressed in costume.

I was the *Capitaine Funèbre*. Etienne was *Woman Fecundus*, with water balloon breasts and high heels. M. d'Aube was *Great Procreator*, with *papier-mâché* testicles the size of basketballs, hair glued on to a broomstick in his belt. Paul Hartmann was *La Putain* in black fishnet stockings. Antoinette Hartmann was Pope Pius XII. She wore a red towel for a cope, pumpkin for mitre, and sprinkled us with Seven-Up. Jack-in-the-Green, Ed Gien, Elvis Presley, bobbed among the lanterns.

Etienne found me. He smelled of cigarettes and wore sunglasses. He took a newspaper clipping from his wallet. A hobo named Kurt Flood had burned to death in Minnesota.

'Thank you,' I said.

'Do you remember, Jean? When we first kissed?'

'Leave me alone. Look!'

A seven-headed mutant lay in a cage with red bulbs winking. It disgorged its meal. A white, lethal light filtered down on its striped back. It stared. Flies danced on its head, because it was meat, and nearly corpse, and the flies needed to lay eggs.

Cousins came daily. Our trailer was packed with Verhaerens. Fighting, drinking, cooking, throwing up. They rode a horse around the paddock. There was a shrimp feast. My father called for Antoinette Hartmann.

'It is not right,' she said gently.

'Antoinette – '

'No, no . . .'

'Please . . . I am dying . . .'

'Naughty Jack . . .'

My mother sat on a folding chair, knitting burial tassels. Dust motes danced behind her head. She sang:

> *'Monsieur d'Marlborough est mort*
> *Mironton, tonton, mirontaine*
> *Monsieur d'Marlborough est mort*
> *Est mort et enterré.'*

'The Duke of Marlborough is dead
Mironton, tonton, mirontaine
The Duke of Marlborough is dead
Dead and in the ground.'

My father looked to Antoinette. It was his turn to sing.

'Antoinette, your pants are wet
I love you yet, Antoinette
I'll bet you wet everybody you met
My lovely freckled Antoinette.'

Antoinette blushed. She left with Paul and Etienne. When my mother wasn't looking I shoved my father's head into the pillow.

'Papa,' I said. 'DID YOU?'

In the second week of his agony there was no bread. Sister Alicia from Catholic Relief brought us two shopping bags of groceries. My mother fried fish. He retched. I gave him rum. He hallucinated. Antoinette and Paul Hartmann, the Pics, and the Leszeks, Etienne Bastide, came to pay last respects. My mother sewed burial booties.

'Death comes in giant steps, Mr Verhaeren,' Paul Hartmann said.

'I am swollen with it.'

'Yes. Your belly is full of wind.'

'They have it up my ass.'

'You decay, sir,' Etienne said, moving away, waving the air.

I played the red accordion for my father. During those long days and suicidal nights I played *La Tempête sous la Lune*, *Miséricorde*, *Les Saltimbanques* and *Le Pendu*. I played Gaspé reels. I was Jean Carrignan. I dressed in Swallowfield grey. He clutched the sheets like a shroud.

'Who will help us?' he asked.

'We are beyond help,' I said.

'Our lives are incoherent.'

'Yes. One moment I'm at Burt Lake. Bang, slam. I'm in Vincent. I don't remember how.'

The trailer began to sink into the earth.

'Now listen,' he said. 'When I was in the merchant marine I saw an ammunition freighter torpedoed. It was in the North Atlantic. The ship rose three feet above the waves, turned inside out, arms and legs flung into the open sea. Orange fire rolled over black oil.'

'It was a vision.'

'At that instant I seized life,' he said.

'I have no vision.'

'You live on other people's visions.'

'Because you had complicated relations with me.'

'I played games with your miserable life,' he said. 'Ha.'

'I tried to be free.'

'You became imprisoned in your liberty. Only in prison are you free.'

'Father, you have confused me.'

I got depressed.

'*Le bon Dieu* was cruel,' I said.

'Don't blame *him*. It was your melancholy friends. Negroes and hobos.'

'I never told you about them.'

He waved a hand.

'Bah. I created them.'

Breezes whispered through the birches. Death rode the sunset. There wasn't much time. I leaned forward.

'But I learned the price of liberty,' I told him.

'How expensive is it?'

'I speak of prison uprisings.'

'You mean – the Kingston riots – ?'

'No,' I said. 'Worse. Bolts driven through heads of wardens!'

'Oh – God!'

'Prison guards sent through saw mills!'

My father clutched at the window.

'Guards clubbed on tree stumps!' I yelled. 'Burned in resin!'

184

'*Where?*'

'Here! In this trailer!'

He arched his back. He was going nowhere. I pushed him down.

'I'm so glad we've had this little talk,' I said. 'We'll talk again, after tea.'

His Missouri cousins Armand and Jim Verhaeren gathered his sweaty pyjamas. They piled his shirts, shoes, tie and prison uniform and made a bonfire.

My father and I played dominoes for quarters and *fan droana* for dimes. He sank into a perpetual twilight. I sponged the corners of his mouth. I inspected his ears. I plaited his hair for the grave. Trees fascinated him. I saw him licking pencils.

'*Qui a fermé ma porte?*' he asked.

'Nobody. Nobody slammed your goddamn door.'

Along the river we heard the *tom tom* beating, slow and steady.

'Death,' he whispered. '*Le grand musicien.*'

Zena Courennes came by that night and examined my father. She leered at him with an ironical, rubbery mouth. Old Woman Dyb had died, but Old Man Dyb practised dance steps in the paddock.

'Jack, Jack, flat on his back. Hang him on the bacon rack.'

Blue bombs exploded. Blue cascades trailed over the Chevrolet. Red bangers sent shocks echoing down the Mississippi River. My father copulated with the pillow. But he couldn't come. He beat himself with a stick. His hair turned white with desire. Red reflections flashed on his blackening eyes. He used mechanical aids: lubricants, batteries, rubber. In the morning he had facial tics.

'You look like turkey wattle,' Zena Courennes laughed.

Doctor Carryfew came to the trailer. My mother served him jelly beans.

'You have depleted yourself,' he told my father. 'The strain of sex has broken you down.'

'Sex?'

'You have contributed to the catastrophe.'

185

'I?'

'The seminal fluid contains large amounts of phosphorus-containing substances which, lost to the body by sexual excess, have to be replaced from the blood. The nervous system also needs that phosphorus. It is thereby robbed. Neurasthenia ensues. Fatigue. Irritability. Depression. Internal explosive pressures.'

'The whores killed me?'

'Just so, sir.'

'And what am I supposed to do now, tie a rubber band around my *zizi*?'

'Now?' Dr Carryfew said. '*Now*? I don't know what to do *now*, Mr Verhaeren!'

The priests came. This time my father let them chrism his forehead. My mother lighted incense. Red candles burned all night. Father Jesnin said the last rites.

'Clocks go wild,' my father said deliriously.

The death watch began. Black beetles clicked on the red divan. His belly turned black. Wax ran from his ears. His teeth chattered. The tax man arrived. My mother drew up a chair.

'My, my,' she said, 'won't this be interesting?'

I raised his feet. Blood rushed to his head and he passed out. He woke.

'I can fight no more,' he said.

'Papa – '

'I am broken.'

I shook him hard by the shoulders.

'Goodbye, Jean!'

I slapped his face.

'Papa!'

I hit him across the nose. Blood spurted from a nostril.

'It grows dark – '

'PAPA!'

I rolled him over and beat him with a broom. He woke an hour later, sore but alive. He looked at my mother.

'We chewed each other to the last days of our lives,' he said.

'Chew, chew, chew,' she said.

All night the fireworks rose. Green arches rainbowed across the pink sky. I beat out firecrackers in the hay bales. Then it thundered.

'Thunder,' he whispered. 'And it's Sunday. A man will die. What day is it?'

'August twenty-fourth. St Bartholomew's Day.'

'*I win.*'

Suddenly his face turned to a mask of horror.

'In spite of everything we were *petit bourgeois!*'

Dreamily he rose. The dance of dust motes swirled apart like a beaded curtain. Ignace's figurines fell in a cloudy light.

'*It is so cold, and I am so naked.*'

'WHO SAID THAT?' he screamed.

His face turned raspberry. I stepped back.

'Jean!'

'Papa!'

The septum of his nose gave way. Flecks of blood spattered his ruined gums.

'*Jean!*'

My father spat blood. As he stretched his skin split. Veins exposed and his hip ligaments split.

'JEAN!!'

'PAPA!!'

Veils of blood blew over the bed sheets. Clumps of flesh flew into the altar.

'PAPA!!'

'*No – !*'

'*PAPAAAAAAAAAAA!!!*'

I ducked. Fingers, toenails, gold molars blew against the windows. Jack Verhaeren collapsed into red meat that grinned. His rubbery spine twisted on soiled white fabric.

My father died 24 August 1955. The cause of death was *exsanguination*. We buried him standing up in the paddock. He was only forty-one years old.

His last words were:

'*Sauve qui peut.*'

SIXTEEN

Liberated at last, I danced down the crossroads. I knifed my father's uniform in the dust.

> 'Antoinette, your pants are wet
> I love you yet, Antoinette
> I'll bet you wet everybody you met
> My lovely freckled Antoinette.'

I built a coffin and carried it across Missouri. Dirt storms were so bad the air was black.

They arrested me in Jackson, Mississippi, and threw me in the women's jail where I slept on a leather pallet. The moon was three-quarters full over the water tower and it lit my cell. I smelled peppers and cold dirt. I looked out and saw nothing else, just the silhouette of the city tower. Gradually I calmed down. I dreamed of Antoinette Hartmann, but when I woke I could not retain the memory.

I just had this fragrance . . .

'You've got a nasty record,' the sergeant said, bringing me flowers.

'Do I?'

'You've broken into cars, gotten arrested for burglary, assault and indecent exposure.'

'Well, it's rough, on the road.'

'And you remember nothing?'

'I am going through hell.'

He wiped my face with a lace handkerchief.

'You should be in an asylum,' the sergeant said. 'How can you not know what you did?'

'No telling what I did.'

'Or will do.'

The sergeant faded in and out in a series of black. I grabbed hold but woke later on the leather pallet in the women's jail.

'Feel any better?' the sergeant asked.

'I think so.'

'Well, you were pretty weird last night. What are you, anyway?'

'Basque.'

I stayed a long time in that prison. Breezes circled through the dusty streets under a full moon. Fragrances of cactus candy, asphalt and horses came to me in the dark. Far away a freight train blew its whistle. I looked a long time into the darkness. On the third day the sergeant took me from my cell and gave me five dollars. He shoved me out the door.

'Believe in God,' he said.

I left Jackson. I became like an unsighted person. There were things, places. But I was not.

American towns were all the same. The same rivers, the red-brick warehouses, garbage. There was always a slaughterhouse, a bridge somewhere, broken walls where Negroes stood. The skies darkened. Everywhere there was broken glass, beer bottles, windows, headlights. Red berries spit poison. Ragweed in a railroad line, heading toward blue mountains, dripped from a rain gone by . . .

'My fingers!'

The bones of my metacarpals came through red splitting skin.

I groped forward, collided – now I was really blinded. Moonlight was dark and day was darker. I refused to look backward or touch a horse or goat. There were no knots in my shoestrings. I was a bird ready for flight. I changed my identity.

★　　★　　★

I was an Albanian.

*My name was John Michaels. When I was twelve my brother
Ignace was shot by a Marseilles policeman named Roger Vaucaire.
My father was Montenegran, my mother from Shkoder. They were
butchered by Turks. I joined the French Foreign Legion, served under
Colonel Canale. I had an affair with a prostitute named Antoinette
Hartmann. I beat up a man in Gulfport and escaped to Florida.*

*I went to Carrabelle, Florida. Across Apalachicola Bay on Dog
Island I set crab traps where the marshes moved. Under lanterns
Negroes pulled fish. Seminoles gunned their boats past the cypresses.
I left for Port St Joe and with three men held up a Greyhound bus,
took a sixteen-year-old girl to the men's room and raped her . . . But
that's one thing they'll never pin on John Michaels.*

I visited the museum of death.

The museum was on Lilac Street in Meridian, Mississippi.
It had been a synagogue and was now in ruins. The slats were
wood, with fallen white cornices. Engravings filled the foyer:
the bleeding of the corpse, flushing the veins, collection of
bodily fluids, wax-stopping the orifices. There was a display
of formaldehyde and resins, a decomposed head.

Light hung in long shafts through the gauze curtains. I
walked alone among the exhibits. A bull skeleton stood by
black velvet curtains. White fish hung from black coat hangers.
In a bell jar rubber tubes curved into the thighs of an infant
mannikin. I pressed a red button. Current ran into the head
plate and the baby was clad in copper.

Mementos littered the tables: china dogs, tickets to Lake
Charles steamers, marmalade jars, fragments of lace, a cloi-
sonnée cosmetic jar, a Negress carrying a clock, death cards.
Upstairs a bog corpse was displayed on a grass mound, kept
wet by a dripping lead pipe. It was tarred, like the dogs Indians
pulled from the swamps.

There was a shooting gallery in the hall. Tin women in
black velvet gowns crossed back and forth in front of my air
gun. When I shot three, the house lights went out.

I walked outside past a skinned goat. Tea roses, calendula,
violets, statice, jasmine, sphagnum, maroon tendrils, yellow

butterflies, all twined upward on the garden walls. There were fountains and an obelisk in an *allée* of chestnut trees. A Negro, the oldest man I had ever seen, served tea by a Sumerian necropolis.

'Warm me,' I begged.

I left the museum of death.

I was a Choctaw.

My name was Gene Vernon. My mother was Seminole. She was killed by a prison guard named Szegy. I sold trailers in Grayton Beach. I married a Catholic girl named Antoinette Hartmann, then robbed gas stations with Kurt Flood. He was clubbed from behind by police in Vincent. Now he's serving five years to fifteen in Pensacola. But they'll never find me, Gene Vernon.

I drifted down the coastline toward the Choctawhatchee. I cut horse bellies in Wewahitchka. I went blind. The sun burned off my lips. I drank with my teeth exposed. I was an alcoholic, a plaything of the Choctaw nation . . .

They called me Handsome Gene Vernon.

Lightning cracked over the water towers . . .

Pzzzzt.

'Antoinette!'

Distances became unpredictable. Words lost their meaning. For example, I asked a carpet cleaner the way to Wolf River and he smiled and handed me his cigarette lighter.

'Keep it,' he said generously. 'It's old.'

I drifted away . . . I snapped behind trees . . . the earth buckled . . . The United States shifted, expanded.

I was a Spaniard.

My name was Jack Castro. My grandfathers were Mayan. My father was killed by a railroad detective named James Barrault. I murdered a derelict on the Escambia River, Ignace Vaucaire, and lived with a fat woman from Chile named Antoinette Hartmann. When she died I tattooed a viper in a heart.

In those days there were lots of Cubans in Florida. I lured them to tenements and stole their money. In San Blas three Cubans caught me and tore out my gold teeth. That's how I got black gums. I fished with refugees on my trawler, the Erland Szegy. We fought the Texans. I killed one with a boulder and ever since took to the road.

I was crazy Jack Castro.

I circled to Camas, Idaho, walked to Malad City, Samaria, Roy and Portneuf, where I stole a porphyry amulet and hung it around my neck. I crossed and recrossed the dark towns, gulleys, buttes, railroad stations like a dog settling down. Leaves in whorls whirled up the branches, owl-shaped leaves, rose and fell as I passed.

A shroud knitted itself overhead in the sky. Below, irises grew between the corn, blue, with crimson pockets. Fields of wheat and rye pollinated themselves out of season. Hollyhocks detached themselves and floated across ponds. Insects began to eat each other. Under blue storm clouds explosive broom darkened the air. Canadian geese flew upside down over the aspen blowing green, silver, green, silver.

I was fruit broken by heavy hands.

'Antoinette . . .'

I dug my grave through the world. Erland Szegy met me at a split oak.

'You look terrible,' he said.

'I am frightened.'

Erland took me down to limestone caverns. Prisoners hung by the thumbs. Men dangled upside down with gunny sacks on their heads, crosses jammed in their handcuffed fists. Ojibways, Fox, Sauk and Menominee crossed stagnant black pools, dripping.

Corpses spat teeth. Orchids grew around their heads. They pointed at the causes of their deaths: a knife in the chest, a corroded liver, a bullet hole in the temple.

'Who are they?' I asked.

'Suicides.'

'Who?'

'You and me.'

'Me? What did I do to myself?'

Black birds swooped down the canyons. A guard beat a boy until the skin burst. A woman gave birth to a hog, screaming. In a tunnel a bull sodomized a child. Trees sprouted fingers where orphans hung by their necks. The rivers of North America, the Missouri, Platte, the Snake, Klamath, dripped through the trembling roof. Screams echoed down the crevices. Erland put on a red-tasselled hat.

'Oh, Jean – what happiness we could have had!'

It rained upward. Men ate clay crying in the rocks. Erland burst into tears.

'*J'me suis fait avoir,*' he said. 'I was had.'

'*T'as ben raison,*' I said. 'You're right.'

Erland turned into a lame rabbit and jumped into a hole. This was my dream of Erland Szegy, 23 September 1955, on the Purgatoire River, Idaho.

I became invisible.

Idaho stank of sweet, choking red clouds. Ribbon fish stirred in the Purgatoire. A black cicada shot apart on the pine bark. The moonlight twined down spikes of hickory trees and told me what to do. I stumbled out of the pines at Heyburn.

I became visible.

There was a black trunk-line shanty, a switchman's shack, with a red lantern in the window. I knocked on the door. A round Polish face, reddened with drink, appeared.

'You must be lost,' he said, with a Polish accent. 'Come in.'

I followed him in. The shack measured about twenty feet by fifteen feet. Calendars of pornographic women lined one wall. He saw me see them. A plate of cling peaches was on the desk by his clipboard, telephone and timetables.

'Gets pretty lonely here at night,' he said.

I sat on a cranberry crate. He drew up his lantern and turned up the flame. He studied my face.

'Where are you going?' he asked.

'As if any of us know where we're going.'

'You must have a destination.'

'Do I?'

'Invent one,' he said.

'Okay. Burley.'

'Well, it's just down the road.'

'I know.'

'You can follow the rails.'

'I can go anywhere.'

'I'd drive you,' he said, 'but I've got glaucoma. I have to be here to answer the telephone. Not that a hell of a lot happens on the trunk-line.'

'No telling what will happen.'

'Wine?'

'Love some.'

The Pole drew back a black curtain and pulled out a jug of red wine. He was embarrassed because there were many empty jugs. He let the curtain fall. He poured wine into two dirty glasses.

'Where are your parents?' he asked.

'My father was a construction worker. He fell to his death. My mother drowned in Georgian Bay.'

'Now a person like me,' he said. 'I've lived my whole life being disowned and I still can't prepare myself for death. I lack contrition.'

'Let's cut the crap,' I suggested. 'I feel like gambling. Do you have cards?'

'I do. In fact, I have a pack right here in the desk drawer. Poker?'

'Five card.'

'Stud?'

'Deal.'

We started drinking. He said his name was Rybczinski. He was born in Poznan. His father had been a railroad switchman. He himself hated the railroads. When they moved to Chicago his father got a job with Union Pacific. They moved to Idaho. Rybczinski fell in love with a girl named Dawn Gilchrist. They didn't have money to marry. Rybczinski went to Bolivia and worked the tin mines. Dawn put his cheques in Twin Falls Federal Savings and Loan. Rybczinski worked one year. Then his contract expired.

Dawn Gilchrist wrote. She asked him to work one more year. They needed seven thousand dollars for a mortgage. Rybczinski cancelled his train ticket and signed for a second year.

'I couldn't trouble you for a bit of red wine?' I asked.

'Not at all, my friend.'

Rybczinski poured the fourth glass. His breath was warm. Black ovals moved in the wall boards behind the pornographic women.

After the second year in the tin mines he received another letter. Dawn Gilchrist said there was money for the house but not enough for an apple orchard. Rybczinski put her photograph back on the table and signed on for a third year.

He worked twelve years in Bolivia. When his lungs filled with the damp they fired him. He came back on a boat to New Orleans, took the train to Twin Falls, and walked to Heyburn. Dawn Gilchrist had four children by James Park and lived in a white Victorian house on the edge of Burley.

'What did you do?' I hiccuped.

Rybczinski shrugged. 'Well, I got a job as a railroad switchman. Same as my father.'

'Why didn't you beat them up? Why didn't you kill her?'

Rybczinski laughed.

'I don't need trouble.'

'It doesn't bother you he's got her?'

'Well. Sure.'

'Daily? Giving it to her in the belly, mouth?'

'Well, of course, sure.'

'Twelve years in Bolivia. You won't get those back, Rybczinski. You won't get her, either.'

'I know.'

'They made an ass of you.'

Rybczinski tried to laugh but it turned into a cough of damp-filled lungs.

'Boy, they sure did.'

'Dumb polack.'

'They don't come much dumber. Twelve years. Making babies with my woman on my money.'

195

I stood up. The cranberry crate fell over.

'You know, you're a stupid shit, Rybczinski,' I said. 'I've got half a mind to teach you a lesson.'

Rybczinski grabbed for me but missed, spilled the red wine on his little red-checked table cloth. He suddenly slipped from his chair.

'I don't need – teaching – from the likes of you – ' he said in his stupor.

I kicked him in the chest.

'Ha,' I laughed.

Rybczinski struggled to his feet. His face was red as a pig's liver.

'I invite you out of brotherhood,' he said. 'You do this to me.'

I kicked him in the chest again to hear him cough. He fell on me and we rolled against his bed. I stood and he hugged my knees.

'I need love.'

'Well, you should have thought of that before you fell in love with Dawn Gilchrist!'

'You're so right.'

'Or Antoinette, or anybody!'

I hit him with the cranberry crate. The crate broke on Rybczinski's head. He stumbled after me and tried to pull himself up by the desk. I threw a jug of wine at him.

'STUPID SHIT!' I screamed.

Rybczinski fell back against the pornographic women. I lost control. I shoved his dirty glass into his mouth and smashed the glass in with a board. Rybczinksi couldn't breathe. He flailed his arms. He tripped over the bed blankets, banging into his table. I hit him again with my fist and broke his nose.

'– uh – hhhhhhh – ccchhhhhh – ughhhh – '

Rybczinski ran me out of the shack, swinging a coal shovel. I danced out into his little garden and threw coal at him.

'Ha ha ha!'

'– hhhhhuchhhhh – me – '

'POLACK SHIT!'

I ran up the railroad embankment carrying two of Rybczinski's gallon wine jugs. The moon glided out. Rybczinski became a staggering silhouette at the shack's door, yanking at the glass in his throat.

It was almost midnight. Dead twigs rolled down the railroad ties and burst into white flowers. I stepped on to the Burley road.

Jean-Michel

I DRANK.

I drank two gallons of red wine. I drank until I drooled and I drank that too. After a while it grew warm. I saw shadows sneaking across the field. The black road wound toward the moon like a dark fish swimming upriver. Branches separated. A stallion pounded across the meadow. Cows turned their backs, tails raised, vermilion fold, black hides.

The earth rotated. Stones suddenly rattled across the dark meadow. I was in ecstasy. I was rich, rich beyond anything my father had dreamed of. I was a windblown seed. Hawks glided past my arms. The moon burned my face.

> 'On danse avec nos blondes
> Vole, mon coeur, vole!
> On danse avec nos blondes
> Nous changeons tour à tour
> Nous changeons tour à tour.'

> 'Dance with the blondes
> Fly, my heart, fly!
> Dance with the blondes
> Change your partner round and round
> Change your partner round and round.'

Death floated up the road. He wore a Militant Lamb sash.

Death glided three feet off the road. His eyes were red rubies. A corpse held him from behind and sodomized him. They passed through me, up the Burley road.

'Hurry up, Jean,' Death said.

I slipped. I stumbled into a grassy ditch. Suddenly Red Two Hats, drunk as a loon, rode from the pines on a black stallion. He carried gourds of blood.

Red opened his mouth.

'*Jean-Michel.*'

But he said no more.

Father Przybilski rode out from the pines. He wore a red cassock with black bullets. A *crème de menthe* bottle banged against his pommel. Wild turkey feathers lined his cope and rodents' teeth his saddle.

Father Przybilski opened his mouth.

'*Jean-Michel Verhaeren.*'

But he said no more.

The Lutheran Ed Gien crashed out of the pines. On his head were moose antlers. He wore a black bandolier of women's hands. He carried a rifle across his knees and females' ears, fingers, teeth, were strung from his red reins. His roan reared.

He opened his mouth.

'*Jean-Michel Verhaeren of St Croix.*'

But he said no more.

Pius XII crashed out through black spores. His blue face was unshaven. His spectacles glittered. Red slippers flopped in black stirrups because the ecclesiastical flesh was rotted. There was a double-headed eagle on his head.

Pius opened his mouth.

'*Jean-Michel Verhaeren of St Croix, Ontario.*'

He pointed with a fish scaling knife at the riders' bulging shrouds. Ignace dripped lake water from one shroud. My father was tied elbows to knees, his khaki trousers dark at the crotch. Georges Verhaeren's fists were tied by barbed wire. Bobo, Estée, Emil, were heaped on a red cart behind Father Przybilski. Erland Szegy was dragged over the rotted logs by rawhide tied to his hamstrings.

Pius stood on his stirrups.

You will die, Jean-Michel. Therefore there is no good in anything you do.

Ed Gien stuck a red feather in his hair. Father Przybilski fired his rifle. Red Two Hats rattled a rope of skulls. Mercury-bright clouds screamed. Pius spurred his horse, whirled, and they crashed back into the pines.

Hot air hissed through my skin. I stuffed my ears with newspaper, my mouth with socks, my nose with candy wrappers. Nothing stopped the hissing from the body. The body crumpled. Jean-Michel Verhaeren died. In a way, in a strange way that night, that very night, in a peculiar way, I escaped and died.

I woke in the morning.

It was hot and muggy. I lay on the Burley road. The fog stank. It was a miracle I hadn't been run over. Pigs wandered down from the farms and ate vomit from my hair, crotch, mouth. I was disgusted but I couldn't move. I was paralysed.

I am swine.

SEVENTEEN

'*J'irai revoir ma Normandie*
C'est le pays qui m'a donné le jour.'

'I'm going back to Normandy
That's the place where I was born.'

I went to Bunco, Louisiana.

Bunco was on the Calcasieu. Negro prisoners filled levee bags. It was September, but the Spanish moss was already grey. A schizophrenic ate yellow dirt on Bell Street. A locomotive crossed a black trestle bridge. The milkman walked past an ice truck. In a slaughterhouse window was a pig's head with sunglasses and aluminium foil hat. On it was a sign:

'Cook me tenderly
Cook me with care
With herbs and green garlic
I'll eat you next year.'

My mother lived in the old slave quarter.

The stairwell smelled of leeks. My ice skates with red pom-poms were in a cardboard box. A jumble of my father's tools blocked a grey door. There was an aphasic in the basement crying. An old dog lumbered to me and gummed my crippled leg.

Pippi was very old. His hair was dirty and he had foul breath. He had grown huge, almost chest high. I knocked. My mother had *progeria*, accelerated aging. She was enormously fat and wore spectacles and heavy shoes. She was a chain-smoking woman in curlers.

'Who are you?' she asked suspiciously through the door crack.

'Jean-Michel Verhaeren.'

'Who was your father?'

'Jack Verhaeren.'

'And he?'

'The murderer of James Barrault.'

'Where is he?'

'Dead.'

'Of what?'

'*Exsanguination.*'

'Who else?'

'My brother Ignace.'

'And he?'

'Drowned.'

'Who drowned him?'

'I did.'

'In what major North American body of water?'

'Georgian Bay.'

'That is correct. You may enter.'

We sat formally with espresso cups, on the old red divan. Her head bobbed slightly. There was the brass floor lamp, Ignace's religious theatre. The apartment was very dark. The portrait of Catherine Labouré had its own lamp on the wall. My mother sat like a mountain. *Progeria* had bowed her legs.

'You have not aged well, Mama.'

'With *progeria* one wins no beauty contests.'

I heard the clangour of irons below.

'I am swine,' I said.

She lit a cigarette with an old one. She blew a smoke ring at a blue chandelier. With her forefinger she poked the smoke hole. I presented a gift of wax flowers I had stolen in Burley. The mirrors reflected variations of a fat woman, an unkempt man with an iron bar on his foot.

'Our values failed,' she said. 'We were deceived.'

'It was just bad luck.'

'Oh, *pauvres Verhaerens!*' she suddenly cried, knocking her head against the table top. '*Enchaînés par le bon Dieu!* All our hopes! Our future crushed!'

'Please – '

'Ignace, everything – swept away – everything finished!'

'Mama!'

'Not even children from the Verhaerens!'

I looked out of the window. A duck ran in terror down the shadows. My mother put on an imitation fox fur. She was cold. I sensed wheels, cogs, threads, all invisible, pulling our heads round and round.

'Raising children is not easy,' I said lamely. 'Nor is it entered into with all the hopes and dreams for a beautiful future as imagined for us when we were first born. There are a large number of myths connected with all this. Our tendency to selectively remember and observe this reality.'

'How would you know?'

I went to the butcher's, bought a small rabbit and spent the afternoon soaking it in boysenberries.

'A man who has been tossed around,' I said, stirring the marinade, 'who is judged crazy, good for nothing, such a man, whether he limps or not, or has a pinched nerve from lying on roads, eaten by swine, might not be a failure, after all.'

'What is he?'

'Exactly. I have lost confidence.'

'So you had a catastrophe. Was it my fault?'

She became angry.

'You're not happy, Michel?' she said. 'Try harder. Multiply your efforts. Work. Get paid. Slave. Like me. My poor little *condamné*. You're in prison? The days harass you? Oh. How terrible. And night makes you worse? Well, let me tell you about charity, Jean. Let me tell you about bandages that leak and throats that rattle. Let me tell you about clogged drains and betrayal and electricity in the forehead.'

'Yes? Well, I could tell you a few things about your friend Zena Courennes!'

She sagged on the red divan.

'There are no moral values,' she said. 'And worse: it looks as though there never were any.'

We went on, talking to each other, at each other, past each other, making no impression.

'Why do we bother?' she asked.

I went from room to room. The pantry was full of *filé*, red pepper, tabasco, onion, bacon strips, the shrimp of the parish. I went into her bedroom. The blinds were drawn. The slime haze of the Calcasieu hovered on blue-grey wallpaper. I ate an *oreille de cochon*. Nothing eased my hunger. I went into the bedroom. Saints and sand, clouds and Saviour, lay on jumbled cardboard.

'Mama!' I shrieked. 'The altar!'

We caught up on news. Canada had a flag. The motel on Abattoir Road was a storage facility for the school district. Highway 17 was complete now from Wawa to Marathon. France had lost Algeria. Ho Chi Minh had beaten the Americans. Danny Auban was a garage mechanic. Father Przybilski had broken both hips in a fall. Paul Hartmann taught school.

'And Antoinette?' I asked.

'Hartmann?'

'Paul's sister.'

'She was a lovely young woman.'

'She was,' I said.

'You should have married her.'

We had many discussions. I emptied her tea cups of ash and butts, thinking, remembering. She listened to the radio, polkas. The apartment filled with cold fog in the morning, stifling heat in the afternoon. You'd have thought we were in Surinam. The sun never quite came through the burnished blinds. Blue vapour curled down the corridor.

'Perhaps we could fit you with an artificial leg,' she said. 'The one you have is for the birds.'

I bought my mother a cane. For her, Bunco turned upside down. All pretty things had turned ugly. I asked her about her pain.

'It is forbidden to die,' she said, 'before Jesu calls.'

'Yet many do it.'

'Their souls are in hell.'

'I lost mine,' I said. 'I didn't know I had one until I lost it. Ha.'

And:

'Ha ha ha ha ha.'

We played poker, sometimes *piquet*. I won the *capot* every time. I had *carte blanche*. I had it all. We played *mah jong*. We forgot what we were playing. My right arm died. I wired a battery to it, tied the wires around the bicep but it flopped like a rubber hose. I was at the end. I was drugged. Periods of hysteria followed fits of dazed stupidity.

My mother sang:

> '*La Pluvoise est coulée*
> *Si léger, si léger . . .*'

> 'The submarine, the Pluvoise, has sunk,
> So swiftly, so swiftly . . .'

Pippi died. I took him to Eliade's taxidermy and brought him home on wooden wheels.

My mother's face became a mask. She developed whip-motions of her head. I bought her a wig, but it was a Negro's and she left it in the box on the dining-room table.

I walked the scummy Calcasieu. I was overwhelmed by the mediocrity of our fates, the unreality of my existence. I caught dragonflies and snapped off their heads. It felt like twenty years since I had first run away. Maybe it *was* twenty years. I went home and looked for a calendar.

Etienne Bastide came, uninvited, to Bunco. He was six feet four inches, thin, abnormally pale. We went to the Fleurs de la Rivière, red chairs in a sunken floor, and had *beignets* and *café au lait*, then oysters in the half shell, barbecued shrimp, *andouille*, *boudin* and *courtbouillon*. We concluded with chocolates in ginger, espresso and cigars.

'It is over for you?' Etienne asked. '*Le grand dérangement*. The great exile?'

'Yes. I swam in deep waters.'

'*Tu sais, t'étais ben malade depuis longtemp.* You know, you were sick a long time.'

'It was a nightmare.'

'Come back with me.'

'Etienne, I don't remember a thing.'

'The United States? Nothing?'

Etienne gave me a newspaper clipping. The retired assembly-line worker Reynolds Kayran had died in Dearborn of emphysema.

'Thank you.'

Etienne gave me a present: a portrait of Philippe, Duc d'Orléans, the transvestite.

'Thank you, sweet Etienne.'

Etienne took my mother to Bunco cafés: *Au petit Elégance, A bon Diable, Au Temples des Douces.* She and Etienne ate *macque-choux*, crawfish, okra. Negroes stood on Charity Road selling red coral, shells, alligators, cinnamon, gum copal, tangena, breadfruit. Etienne and my mother sat on crab boxes and watched Negroes work the grey Calcasieu. Etienne sang:

> '*Un' belle Marie coolie*
> *Un' belle Marie coolie*
> *Un' belle Marie coolie*
> *Vous belle dame, vous belle dame pour moi*
> *Mama est an African'*
> *Un belle coolie*
> *Vous belle dame, vous belle dame pour moi.*'

Gumbo bands came to the Calcasieu. Drunk Cajuns, speaking Congo French, pounded on doors demanding live chickens, danced on Pork Street. Blind from gin they staggered through the slave quarter.

'*Hé quoi! Citoyens! V'en faire de la music.*'

Etienne and I rowed the marshes around Lake Calcasieu and slept in the *marais*. Boats bumped past the cypresses: *La Jeunesse,*

L'Enfant du Paradis. We caught a *grosbec* and roasted it on firm ground. Etienne showed me how to prepare salt bindweeds. There were specklebellies, snows from Canada. In the morning we were covered in the sickly smell of crushed vines.

We explored a ruined house. *Cheveux de frise* hung over a ruined gate where ivy broke through the walls. We found old ammunition. Water lilacs covered the cistern. Light flashed deep below. Etienne kept trying to seduce me with *joual.*

'*Une p'tite lumière qui brille au bord de la nuit,*' he said, looking through the lilacs. 'A flicker of light shining on the edge of night.'

'*Oui, cé belle.*'

'*Un bec, a noirceur, cé tellement excitant,*' he said, turning to me in the shadows. 'A kiss, in the dark, it's very exciting . . .'

'Etienne,' I interrupted. 'I had an episode – '

'A bad one?'

'In Idaho. A crime – '

'What?'

'I may have – killed – somebody – '

Etienne kissed me.

'Poor, sweet Jean. *Ch't'é cru,*' he said. 'I believed in you.'

'I was hammered about.'

We went out into the bayou where the mirlitons grew. We stayed out in the rain squalls, equally in the warm red twilight. Light came from the swamps and followed us down the road. The tide became luminescent, rolled under the reeds.

I became worried.

'See?' I said. 'Wilted celery.'

'Not even a salute,' Etienne said.

'Etienne. It's serious.'

'*You* should have been the Jesuit!' he laughed.

Now I was really depressed.

'Etienne,' I whispered. 'I'm limp.'

'A limp imp.'

His baritone laugh boomed over the Calcasieu.

'For this I came to Bunco!'

Etienne suddenly spat and turned around three times clapping his hands for grief.

'When I think of the pain!' he cried. 'Loving you!'

Bunco was invaded by *les hurlants*. Choctaw corpses, wearing blue, opened their mouths and hissed. They wore heifer hooves. A Catholic church was vandalized. They pissed in the soup kitchen, humped the pews. They came out when the twilights rolled in. We carried pistols because of *les hurlants*.

Artichokes grew woody. It thundered heavily on Sunday.

'Somebody will die,' Etienne whispered, and crossed himself.

My mother told me her idea.

'We make a Catholic city of Bunco,' she said. 'Nurse the sick. An almshouse for women, you see, rich as Cluny. Cleanse each other with aloes. We send *bons garçons* through Louisiana.'

'I have *my* idea.'

'Yes?'

I drummed my fingers excitedly.

'I will go to Haiti. I will set up a museum of the Verhaerens.'

She clapped her hands excitedly.

'At last! Jean-Michel formulates a plan!'

In fact, we wrote right away to the Sisters of Charity in Haiti, because my mother had a cousin in Gonaïves.

'Oh, Mama! We will drink *paiwori* and wear bells in our lips!'

She took morphine at night, capsules in grey tubes that she dissolved in water. In the morning she woke dreamily, sliding around the apartment. She watched the grey dawn breaking through the mirage of Bunco. She dreamed the Verhaerens rose from the sea, silver streams pouring from their wounds.

'Morphine,' she slurred. 'God's aperitif.'

Progeria accelerated. Her flesh dropped off and fell on the floor. I found scraps of yellow skin, whole tendons, a broken tooth.

'Mama! *Your ligaments!*'

Finally her leg fell off. I worked the bone back in with a ballpeen hammer, two screws, and varnished the joint.

I stepped back.

'Woman,' I said. *'Reassembled.'*

It came time. After all the consultations, operations and pro-
cedures, there just wasn't much left. I drove her to the Gulf.
Clouds tore over palm fronds shivering. One had to go forward
by smell. There had been a strong gale last night and the water
heaved and flashed. The sun was green over the Gulf of Mexico.
The clouds choked a lighthouse. I put my arm in hers.

'Lâche-moé,' she said.

'I'd like to help, Mama.'

'Please don't.'

I strapped her down in her wheelchair. We went down wood
stairs and came out into flashing, sodden cane. Big storm clouds
came up the Caribbean. I tucked a plaid blanket around her
slumped shoulders, a bonnet over her rubbery ears.

'LÂCHE-MOÉ!'

'Okay, *okay,'* I said.

I cupped my hands lighting a cigarette. She stepped over wet
sands, heavy as a manatee. Red kelp curled at her legs. The skies
grew complicated. A million waterfowl suddenly darkened the
sun. Her knee floated away.

'Perhaps you could fetch it for me,' she asked.

'I'm getting it. See?'

I went far out but she went farther. When I looked up she
was beyond the lighthouse.

'Mama – forgiv – '

Ether bubbled up through the boiling ocean. Lavender
mist circled her singing over white dolphins jumping out
of black waves. Bleeding hearts flared in the palms. She
twirled into a black hole in the clouds and disappeared.
I heard:

Yvonne Krems, thou art blessed.

At least, that's what I told Etienne Bastide.

'Jean. Your mother died on the operating table at Lake
Charles Hospital.'

'The surgeons butchered her.'

'You were *there,'* he said. 'With *me.'*

208

'I'm *telling* you what I *saw*. I'm *telling* you what I *heard*.'
'Frankly, this casts doubt on everything.'

I worked the Verhaeren museum.

The smells of glue, wire, cotton and paints filled the apartment. I repaginated scrapbooks. I painted Jack Verhaeren, Gruel, Barrault, Father Przybilski, Swallowfield prison, St Bonaventure, Erland Szegy and his shotgun. A fierce wind came through. Exhibits flew out the window.

'Jean,' Etienne asked. 'This museum. Is it worth it?'

'Anything is, if you believe in it.'

'Jean, you didn't even come to the *funeral*.'

I carried the museum to the train station. Etienne double-stepped to keep up. Exhibits tumbled into the gutter.

'Jean – *Cé-tu bye-bye pour toujours?*' he asked. 'Is this – goodbye for ever –?'

'Yes.'

'Not even – an embrace – ?'

'In the scheme of things,' I said, 'what is an embrace?'

I went south, he went north. It was the last I saw of Etienne Bastide. It was the last anybody saw of Etienne Bastide.

EIGHTEEN

I was a prison guard.

I worked in Gonaïves, in the prison between the cemetery and the cathedral. I invented an *oubliette* and a machine that fed prisoners. I was a *separatiste*, and sent part of my salary to Quebec. I ate no meat on Friday, in the old style.

My house had French iron grilles on a balcony. The floorboards were maroon, sun-spotted, brightly varnished. I could see from Cap-a-Foux to St Marc. I took a boy, René Haraucourt. He was an orphan and used to live on rue Cardinal, in the shadow of my prison. Orchids grew in from our Guatemalan ceramics. Behind our white stucco house were black cobblestone stairs leading uphill.

I built the Verhaeren museum. I put the portrait of Catherine Labouré on red velvet. Ste Dymphna's card, all the cards of the saints, were spread in fans. My father's ammunition belt hung on a peg, his red accordion from a strap on a nail. I built a table of marble and laid out Ignace's baptismal gown, stained amber. Postcards from St Lazare lined the wall. Pippi-on-wheels stood by green curtains that never moved.

My living room contained pig's blood in pewter, *gris-gris* dust, ceramics from New Orleans: Death poured beer for Satan, a male bride rode a black horse. A wooden German knight killed a dragon behind a stairwell. On the door was my votive painting of St Michael Archangel, who saved me from being run over on the Burley road. I had drawings of Black Hawk and Leith Anderson. I had a bird that whistled, a bird that sang.

I had everything.

I started a museum of my generation, but it depressed me and I threw it away.

I dressed René like Antoinette Hartmann. Roger Vaucaire, too, and Colonel Canale, Reynolds Kayran, and Kurt Flood, all those who had been kind or cruel.

I made René massage my deformed foot.

'Such pain!' I yelled.

'Only I know where you hurt,' he said.

'You do – oh – God – that hurt – felt wonderful!'

I kept a coffin under the bed.

I played my father's red accordion. René danced a bastard flamenco. I decided to blend the accordion with rock and roll and become an international sensation, but I got tired and put the accordion on the bed. René brought the mail. Danny Auban sent me a newspaper clipping. Etienne Bastide had hanged himself in Windsor, Ontario.

'Who was Etienne Bastide?' René asked.

'Nobody.'

René regarded me suspiciously, big eyes, furrowed dark forehead, hair bristled back.

'*A la ti monde malhonnête,*' René said. '*– ti Jean-là.*'

'Who? Me?'

'Yes. My little dishonest, my dear, Jean.'

'Me?'

'*Mo' che*',' René asked. 'My dear friend. Why with you, this feeling, like – death – ?'

I signed my death certificate.

Rain drenched the wildly overgrown gardens. Decayed French buildings sagged. Cemeteries ran with water and the corrugated roofs of the market rattled. One bought oranges down there, tobacco, donkeys, allspice, red peppers on strings, chicory, apricots, peaches in wooden boxes, spinning metal toys and hair straightener.

'Remember the day we met?' René asked. 'In the market?'

'I do.'

'You interviewed me right there on that bench.'
'I did.'
'And now. Everything is so – difficult – isn't it?'
I wore a knife because of all our fights.

René and I walked past the beggars outside the museum to the marina. We smoked cheroots and watched wet sailboats: *La Bataille, Mon Pouvoir, L'Enfance Perdu*. Sun came suddenly onto the bright cathedral. A square-faced man jumped from the alley. His black tongue pointed at me.
'*Śmierć!*' he yelled.
I hurried René onward.
'Who was that?' René asked.
'Nobody.'
'What did he say?'
'Nothing.'
We walked and smoked. Gradually our hopes revived. We decided to move to Venezuela. Tourists from America came off the boats in white slacks and striped green designer shirts. The ingénues never looked at us.
'We stink of the mattress,' I said.
'*You* do.'
'You too.'
'I'm young,' René said. 'They like the way I smell.'
René slapped his thigh and laughed.
'Crazy Monsieur Verhaeren!'

We went to the Queen of the Night night club.
'What does *śmierć* mean?' René asked. 'It's Polish, isn't it?'
'*Śmierć* means death.'
Lights came on in the marina. Boats moved in black swells. Inside the night club, red lights circled a caged monkey on the dance floor. Gonaïves's black women danced.
'In Polish,' I added smugly, 'death is feminine.'
René insisted we go out on to the balcony. There must have been a party last night because glass beads hung over the balcony rails and on the palm trees. I snapped my fingers. A Cuban girl took our order. René winked at her.

'Stop it, René.'

'I can smile at a girl.'

'Not when I'm paying.'

There was a *fiestecita* far away on a different island. Bonfires rose in a different harbour. There was a competition of bands. Silhouettes danced. I looked inside. The caged monkey beat against his bars. I looked up past the insect-blotted light. There was a heavy rain coming.

'Who said that?' René said suddenly, looking around.

'Nobody said anything.'

'No? I thought . . . somebody was listening . . . women . . .'

René leaned forward, nursing his drink.

'Monsieur Verhaeren,' he said. 'I have a feeling.'

'Yes?'

'Some day – maybe tonight – something extraordinary will happen and my soul will be revealed to me.'

'Good luck.'

Inside the nightclub Ignace rode his tricycle around the monkey and Erland Szegy winked at me, his forefinger sliding across his throat. René dropped my hand. He watched the Cuban girl. Birds settled in the trees. The sea mist turned black.

'Where am I?'

'Gonaïves, Monsieur Verhaeren.'

I wrote *I was cheated* in spit on the table.

'Maybe if we'd been able to resupply Dienbienphu,' I said.

'You're drifting.'

'Or if *crème de menthe* hadn't tasted so sweet.'

'Drifting.'

René faded into the black haze. Everything was slipping away.

'Maybe if Antoinette Hartmann had loved me.'

'You?' René laughed.

René brought his swizzlestick to a moth. The moth stiffened, then fell apart, all over the table.

'See?' he said. 'No oxygen.'

Caribbean breezes suddenly separated the palm fronds. Red geraniums trembled. The monkey escaped from its cage and committed obscenities. Gonaïves's black women laughed and came out behind me on to the balcony. Palm fronds shivered, birds flew away, red geraniums, beads, everything moved in the shadows of *négritude*.